Mom

AMONG THE LIARS

Also by James Yaffe

Mom

AMONG THE LIARS

JAMES YAFFE

ST. MARTIN'S PRESS • New York

Design by Judy Stagnitto

Library of Congress Cataloging-in-Publication Data

Yaffe, James.
    Mom among the liars / James Yaffe.
       p.   cm.
    "A Thomas Dunne book."
    ISBN 0-312-08264-9 (hardcover)
    I. Title.
    PS3547.A16M6   1992
    813'.54—dc20   92-26153
                                                               CIP

First Edition: November 1992

10 9 8 7 6 5 4 3 2 1

Mom

AMONG THE LIARS

PROLOGUE

Excerpt from Mom's diary

Dear Diary,

I'm feeling foolish already, and I only wrote two words in you.

When I was a girl I never kept any diary. Plenty girls that I went to school with had them, with fancy leather covers and locks on them. These emptyheads wore the key on a chain around their neck, they made a big *schmeer* out of how secret it was. The idea was, you ask them what they're writing and they say, "I'll never tell you in a million years!" so you go on asking and finally they tell you, naturally swearing you to secrecy. By me this wasn't such an interesting game, so I never bought a diary.

So tell me please, what am I doing with one now? At my age, after seventy-five years keeping such foolishness out of my life? The answer is, since I moved to this little town called Mesa Grande, in the shadow of the Rocky Mountains—where my son is investigating murders and other crimes for the public defender—I'm giving him more help with his cases than I used to do back in New York even. In New York, where he worked for the Homicidal Squad—the youngest man that ever got promoted to inspector, it was a big honor—he told me about his cases every Friday night, when he came to the Bronx for dinner. Here I'm seeing him a lot more often than once a week, so a lot more cases I'm hearing about.

And it sometimes happens there are deductions I'm making about these cases, ideas coming into my head that I can't tell him about, it would be dangerous or embarrassing he should know them. But I have to get them off my chest, no? Everybody has things they have to talk about to somebody. So that's you, dear diary, you're the one I'll be doing my talking to.

Like now, when I know something I never want Davey to know, concerning these murders that all the politicians got mixed up in. . . .

DAVE'S NARRATIVE

ONE

I don't like politicians. I never have. Back in New York, when I was working with the Homicide Squad, I couldn't step out of my office without tripping over one. We'd arrest some hood, we'd have him dead to rights, we'd turn him over to the DA's office—the next thing we knew, they were letting him plea bargain for a suspended sentence or dropping the charges altogether. Nobody had to spell it out for us. Behind the scenes some politician's greasy fingers had been pulling the strings. One thing I was looking forward to when I took this job out here in the West—no more politicians in my hair.

It hasn't exactly worked out that way. This murder I'm about to describe was full of politicians. I won't be able to make sense out of it, in fact, until I fill in some background on our local political situation.

Outsiders coming to this town might be deceived into thinking that our politics is the easygoing, old-fashioned type, nice gentlemanly candidates kissing babies, delivering homespun speeches from their front porches, and refusing to soil their lips with abusive remarks about their opponents.

This picture gains some plausibility from the looks of the town. Though in the last decade malls and shopping centers and rows and rows of jerrybuilt clones often advertised (by developers who have taken vacations to London) as "housing estates" have been spreading like crabgrass, the center of Mesa Grande, consisting of the so-called downtown area and the residential areas next to it, remains pretty much what it's always been. It includes the oldest, most beautiful houses in town, the four acres on which our local ivy-covered liberal arts college sits, the upper-crust churches, and the elegant central branches of banks, insurance companies, and other long-established business firms. Separate all this from the other 90 percent of the town, and you've got the set for an old Andy Hardy movie right off the studio lot.

Furthermore, there is the constant presence of the mountains, which you can see from almost every street corner if you face west. Especially in sunny weather, when they are at their most beautiful and majestic, they seem to be reminding us how unimportant human scrabblings and graspings are in the grand serenity of Nature. They make it easy to believe that the political sleaziness of other sections of the country couldn't possibly have found its way into this paradise. Honesty, integrity, civility, and good sense must have managed to survive and flourish here.

A quick look at our local system of government might tend to reinforce this belief. Mesa Grande's chief elected officials are the seven members of the City Council. Each represents a different section of the city, and their campaigns are not identified with political parties; they run for City Council as individuals, not as Democrats or Republicans, although their political preferences are no secret. (Republicans do tend to get elected more often than Democrats, but then there are a lot more of them around.) City councilmen get no salary for their work; they are given "expense money" for each day the council is in session, and this stipend amounts to a little more than citizens receive for jury duty.

The mayor of Mesa Grande is elected at the same time as the City Council, but he (as yet the mayor has never been a she) has no special executive powers or privileges. He presides over council meetings, where his vote counts the same as all the others; he cuts the ribbon at public functions and makes boring speeches on holidays. But he gives out no jobs, initiates no legislation, and has no right to veto the laws that the council passes. The other important elected officials in town are the district attorney and the members of the school board for District Nine—the district that coincides exactly with the boundaries of Mesa Grande. So it seems maybe that our system of government, even though more than two hundred and fifty thousand people live here now, is as simple and laid-back as if we still *were* in the world of Andy Hardy.

Do I have to point out that this appearance of innocence and serenity is strictly an illusion? Mesa Grande is a real estate town. People come here to retire, especially from the military, which has three bases nearby; the population is older and richer than the national average. In recent years computer companies have moved in, in a big way, and so the malls and shopping centers have grown. Last year's economic dip shook us badly and created a lot of foreclosures and bankruptcies, but until that happened Mesa Grande was a success story, a town with a lot of money in it.

Where there's money the vultures gather, and their first move is to get their claws on the machinery for putting that money in their pockets. The machinery here as elsewhere is political. The City Council has contracts to award, decides what new real estate developments to approve, sets up conditions for the settlement of new business, and through its appointed City Planning Board controls the zoning laws—and the exceptions to them. The council being instrumental in dividing the pie, there is no shortage of special interests to put on pressure to get that pie divided their way.

Because a great deal is always at stake in our local elections, they can be lowdown and dirty. They haven't usually involved murder—like the election I'm about to describe—but there's no reason, when you think about it, why they *couldn't* have. We can point with pride to the fact that our politicians are just as coldblooded as the ones they have back East or anywhere else in the world.

Anyway, the election I'm referring to was in an odd-numbered year, so there was nothing presidential or congressional or even state-legislatural to distract us from local politics. A couple of city councilmen were on the ballot, but there was only one genuinely dramatic race. Our district attorney, Marvin McBride, was running for reelection. Ordinarily nobody would interrupt a yawn over this, but for the first time in the twelve years he'd been in office—his term runs for three years, and he was finishing up his fourth one—he was being challenged by a genuinely formidable opponent.

I've had occasion to mention McBride before: that belligerent little bulldog, with his bloodshot eyes and the thin red veins crisscrossing his cheeks. I've explained that McBride hardly ever tried any cases personally; he usually turned them over to his assistant DAs. This was because judges insist on convening their courts at 10 A.M., and McBride was seldom in condition to appear at such an early hour; it took him the whole morning to blink and cough away his hangover from the night before.

His opponent in the upcoming election could hardly have presented a more extreme contrast. She was Doris Dryden. For the last ten years she had piled up an admirable record of acquittals as a criminal lawyer, making herself almost as big a thorn in McBride's side as my boss Ann Swenson, the public defender. The difference, of course, was that Dryden pocketed huge fees for her efforts while Ann pocketed nothing but her modest salary from the city.

Dryden was half a head taller than McBride (maybe more; we all suspected Marvin of wearing elevator shoes) and beautifully turned out, her hair always impeccably coiffed, her clothes clearly coming from the best stores in town, and some of them imported from New York or Paris. She had come to Mesa Grande from the East and had been married once; the rumor was that her affluence was founded not only on her success as a lawyer but on a spectacular divorce settlement, which she had won for herself in court.

Her decision to run against McBride was announced early in September, and his first public reaction was to say to some reporters, off the record, "She's a nice lady, but let's face it, she just doesn't have the balls for this job!" Since her announcement, however, Dryden had been putting on a whirlwind campaign, with a real genius for getting her name and face in the papers. And her efforts were paying off; according to the latest poll, conducted by *The Republican American,* our only local newspaper (which supported McBride), the two candidates were now neck and neck.

"How do you explain, Mr. DA," asked old Joe Horniman, *The Republican American*'s veteran political reporter, at one of McBride's press conferences, "that Mrs. Dryden seems to be growing balls?"

Evidently McBride didn't hear this question, because he went right on to the next one.

It was Saturday night, the end of October, ten days before election. We had been having one of those autumns that the human race dreams about: temperatures in the seventies, plenty of sunshine, gentle balmy breezes. But this afternoon a suspicion of a chill had come creeping into the air, and the TV weathermen were putting anxious looks on their faces.

On this particular Saturday night the local chapter of the League of Women Voters held a dinner at which the two candidates for district attorney were the guests of honor. Each of them would be addressing the assembled diners, who had paid fifty dollars a plate for the privilege—except for a few who had special connections and had been invited gratis by the League. This included Ann Swenson, because she was the public defender, and me, because I was her chief investigator.

Along with the other freebie recipients, we sat at a table off to the side of a banquet room in the Hotel Richelieu, our local resort, which occupies a few acres on the outskirts of town. Joe Horniman from *The Republican American* sat at this table with us. So did two anchormen and one anchorwoman from our three TV stations. So did McBride's number-one assistant DA, Leland Grantley III, whom Ann and I had come to know all too well in his official capacity.

The speakers' table was halfway across the room, but I had a good view of who was sitting there. In the center spot was the presiding officer from the League of Women Voters, a heavyset, organ-voiced lady with gray hair and glasses and the no-nonsense look of my third-grade teacher. McBride was on her right, and next to him was Ed Brock, his longtime campaign manager. Ed's massive fleshy face and knobby bald head were familiar sights at most of Mesa Grande's political events. He had been in the insurance business years ago, but he was long retired, and he now officially listed himself in the yellow pages as a "consultant." In fact, it was only politicians who consulted him. He had plenty of wins to his credit; he turned away business.

The last time the League of Women Voters had thrown an election dinner for district attorney candidates—three years ago, just after I moved to town—McBride had been flanked by his wife and his thirteen-year-old daughter. They weren't in attendance tonight though. A messy separation had taken place in the interim.

On the presiding officer's left was Doris Dryden, McBride's opponent, looking trim and elegant in a greenish suit. No campaign manager or other assistant sat with her. This was deliberate on her part. She had gone out of her way in these last months to let the world know that she had no entourage, no political connections, nobody to help her with her campaign. Her strategy was to push the David and Goliath image hard.

We ate the usual institutional dinner—fruit cocktail, breaded chicken breasts, french fries, and broccoli—and washed it down with our choice of wine and beer. Coors beer, it's practically illegal to drink any other brand in our state, and California white wine, not exactly the best vintage either.

McBride wasn't turning up his nose at it though. Practically every time I looked at him, he had his glass up to his face. A characteristic position for him to be in.

Ann Swenson, my boss, wrinkled up her nose. "I don't have any moral objections to the way he laps up the stuff," she said. "It's the smell that gets to me. I must be allergic to it. I feel like throwing up whenever he gets within a foot of me."

"From what I hear," said Joe Horniman, "his wife developed

the same allergy. Only it took her twenty-five years to throw up."

Joe Horniman had turned gray at his job with *The Republican American*. There was no human being or institution in Mesa Grande, including the newspaper that employed him, about which he didn't know everything and respect nothing.

Cake and coffee came, and with it the speeches. McBride stood up to give the first one. He was wearing a conservative gray suit, and for once it didn't look as if he had slept in it all night. He was also, untypically, wearing a tie, a red, white, and blue one, with some kind of repeated design on it; I was sitting too far away to make out exactly what this design was.

The loudspeaker system, at least on our side of the room, left a lot to be desired. His voice came to us in waves, some sentences ringing out sharp and clear while others turned into incomprehensible squeaks.

He started off with the prologue he gives to every one of his political speeches—how pleased he was to be there, but also how surprised, how positively amazed, because who ever would've thought that a poor farm kid who grew up in the mountains south of Mesa Grande, whose folks sometimes didn't have enough food in the house to feed the cows and the kids both—so guess who went hungry? it sure as hell wasn't the cows!—well, only in America could a barefoot ragtag kid like that end up getting himself a law degree from a Great University (actually the University of Northern Michigan), and holding down the solemn office of district attorney in the very county where he was born and brought up, and addressing a body of distinguished ladies and gentlemen like he saw before him tonight?

The squeaks and squawks were particularly active during this prologue, which gave the rest of us a chance to relax and guzzle our wine. But they cleared up for the next part of McBride's speech.

"My opponent's long association with the criminal element, though strictly legal in every respect, I don't want to give you any wrong ideas about that, has nevertheless had its effect on her attitudes and her philosophy. She's devoted her life to throwing roadblocks in the way of law and order, so without even being conscious of it she's absorbed the criminal point of view. In all her public statements so far she has made it clear that she'll be soft on crime—"

The rest of his sentence was lost in loudspeaker's noise. "If your job is to investigate and prosecute crimes," said Joe Horniman, addressing nobody in particular at our table, "wouldn't it be a good idea to understand the criminal point of view?"

"No, no, you've misunderstood Marvin's point completely," Assistant DA Grantley put in. "He's not just talking about understanding, he's talking about the regrettable tendency of criminal lawyers to identify with the people they defend, to accept their rationalizations and excuses."

Grantley came from a well-to-do Mesa Grande family and was married to a young woman from old New England stock, reputedly very high up in the most impeccable social circles of Rhode Island; as a matter of fact, the reason she wasn't here tonight, he told us, was that she had gone back to Newport, with their two small sons, for a month's visit to her impeccable relations. After graduation from Harvard Law School, Grantley had returned to his hometown because he "felt the need to give back something to the community which gave so much to me." You wouldn't know from Grantley's stiff manner and his pedantic vocabulary—or from the staid dark Brooks Brothers suits, vests, and ties he always wore—that he was still in his thirties.

By this time McBride had come to the end of his speech and sat down to genteel applause. Grantley was the only one at our table who contributed to it.

Doris Dryden was introduced now, and her speech was subject to the same arbitrary censorship from the loudspeaker system. "Mr. McBride accuses me of associating with the criminal element," we heard her say. "Is he referring to the people I've defended in court against him, people whom juries have seen fit to find not guilty? There *have* been a great many of them, I admit." Laughter from the audience and from everyone at our table, with the exception of Grantley.

"I would like to point out to Mr. McBride," Dryden went on, "that criminals are people who have been convicted of crimes. In our society, people who have been *acquitted* of crimes are not considered to be criminals—not yet anyway—though Mr. McBride would no doubt like to change all that, and make himself judge and jury as well as prosecutor. As for the charge that I'll be soft on crime—a prosecutor who loses as many cases as Mr. McBride does can hardly be said to be *tough* on crime, can he? In convicting criminals—just as much as in defending them—you have to hit your target with everything you've got, you have to bring up your big guns, you have to be a fighter, like me—not a bumbler, like my opponent."

And so on, until the squeaks drowned her out too. "Of course," said Joe Horniman, "Dryden never had a client who was guilty, did she? They've all been pure as the driven snow. For instance, that oil man's son a couple years ago who ran over those two little kids in his Porsche while he was drunk—"

"Absolutely right," said Grantley. "What she specializes in is taking advantage of legal loopholes."

"And what your boss specializes in," Joe said, "is opening up the loopholes so that defense attorneys *can* take advantage of them." Joe gave a little wink at Ann Swenson, as if to acknowledge her superior skill along these lines.

The loudspeaker broke in again, letting through some more of Dryden's words.

"—callousness and carelessness, those are the two Cs that have characterized the way Mr. McBride has done his job. *My* way of doing the job will be characterized by two entirely different Cs—competency and compassion. From now on the district attorney's office will be a kinder, gentler place for everybody, accused and accuser alike—"

Squeaks again, then the loudspeaker allowed the end of Dryden's speech to come through. "But I realize I've made one innacurate statement in my description of my opponent," she said. "I've talked about defending my clients in court against him. Actually I can't recall *ever* defending a client in court against Mr. McBride personally—though sometimes I've had to defend them against the accusations he throws around so liberally in his statements to the press. As everyone in this room knows, Mr. McBride seldom appears in court, seldom takes personal charge of any of the cases his office handles—especially the cases that involve serious crimes. He turns all that over to his assistants. For a long time what we've had here in Mesa Grande is an absentee DA."

A kind of half growl, half yelp burst out of McBride. I could see Ed Brock putting a hand on his arm.

Dryden sailed on calmly. "I'd like to offer Mr. McBride a suggestion—no, let's call it a challenge. The next murder case that comes along, Marvin, how about you taking charge of it yourself, right from the start, and seeing it straight through to the finish? Just to show the citizens of Mesa Grande that you haven't forgotten how to do it."

McBride's head snapped up. "That's a lot of bull, Doris, and you know it! It's always been my policy to give my associates as much experience and responsibility as possible. That's how an efficient office ought to be run. I oversee everything myself, I'm on top of every detail, whenever there's any disagreement my judgment prevails—but you have to know how to delegate authority, how to work with a team. You can't be a grandstander. That may be okay for you criminal attorneys, but in the DA's office you have to be above ego—"

"In other words," Dryden said, grinning out at the audience, "our district attorney isn't going to accept my challenge. He doesn't have the guts."

"Guts! You're saying I don't have guts?" I could see McBride's eyes flashing and his lips quivering. If there's one thing little bantam cocks like him don't like to have doubts cast on, it's their manhood. "Damn right I'll take charge of the next murder case that comes to our office! And incidentally, it would give me the greatest pleasure if you turned out to be the defense attorney for the killer! Like you've defended so many in the past—"

It was hard to say who won this little duel of words. Dryden had McBride on the ropes for a while, but he didn't stay down for long. You had to give the little shit his due, his powers of recovery were phenomenal.

Anyway, the fur soon stopped flying, and the mayor made a smarmy little speech about the free exchange of opinions being the lifeblood of democracy. Then the presiding Woman Voter intoned a few peremptory thank yous to the guests of honor, and no waiters appeared to pour more coffee, so everyone reached for coats. It was close to eleven, according to my watch.

In the anteroom outside the banquet room, there was a large crush of people. Ann and I found ourselves pushed up against McBride, and I could see now that the design on his red, white, and blue tie consisted of a lot of little American flags. Just like him, I thought, during a political campaign he *would* wrap the American flag around his neck.

"Glad to see you, Dave," he said, without much gladness in his voice. But to Ann he gave a big broad smile and grabbed her by the shoulders. "Ann, sweetie, you're looking great! I can't figure out why that husband of yours spends so much of his time in the operating room. Believe me, if *I* had a beautiful creature like you waiting for me at home—" Then McBride threw his arms around her, stuck his face next to hers, and gave her a big hug. Over his shoulder I could see Ann sighing, with an amused philosophical twist to her lips.

"Oh, by the way, honey," McBride said, when he finally freed Ann from his embrace, "I don't like to throw cold water on a happy occasion like this, but I've been looking over that budget of yours for next year, the one you'll be submitting to the City Council in a month. I notice you're asking for a big increase for your department."

"We need the money, Marvin," Ann said, her voice perfectly steady, but my hand was on her arm and I could feel the muscles tightening up. "Everything's costing more these days."

"That's exactly the point," McBride said. "Everything's

going up in *my* operation too. Something's got to give, the deadwood has to be pruned, right? Anyway, I don't want it to catch you by surprise, I'll be opposing this increase of yours. In fact, I'll be recommending to the council that the public defender's budget be decreased."

"You don't mean that!"

"It's a question of priorities, sweetheart. Do we spend the taxpayers' money to catch the crooks or let them go? Besides, admit it now, you've got a lot of padding on that budget of yours. For instance, Dave has this kid working for him, you just put him on the payroll, this assistant investigator. Now come on, Dave, just between us, what do you need an assistant investigator for? We all know what a terrific job you do, you're worth at least two men—" McBride broke off. "Well, this is no place for us to talk business. You want to thrash this all out, Annie, I'll be available at the same old stand, just as soon as I've got this election behind me."

"Or maybe not," Ann said quietly.

"What do you mean— Oh, I get it!" McBride gave out one of his most explosive guffaws. "I wouldn't worry about *that* if I were you! I'm not sure of much in this world, but the one thing I *am* sure of is how the voters of Mesa Grande feel about me. We love each other, don't you know that? It's a marriage that was made in heaven."

"There's a lot of divorce going around these days," I said. Which you may think was an unfair crack, hitting a man when he was down. But from the rumors I'd been hearing, McBride wasn't having much trouble consoling himself since his wife kicked him out. Or before, for that matter.

A little later Ann and I made it to the Richelieu lobby. We could see through the revolving doors that the weathermen's anxiety had been justified. The balmy spell was over; thin icy slivers were shooting down; they might or might not develop into snow. As we started out, we met Doris Dryden putting on her coat. It was a black coat, sleek and simple and beautifully cut, covered with the kind of fur that costs a bundle but doesn't call attention to itself.

Ann greeted her with congratulations. "That was lovely, the way you maneuvered McBride into putting himself on the line for the next murder case that comes along."

"Oh, that wasn't hard," Dryden said. "He's so pathetically vulnerable. He can't bear the idea that anybody might think his balls were smaller than King Kong's. I'm always suspicious of these macho types who go around flexing their genitals. McBride's wife kicked him out of her bed ten years ago, did you know that—long before their current separation? Now was that because he wanted too much from her, or because he couldn't give her as much as she wanted? I've never had the pleasure of meeting the woman, so I can't say for sure." She laughed, then she sighed. "Given the odds, though, there won't *be* any murders before election day. We never get more than two or three a month so how can we expect to be lucky enough—"

"You're not throwing in the towel, I hope," Ann said. "A nice clean knockout a week from Tuesday—I'm depending on you more than ever, Doris."

"Oh, I intend to give you something a lot bloodier than that," Dryden said. "Those balls McBride's always bragging about—the day after the election he'll be eating them, scrambled, for breakfast."

The tight little smile on Dryden's face made me glad *I* wasn't running against her for anything.

TWO

Since Mom moved to Mesa Grande, it has become a tradition that I go over to her house on Sunday morning and she serves me breakfast.

Her house was a compact little two-story structure, white with red shutters, in a pleasant but modestly priced neighborhood; a surprisingly large number of them were still left in town. I had tried to persuade her not to cut into her savings to buy it. My own house, located a few miles away, had a couple of extra bedrooms I never used. Mom could easily have moved in with me. But she had vetoed this idea from the start. "Positively not," she said. "I believe in the declaration from independence. People should have privacy, they shouldn't have to give up their freedom to their loved ones."

"But I wouldn't do that, Mom, I promise you. I'll come and go as I please. I'll live my life the same way I would've done if you hadn't moved in."

"Who's talking about you? *I'm* the one that's declaring my independence. For twenty years I worked my elbows to the bone keeping house for you and your father. Then your father died, and you moved out, and for the last twenty years I'm living alone and liking it. So now you want I should go back to working my elbows again?"

So she bought the house, and also a car, a snazzy little Japanese sports job that was painted bright red, and she quickly established for herself a nice independent social life. It centered on the synagogue sisterhood, the Senior Citizens Bridge and Canasta Club at the YMCA, and her neighbors, whom she got to know by name after a couple of weeks.

I've been living in *my* neighborhood for three years now, and I haven't set foot in any of the neighboring houses, and the neighbors haven't set foot in mine. But Mom has this knack for getting people to open up to her after two minutes' acquaintanceship. She listens to them talk about their troubles, nods and looks sympathetic, and they never find out how sharply, unsentimentally, and worst of all accurately she's sizing them up and making her judgments.

Her Sunday breakfasts are lavish, consisting not only of the usual eggs, sausages, and pancakes, but also of three or four kinds of fresh fruit, homemade pastries, chicken salad, and some variety of smoked fish. She will never, however, let me refer to this feast as "brunch." "Brunch yet!" she says, with one of her magnificently contemptuous snorts. "This is a word I never heard when I was a girl. It was invented by lazy good-for-nothings who wanted to lie in bed on Sunday mornings. Brunch is what you eat after twelve noon. In this house, if you came so late, there wouldn't be any food left."

So I arrived for breakfast that Sunday morning at my usual time, eight-thirty. Last night's icy drizzle had petered out without turning into snow, but there was still a sharp chill in the air. Nothing in the world except Mom's cooking could have got me out of bed this early on such a Sunday morning.

Roger Meyer showed up too. Roger is my chief assistant in the public defender's office. "Deputy investigator" is his official title, and what it means is that he takes care of a lot of the legwork: an important responsibility, since my legs have started letting me know recently that fifty-four years is a long time to be subjected to constant use. Roger is also my soundingboard when a case confuses or baffles me. He's a smart kid, a Yale graduate of two years ago, with a degree in criminology. He has brains and commonsense, when they aren't undermined by his only real fault: He goes to the movies too much, so sometimes his ideas about life come less from experience of the world than from Hollywood's version of it.

He'll grow out of that though. Since he took this job under me he's already gone through a few things that have shaken him into reality in spite of himself.

One of those things had happened about six months earlier. It involved a girl, and I've gone into the details of it elsewhere. But Roger was still feeling depressed over it, so Mom was trying to make up for it in the best way she knew. She piled food up on his plate. "Eat, eat," she kept saying to him. "You don't take seconds from my blueberry pancakes, you'll fade away, your mother will never forgive me."

Roger was tall, his shoulders were broad, his face was shining with sun and good health. The danger of his fading away in the near future seemed negligible to me.

Once he was stuffed to Mom's satisfaction, we got back to the discussion we had been having. I had told Mom and Roger all about the League of Women Voters dinner last night, and McBride's talk with Ann and me after it was over. Roger began to look depressed, so I quickly added that of course his job wasn't in any danger. Nobody was going to cut the public defender's budgets, McBride was just giving a display of wind.

And the same was true, I went on, about his accepting Doris Dryden's challenge. "If he ever did have to face her in court," I said, "she'd wipe up the floor with him. Even if there's a murder case tomorrow, even if he makes a big noise about taking charge of it personally, it couldn't possibly go to trial till after the election. By that time he'll be safely reelected, so he'll find a way to weasel out of it."

"Why wouldn't he take charge of the next murder case strictly out of pride?" Mom said. "You told me already many times what a swelled-up head he's got, what a high opinion of himself. So maybe he wouldn't agree with you Doris Dryden could wipe up the courtroom floor with him. Maybe he thinks *he'll* wipe up the floor with *her*. For making a man deaf and blind to what's real and what isn't, a big ego is better even than a big bank account. You never knew your Uncle Hymie, but he's a perfect example. He had both, as a matter of fact—"

Mom expounded for a while about her late brother-in-law Hymie, who made a fortune in the junk business and tried to get himself elected into the New York Athletic Club, which back in the 1930s was strictly closed to Jews. The story, I have to admit, was fascinating; it showed what lengths a man will go to so he can play cards with people he doesn't like and who he knows don't like him. Maybe the story was even true. But eventually I pulled the conversation back to the point.

"Even if McBride *was* egotistical enough to make a fool of himself in court," I said, "Ed Brock would never let him do it. Ed isn't blinded by ego, or by anything else. Marvin McBride is his creation, his brainchild. He's spent the last twelve years making sure that his child smells like roses, and he wants it to go on for another twelve years. He won't let McBride do anything to throw all that away."

"The voters won't stand for that," Roger said. "When he runs for reelection the next time, they'll remember how he broke his promise."

"The next election is three years from now," I said. "Voters never remember anything that far back. Voters forget what happened three *months* ago."

I could see how disturbed Roger was. I had hit him where he lived, in his idealism. "If that was true, there'd be no hope for democratic government. I mean, democracy depends on an informed responsible electorate. Sooner or later the voters will get wise to McBride, they'll rise up and kick him out!"

"Like in that movie?" I said, and I couldn't help putting a load of sarcasm into the word movie. "Sorry, kid. If Mr. Smith *really* went to Washington, they'd kick his teeth in. Or buy him out after the first reel."

"I remember that movie," Mom said. "With that tall actor who opens and closes his mouth before he talks. A nice-looking boy."

"Jimmy Stewart," Roger said. "Of course I know it's only a

movie. Our system won't change that easy in real life. But still, in principle, there's a lot of validity to—"

"It isn't just our system," I said, "or any other system. It's the basic nature of politicians. There's only one fundamental for politicians. Get elected. They'll do anything and say anything to bring in the votes. They couldn't care less what anything really *is*, only how it *looks*. For politicians image is everything. In other words, basically, all politicians are, by definition, liars."

"You don't think you're just a little bit exaggerating?" Mom said. "I never met any politicians personally, but it don't make sense to me they should be different from other types people. Don't they have to take off their clothes from the outside in? Didn't every one of them have a mother once? So why should you turn them into the Abdominal Snowman or the Lox Ness Monster yet? There have to be good ones and bad ones, and plenty with the good and the bad all mixed up together."

This was an argument that Mom and I had gone through many times. It always surfaces at election time, or when some particularly juicy political scandal breaks in the news.

"There *can't* be any good ones," I said. "Because they have power. That's what they're out for, that's the whole purpose of their lives. And it's a well-known fact, power corrupts and absolute power corrupts absolutely."

Mom just gave one of her gentle, infuriating smiles. *"Everything* corrupts. It isn't only power. Look at what happened to my nephew Bernard, your first cousin, when all of a sudden he won the slogan contest for the soap company. A trip to Bermuda was the prize. Such a sweet modest boy until then, but after he got back from Bermuda he's suddenly wearing sunglasses inside the house and bringing home all types women. His poor mother couldn't look the neighbors in the face any more."

"Okay, I get it. This is your basic philosophical position again. All human beings are the same as all other human beings. But let me tell you, politicians are *worse!"*

All this time Roger's mouth had been working silently—

somewhat like the mouth of Mr. Smith when he first discovers corruption in Washington—and now the words burst out of him. "But what are you saying, Dave? It doesn't really matter who you vote for? It turns out the same either way, so why bother?"

"There's a lot of truth to that," I said. "At your age, you can't still be naive enough to believe that an election campaign is a reasoned debate over issues. It's a big expensive advertising war between two competitive products."

"But *this* election is more than that, isn't it? Mrs. Dryden has ideas, she has compassion, she really *stands* for something. I don't see how anybody could possibly vote for—" He broke off, his eyes widening. "You *are* going to vote, aren't you?"

I gave a shrug. "I'm registered. I'll probably go to the polls on election day. But that's strictly force of habit. I do it because I've *always* done it." I turned and faced Mom squarely. "You don't have any more illusions about politics than I do, Mom. Be honest, admit it. You know too much about human nature, you *can't* kid yourself into thinking that your vote is going to change the world."

"Changing the world—who ever voted for such a cockamamie reason?" Mom said. "You don't change this world, you figure out what's the best way to live in it. This is why I vote, if you want to know. Because, if you're a human being living in the world, all the time you have to make a choice between things. In the supermarket I choose one artichoke instead of another artichoke. How do I know if I'm right? Maybe they're both the same. But I can't sit back already and say who cares, I have to *do* something. Otherwise I won't get to eat *any* artichokes, somebody will come along and force me I should eat squash. And like you know, Davey, I'm not so crazy for squash."

I shook my head, in great sadness. "You're worse off than Roger. *He* can't see anything because his eyes are shut. *Your* eyes are wide open, you blind yourself deliberately. Well, that simply proves what I've always believed. We can't stop having elections, no matter how meaningless they are. People need the illusion that they've got a choice. It isn't freedom that makes people happy, it's the *illusion* of it. Which means we're stuck with politicians whether we like it or not. They're a necessary evil. The chances are it's always been that way. Since prehistoric days, the first time one caveman hit another caveman over the head with a club and said, 'You just voted for me!' "

Roger looked so stricken I began to feel a little ashamed of myself. Evidently Mom felt sorry for him too. She didn't try to answer my diatribe. Instead she offered Roger a refill on his coffee, and that was the end of our argument for that morning.

A little later Mom turned to me. "So you didn't ask me yet, have I got any ideas about this dinner you went to last night?"

I gave a sigh at that one. Mom likes to see mysteries everywhere. There didn't happen to be any murders on my schedule at the moment, but she still had to keep her hand in.

"What ideas *could* you have? There was nothing peculiar about that dinner."

"You didn't find it peculiar about McBride's drinking?"

"What about it?"

"He's such a big drinker, like you're always telling me. And this dinner is going on how long last night—three hours, three and a half, it isn't over till eleven. And all this time, McBride isn't drinking any liquor."

"But he *was* drinking. I told you, every time I looked at him he was guzzling from his glass of wine."

"Only in his glass there *wasn't* any wine. It was the white type, so nobody could notice he was actually drinking water."

"What on earth makes you think that?"

"Your boss, Ann Swenson—she hates the smell of liquor on people's breath, she's allergic to it, it makes her sick. But five minutes after the dinner is over last night, McBride is hugging her, putting his face in hers, breathing on her—and her reaction is, she's giving a smile of amusement, a philosophical smile, this is what you called it. She's a polite person, but if she was feeling like she wanted to throw up, wouldn't she show *some* sign of it on her face? Wouldn't she screw up her nose or pull back from him a little? The explanation is, on McBride's breath was no smell of liquor—even though he was guzzling all night long from his glass of wine."

I stared across the table at her, and so did Roger. Neither of us could say a word. She was right, and I should have noticed it myself.

"All right, I guess he wasn't drinking," I finally said. "But so what? I don't see why it matters."

A small gasp of exasperation, which wasn't actually a Yiddish word but sounded as if it might be, came out of Mom. "You got any idea what an effort it had to be for such a man, such a heavy drinker, to sit through this whole dinner without putting a drop of liquor into himself? Such willpower, that's amazing. In the past McBride seemed to you to be a man with willpower?"

"Of course not. But there *is* one pretty obvious explanation, isn't there? McBride's beginning to think he could lose this election. *The Republican American*'s poll has got him worried. So it was important to him to make a good impression on the people at that dinner last night. Ed Brock probably told him he better lay off the booze."

"Maybe so. But the people that gave the dinner, this League from Women Voters, *they* don't have anything against liquor. They were happy their guests should drink, they served wine and beer at the tables. In this group of people McBride could drink as much as he wanted to, and nobody would be upset at him. And in fact, they *thought* he was drinking, didn't they? He *pretended* he was drinking so he wouldn't hurt their feelings. He even got the waiter to pour water into his wineglass."

"Maybe he was afraid that if he drank too much he'd lose control of himself and act badly in some way or other."

"Why should he be afraid of this? This is another thing you told me about him plenty times. In the morning, with his hangover, he don't operate so good. But the hangover goes away by lunchtime, and he starts drinking again, and he don't show any signs of it on the outside, he looks like he's absolutely under control. This is true about a lot of experienced drunks, isn't it? My cousin Sidney the brain surgeon, for instance. In liquor they can practically drown themselves, and who would know it? For the whole day and night they could be drinking, and their hands wouldn't even shake. Only the next morning, when they wake up sober."

It was certainly true that McBride was adept at putting up a sober front while he sloshed the sauce down as if there was no tomorrow. I had seen him do it plenty of times at other public occasions.

"Maybe he's gone on the wagon," I said. "Maybe he went to a doctor who told him he had to stop drinking."

"It's possible," Mom said. "Only, if he's been sick enough to take such a big step, how come nobody's noticed any signs of it up to now? This election campaign, hasn't he carried it on with as much energy like always? I didn't read anywhere that he collapsed at a meeting or had to call off a speech on account of illness. All right, all right, there isn't enough information to clear up the mystery. It's very sad. The chances are we'll never know—"

She was interrupted by the ringing of the phone.

I answered it and heard the voice of my boss, Ann Swenson. "I'm glad I caught you, Dave."

She knew about my Sunday morning breakfasts with Mom, but this was the first time she had ever interrupted one. That circumstance alone, even if I hadn't heard the urgency in her voice, would have told me that something big was up.

"I know it's a pain in the ass," she said. "If there was any other way— You and Roger will have to meet me down here right away. I'm not at my office. I'm at the jail."

THREE

Ann was waiting for Roger and me on the front steps of the city jail.

This is an outstandingly ugly three-story building, brown and grimy, located next door to the new courthouse. It was put up in the 1930s, so naturally it's overcrowded, dirty, and badly lit, but we're not likely to get a new one in the foreseeable future. The city shot its budgetary load on the new courthouse a few years back, and the economy is in no shape for any further loads of comparable size. In our conservative mountain fortress, we're willing, though not enthusiastically, to spend money so that lawyers, judges, and other servants of the justice system can work in comfort—but does it make sense to throw money away on enemies of society? If they couldn't stand a little squalor, why did they break the law in the first place?

In the dim reception room of the jail, Ann and Roger and I were met by Leland Grantley. It was a little after ten in the morning, but he was dressed as neatly and somberly as he had been at last night's dinner.

"You've got a new client, I think," he said. "Sorry to bother you on a Sunday, but he refuses to talk to us any more until he talks to his attorney. Well, we've got all the information we need anyway—still, we thought we'd better not wait till tomorrow before we called you."

"That was good of you, Leland," Ann said. "Especially since you'd be violating the defendant's rights if you kept him from seeing an attorney for twenty-four hours. And that could compromise any case you might make against him."

"That's true," Grantley said, nodding solemnly. Sarcasm had to get pretty heavy before it would penetrate Grantley's invisible shield of humorlessness. "And it was very much on my mind, I assure you. As you know, I'm a firm believer in respecting every one of a defendant's rights. What else is a democratic system all about?"

"So who *is* this defendant? What's he charged with?" Ann asked.

"His name is Harry Stubbins. The charge is first-degree murder."

I've heard it a thousand times, of course, but it always sends a little shiver down my spine.

"Who got murdered?" said Ann.

"The woman's name was Edna Pulaski. She was a— She operated a— Well, not to put too fine a point on it, she was a madam, she operated a massage parlor on South Arizona Avenue. Three or four girls work for her, and she serviced some of the customers herself. She owned the house, the first floor is where she did business, and her own apartment is on the second floor.

"Actually, though you certainly wouldn't guess it from her name, the woman was Asian—Korean, to be exact. She was married for a while to a man named Pulaski. She came here from Korea ten years ago, with her mother. As you know, a great many Asians have moved into this town—"

"Why do you say this Harry Stubbins knocked off the Pulaski woman?" I put in. "Was he one of her customers?"

Grantley gave a little smirk. "Well, that would be rather surprising. Wait till you see him."

"You do realize that you're wasting our time," Ann said, "if he can afford an attorney of his own. The statute is pretty clear—"

"Nobody's going to claim you're violating the statute with *this* client." The amusement was still on Grantley's face. "I promise you he can't afford an attorney of his own. He can't afford a shoelace of his own. Now I don't want to talk to you about this any further till you've had a conference with your client. After that I'm at your disposal. I'll be across the street, in the courthouse, just drop up to my office."

Grantley signaled a uniformed officer to take care of us, and he was out of there.

In the basement of the jail is a small room where lawyers can have private conferences with their clients, if those clients happen to be guests of the city. This room has a table and three hard wooden chairs, no windows to the outside, only one little barred window on the door. On the other side of this door a guard with a gun is stationed.

Ann and Roger and I waited in this room for our client to be brought in. Ann sat behind the table, I sat next to her, and the chair facing us was left empty. Roger, on account of his low seniority, had to stand against the wall.

As soon as the guard led Harry Stubbins into the room, we understood why Grantley had been grinning. I didn't feel any temptation to grin myself. I don't find much entertainment value in bums from the street, in overcoats that are only one small step up from rags, in pants and shirts that look like they've been slept in forever, in shoes with holes in them, in the thick sick smell of dirty flesh.

Stubbins sort of crumpled into the chair across from Ann and me, and the guard let him know he'd be right outside and left us alone. The door clanged shut, which made Stubbins give a little twitch in his chair.

"How do you do, Mr. Stubbins?" Ann said. "I'm Ann Swenson, the public defender." She introduced Roger and me, then she held her hand out in Stubbins's direction. I wouldn't have done it myself, believe me. Who could know what that hand of his had been rummaging into? But Ann treats every client the same—she's always businesslike and respectful—and believe me, we've had plenty who barely seem to qualify for membership in the human race.

Stubbins blinked down at her hand for a moment, and then

he reached up, trembling a little, and completed the handshake. His fingers were stubby and black; his nails looked as if he chewed them whenever there was nothing more nourishing available.

"My pleasure, Mrs. Swenson," he said.

The voice was hoarse and shaky—from too much alcohol or too little food or sleep, I couldn't be sure. But the formality of his words caught me by surprise. They made me look at him more closely, but I didn't see anything different from what I expected to see. He had a roundish face, puffy and red, pounded into the anonymous expressionless mush of most faces that have spent too many years on the streets, in all kinds of weather. He might have been fifty or seventy, there was no way of telling—there never is. The eyes looked as dull and bloodshot as such eyes invariably do. His teeth were yellow, and a couple of the front ones were missing. Though he wasn't exactly wearing a beard, he looked as if it was a long time since he had shaved.

"We're here to help you, Mr. Stubbins," Ann said. "Every accused person is entitled to his day in court. If you don't have the resources to hire a lawyer, the public defender's office will serve you at no cost to yourself. And we'll give you a good shot, I can promise you that. Do you want to avail yourself of our help?"

Stubbins hitched himself up in his chair a little, gave those bloodshot eyes a few fast blinks, and managed to put a little more volume into his voice. "Very young, aren't you? For doing this kind of work. Ought to be out making a career for yourself. Building up a practice, driving for a partnership, taking on paying clients. Terrible waste. If I were your father, I'd give you a talking-to."

"I've got a rich husband," Ann said. "I can afford to play around. Now suppose we talk about you, Mr. Stubbins. Where is your place of residence?"

"Place of residence." Something like a smile wobbled on Stubbins's red squashy mouth. "Oh, I like that. Sounds beautiful. My place of residence, young woman—South Arizona Avenue, and—is it Twelfth or Thirteenth Street? Twelfth, definitely Twelfth. Turn left and go up the alley." A kind of laugh, more like a thin cackle, came out of him. "Yes, that's my place of residence, my dear Mrs. Swenson. Been in occupancy there for—how long is it now? Three, four months, since the weather started turning warm. Nice little place, smooth concrete, room enough for my mat, my pillow—which serves as my sweater or, if you will, my undervest during the daytime hours—a few other necessities. Unpretentious, but I call it home. Have to be moving out of there pretty soon though. Feeling a nip in the air these last few days, one great disadvantage of my alleyway— no central heating. Time to head for my winter quarters."

"Where would they be?"

"Wherever, wherever." He made a vague gesture in the air. "There's a pleasant little living complex under the bridge. You know the Pinecreek Bridge, in the west side of town? Excellent accommodations, southern exposure, decent shelter from the wind. Problem, of course, is finding a free spot. Much in de-mand as the days grow shorter."

"You know what the district attorney's office is accusing you of, don't you?"

"Oh yes. Yes." His voice was down to a hoarse mutter. "They say I killed her—that's it, isn't it?"

"Why would they think so? What's your connection with Edna Pulaski?"

"Pulaski? Yes, that was her name. Policeman told me it was—this morning, when they put me in the car. Funny name for a Chinese woman—wasn't she a Chinese woman?"

"Korean. Pulaski was her husband's name."

"Oh yes. Well, that explains it."

"So how did you come to know her?"

"Didn't know her. Never said a word to her. Till last night. Used to see her, from my alleyway. She lived in the house two doors down—used to see her coming out the door, walking along the street. Attractive woman. Late thirties, early forties. Difficult to tell with Oriental women. Small. Not exactly my type—prefer the tall ones myself, big bones, big busts—doesn't prevent me appreciating other types though. Truly good taste is inclusive rather than exclusive—what I always say."

"Did you know who she was when you saw her walking along the street? What she did for a living?"

A little sigh came rasping out of him. "Had a good idea. Something about the look of her. Way she walked. The paint on her face. She was a whore. Am I wrong about that? Hope I'm wrong, poor woman. No sort of life for anybody."

"You were close, I'm afraid," Ann said. "But I take it you never had occasion to . . . make use of her services?"

Stubbins produced the thin cackle again. "Alas, even if I had the means, it's been many years since I had the *means*—if you follow my drift. But I thank you for asking the question, most flattering of you."

"How *did* you get involved with her then?"

"Damned if I know. Used to see her on the street off and on—already told you that, didn't I?—never exchanged a word with her. Not even the ritual 'have a good one'—so pervasive in this part of the world, you know. Until last night." He stopped talking and a shudder came over him. Because of what he remembered? Or was it just a sudden chill?

"What happened last night?"

"It starts when I'm fast asleep. Suddenly I'm awake, somebody's pulling me by the shoulders, telling me to wake up. It's her. This Chinese woman—Korean woman—Pulaski? 'You can't stay out here,' she's saying to me, 'you'll catch your death of cold.' It's raining, you see. Rain like ice, cold as a witch's tit. Pardon the expression, madam. 'Come in to my apartment,' she says, 'I'll give you a cup of coffee.' I have some small difficulty understanding her—her English isn't very good, Chinese accent—Korean accent, I suppose—not that I'd recognize the difference. But soon she had me by the arm, leading me into the house. Titania leading Bottom to her bower, that sort of thing. Went up some stairs, into the bower. Big room, Oriental decorations. Pictures of birds and fish and bamboo trees. Big bed, dragons on it. Drapes were pulled shut, only light from a couple of lamps on the mantelpiece—lamps had dragons on them too. She sat me down, nice comfortable easy chair, cushions trimmed with beads. In Xanadu did Kublai Khan—"

"How was she dressed?" Ann said.

"Dressed? Dear young lady, what do I know about how women are dressed? Nicely dressed—yellow and pink kimono, bit of jewelry too. Pearl necklace, earrings, ring on her finger with a big green stone."

"Did you get the impression she had dressed up for you, or was this what she ordinarily wore at night, even if she wasn't expecting a visitor?"

"Didn't get any impression one way or the other. How should *I* know what she ordinarily wore at night? Don't go out much in genteel female society these days. Lead a rather retiring life."

I spoke up, a little sharply. "She came out to your alley in the cold rain, wearing nothing but a kimono?"

"No, no. Had a raincoat too. Took it off when she got into the apartment."

"So what happened then?" Ann said.

"Asked me if I'd have a cup of coffee. Naturally I accepted the offer. Never turn down a free cup of coffee, a principle with me. Or any of the hard stuff either. She went out in the kitchen, came back with a cup of coffee, said there was only enough coffee in the pot for one cup, said she could make more later if she wanted any for herself. Kind young woman. Very kind. Pretty little thing too."

"She came back into the room with your coffee?"

"Yes, put it on a little table—Chinesey sort of table—next to the chair. She sat down on the bed—crossed her legs—facing me. She turned down the sound on the television—"

"Television?"

"Didn't I say? Had the television on when I got there. Watching some movie."

"What movie?" Roger said. Usually, when he sat in on an interview with Ann or me, he listened pretty much in silence. But he couldn't keep his mouth shut when the subject was movies. They were the passion of his life. Sometimes I thought he had seen every one that was ever made, including the ones that were made fifty years before he was born. I used to tell him what a shame it was that he had wasted his childhood and adolescence on such a frivolous hobby, but Mom always came to his defense. "Better he should've taken drugs and drank whiskey and ruined his eardrums with this loud music?"

"Old movie," Stubbins said, scrunching up his nose in thought. "Remember seeing it years ago, when it first came out. Those three crazy brothers—one of them had a mustache, one of them had an Italian accent, one of them didn't talk—"

"The Marx Brothers," Roger said. "Which Marx Brothers movie was it?"

"Never remember the names of them. They're at the race-track. The one that doesn't talk with the blonde curls, he's the jockey, galloping on the horse—"

"*A Day at the Races,*" Roger said. "It's got that hilarious scene in it where Chico is selling ice cream—" He broke off, blushing, as if he had suddenly remembered where he was. You do a lot of blushing when you're twenty-three.

"So she turned down the television," Ann said.

"Yes, just the sound, didn't turn off the picture. Got very upset actually. Said she'd seen this movie before. 'All reruns,' she said. 'On television are nothing but reruns.' Then she started talking."

"What about?"

"What about? Difficult for me to remember exactly. Men. Yes, she talked about men. Rather bitterly, yes. They use you, and then they betray you. But she wasn't going to let them get away with it, she said. She told him she was going to expose him to the world."

Ann leaned forward a little. "Sounds as if she wasn't talking about men in general. Was she talking about some specific man?"

"Could be. Who knows? Didn't mention any names. Tell you the truth, wasn't listening so carefully by then. Head beginning to spin a bit. Getting dizzy. Voice going in and out, room swaying up and down like water. Then I heard the noise."

"What noise?"

"Rapping noise. Rap, rap, rap."

"Somebody knocking on her door?"

"Yes, that was it. She got up from the bed, went across the room. I saw the door opening, somebody coming in. Heard her calling out—angry. 'Rerun! Had enough rerun! No more!' Odd thing for her to say, I thought. Somebody comes to visit her, first thing she does is complain about television shows. Was it somebody who worked for a television network? Producer, writer? Last thought I remember having. Next moment I was out like a light."

"Can you describe the man who came into her room?"

"Can't even be sure it was a man. Could've been a woman. Or a small child. Never got a real look at this person at all." He looked puzzled for a moment. "You suppose—this was the one that killed her?"

"It seems very probable," Ann said.

"Didn't kill me though. Let me sleep there all night. How come?"

"Maybe because he—or she—saw you were out like a light," I said, "and knew you couldn't make an identification."

"What time was it when this person got there?" Ann asked.

"Time? Yes, I can tell you that. Eleven thirty-five."

"You don't have a watch, do you?" I said, sharp again.

"No, no, no. Once I did—dear dead days beyond recall. What ever happened to that lovely watch? Inscription on the back of it too. Hope it found a good home. No, I saw the time on her clock—big clock on the mantelpiece, gold numbers, Oriental designs all over it. Clock said eleven thirty-five."

"Now tell us what happened when you woke up," Ann said.

"First thing I noticed, terrible headache, somebody jumping up and down on my head. Then the light coming through the windows, coming around the sides of the drapes, lamps weren't turned on any more. Staring into that dead television screen— then I heard the screaming. Lot of words I couldn't make out, didn't sound like English. Little old lady, Chinese lady, in the doorway, screaming her head off."

"What time in the morning was this?"

"Didn't notice, didn't look at the clock. They told me later, though, it was seven o'clock."

"Did you say anything to the old Chinese lady?"

"Korean actually. Found out later it was the mother, the Pulaski woman's mother. No time to say anything to her. She ran out the door, heard her running down the stairs. Then I realized I was on the floor, next to the easy chair. Tried to get up—then I saw her. The woman—stretched across the bed, sheets all bunched up around her. Knew right away she was dead. Seen plenty of dead people since I moved onto the street."

"Could you tell the cause of her death?"

"Couldn't tell. Face all blue and bloated, eyes bulging out. Policemen told me later she was strangled. Didn't examine her at the time, got the hell out of there. Down the stairs, out to the street—right into the arms of the policemen. They put me into the police car—here I am."

We looked at him a while in silence. There isn't much to say after you hear a story like that.

He spoke up again, hesitantly. "Thing I've been wondering about. Over and over, going through my head. Do you think— Was there some kind of drug in the coffee she gave me? Come to think of it— Why only one cup? Why didn't she drink any of it herself?"

"You think you were drugged?"

"Knockout drops, something like that? Happened so fast, you see. One minute I'm wide awake, next minute—"

"Why should Edna Pulaski want to give you knockout drops?" I said. I'm afraid I couldn't keep the skepticism out of my voice.

"Don't know, don't know." He shook his head, looking very troubled. "Can't believe it really. Such a kind lady. Why should she bother to be so kind? Most people aren't. Hold their nose, throw a quarter in the hat, run in the other direction. Can't blame them actually. Kind lady like that—can't believe she'd want to hurt me."

"Do you have any reason to think," Ann said, "that anybody else was in the apartment when Edna Pulaski brought you there?"

"She said there was nobody else in the house."

"Could somebody have been hiding there? Did you hear any noises—from a closet or the bathroom maybe? From the kitchen?"

"Didn't hear a thing. Isn't a very big apartment, you know."

"Until last night," Ann said, "you and Edna Pulaski never said a word to each other?"

"Never. Told you that already."

"You never knew her at any time in your past life? Because if you did, Mr. Stubbins, I promise you the district attorney's office will find out about it. If they dig up any past connection between the two of you, that'll be the end of our case. You'll go to prison, maybe even the gas chamber."

"No connection. Assure you. Word of honor." He drew himself up a little. "Gentleman and scholar."

Ann said nothing for a moment. Then she said, "What *is* your past life, Mr. Stubbins? Where do you come from? How did you get— What did you do before you came to Mesa Grande?"

Stubbins's red eyes shifted away from Ann's gaze. His voice lowered to that hoarse mutter again. "Didn't do anything. Didn't come from anywhere."

"You must've had a home once. A job. A family. If you tell us something about yourself, we might be able to use it in court, the information could help you."

"There's nobody!" His voice got louder, and his eyes flashed up at us. "No name! Irrelevant! Don't ask me about him, no more questions about him—" He lowered his head again, and it was clear we weren't going to get anything else out of him.

Ann sighed and got to her feet. Roger and I stood up too. "Just one more question," Ann said. "For the record. Mr. Stubbins, did you kill Edna Pulaski?"

His head was up again, and the eyes were full of pain.

"Wouldn't do it. That pretty little thing. Didn't kill her. Never killed anybody in my whole life. Except—"

He stopped and shifted his eyes away.

"Except who?" Ann said.

"Except what's-his-name," Stubbins murmured. "Killed *him* all right. Doesn't matter though. Nobody ever goes to jail for *that.*"

We took the underground passageway that connected the jail to the courthouse. While we walked, I sounded off. Frustration makes it hard for me to keep quiet.

"What do you think?" I said. "Is there one chance in a million that he's telling the truth? I haven't heard such a crazy whopper in twenty years! Here's this madam, this hardboiled flesh peddler, and all of a sudden, out of the kindness of her heart, she feels sorry for a homeless old man on the street and takes him into her house to rescue him from the cold! My God, it's like a bad Christmas special on TV! God bless us every one!

"And what's the first thing she does when she gets him into her room? She sits down on the bed cross-legged and tells him—a complete stranger—about her unsatisfactory love life, and how a man has betrayed her, so she's going to get even by exposing him. And at that very moment, there's a knock on the door, and her murderer walks in—but our hero can't describe this murderer because he, very conveniently, is knocked out by a mickey in his coffee.

"You've pulled some rabbits out of your hat before, Ann, but this time you're going to need a genuine miracle."

"Maybe the implausibility of his story is the best thing that's going for him," Roger said. "I mean, would anybody invent such a fantastic story if it wasn't true?"

"An old bum whose brain has been turned to mud by alcohol—or malnutrition—or misery—why not? It's probably been a long time since he could tell the difference between fantasy and reality."

"You don't know that for a fact, Dave. Don't we have to give him the benefit of the doubt? You and Ann have told me plenty of times that every defendant is entitled to his day in court. He's presumed to be innocent until he's found—"

"That's a beautiful ideal," I said. "Until you run across a disaster area like Harry Stubbins—"

"Gentlemen." Ann broke into our argument with one quiet word, but it was enough to make us both shut up. "Not much use in fighting about this, is there?" she went on. "Our job right now, I would think, is to *do* something. We need facts. We need evidence. We need to start digging. Roger, why don't you spend the morning looking into a few things—find out if any of the TV stations really did show that Marx Brothers movie at eleven-thirty last night, find out how long Stubbins has been living in that alley and whether anybody has seen him hanging around Edna Pulaski, see if you can come up with anything about Stubbins's background.

"We'll go right up to Grantley's office, Dave. He loves to hear the sound of his own voice. Shouldn't be too long before he tells us everything they know."

We took the elevator at the end of the underground passageway and stopped at the second floor, the DA's floor. Ann and I got out, and Roger stayed in the elevator to go on up to the fourth floor.

Ann and I started along the corridor, hoping the assistant DA would be waiting for us as he had promised. Consideration for the public defender's convenience isn't a high priority in our city administration. Not too many of our clients are regular voters.

Grantley was there. His office wasn't as spacious as McBride's, his desk wasn't as big, the wall paneling wasn't as oaky and the chairs as large and leathery. But it was snazzy enough compared to what Ann and I had to live with.

And the room was filled with Grantley's style and personality. The walls were decorated with prints of modern paintings: landscapes that looked like geometry, portraits of women with two noses, that sort of thing. It would never have occurred to McBride to put up such pictures in his office. His walls were covered with photographs of himself grinning at political celebrities—presidential candidates, congressmen, state legislators, many of them long forgotten. Whenever people like that passed through town—usually on the campaign trail—McBride made sure to get his picture taken with them.

"Come in, come in, so glad you could spare the time," Grantley said, rising up from his desk, going around to shake hands with us. "Please make yourselves comfortable. I'd send the girl for coffee, only there *is* no girl today, is there? We're all on our own. This working on Sunday is a real burden, isn't it? That's a lovely dress you're wearing, Ann, if you don't mind my saying so."

His words were accompanied by an earnest look on his face, letting us know that our interests were what he cared for most in the world. This was Grantley's peculiar form of camouflage. I had enough experience with him by now to discount it completely. He could play just as dirty as Marvin McBride; he simply covered it up more smoothly. That's what they teach you at Harvard.

"Well now." Grantley settled back in his chair, beaming at us. "You've had a chance to talk to your new client, have you? Poor old fellow. How do people manage to fall so low in the world? And he's going to fall even lower before long, I'm afraid."

"Why so?" Ann asked.

"What I mean is, he'll end his days in a prison cell, won't he? If not worse. We'll go for first degree, of course, but I grant you the jury may feel a certain sympathy for him and recommend something less than the death penalty."

"You're convinced it's an open-and-shut case, are you?"

"Oh, I wouldn't go so far as to say *that.* No case is open and shut, is it? You can never be absolutely sure what juries are going to do. But I *will* say one thing—we don't often get a murder in which the guilty party is waiting for us patiently at the scene of the crime."

"That doesn't bother you just a little bit? If Harry Stubbins killed the woman in the middle of the night, why wouldn't he get out of there as fast as his legs could carry him? Why take a snooze right next to the body, and stay there for seven hours, as if he *wanted* to be found there in the morning?"

"Naturally we don't believe Stubbins *meant* to fall asleep by the body. He'd been drinking all night. And he was exhausted from the strain of strangling her. He intended to get out of there right away, but he passed out."

"And why was he there in the first place? Have you figured out what motive he had for killing her?"

"He broke into her room to rob her. These derelicts are always badly in need of money to support their drinking habit, and Edna Pulaski used to wear a lot of jewelry, right out in public. I saw her body myself, earlier this morning, just before the morgue people took it away from the scene. She was wearing several valuable-looking pieces—earrings, a necklace, a ring with a large green stone on it—quite a temptation for somebody like Stubbins. What happened, of course, was that he didn't think she was in the house when he broke in, she caught him at it, he panicked and killed her."

"And it doesn't bother you that Stubbins is small and old and a physical wreck, not exactly the type who's likely to strangle somebody very effectively?"

"The victim was small too, smaller than Stubbins. And of course we all know how much strength people can summon up if they're desperate enough. The desire to commit murder produces a surge of adrenaline—"

"*Did* he rob her?" Ann said. "I assume the police officers searched him when they arrested him. Did they find any of her valuables on him?"

"No, they didn't. That's not at all surprising though. He didn't have time to take anything from her apartment. He passed out before he could."

"Stubbins thinks he was drugged. He thinks there were knockout drops in the coffee she gave him."

"Oh, really, Ann." On Grantley's face was the kind of smile that makes you wish somebody would plant a bomb under the

Harvard Law School and blow it all the way up to heaven where it likes to think it came from.

"Did you test what was left in that coffee cup? Did you make any tests on Stubbins, to determine if there was any drug in his system?"

"Naturally we did. We've taken samples of blood and urine from Stubbins, and we've sent the coffee cup and the pot down to the lab. We'll have the report first thing in the morning, and of course we'll pass the results on to you immediately. We *aren't* trying to railroad anybody, believe me."

"What about fingerprints? Stubbins's prints would be in the room, and so would Edna Pulaski's—but maybe there are others. For instance, the prints of the person who came through the door just as Stubbins was passing out."

"That person is obviously a figment of Stubbins's imagination. Figments don't usually leave fingerprints. However, we *did* give that room, and in fact the rest of the house, a thorough dusting for fingerprints, and we'll have *that* information tomorrow morning too. Anything else you'd like to know?"

"Have you established the time of death yet?"

"We've been in touch with the coroner, but he can't perform the autopsy till early tomorrow morning. You wouldn't expect him to give up his Sunday poker game, would you?"

"What about the murder weapon?" I said. "What was she strangled with, or did the killer use his bare hands?"

"The killer used some type of heavy cloth. We don't know what exactly, because it was removed from the woman's neck. Small traces of fabric were found in the bruises. We've sent them to the lab along with everything else."

"Why would Harry Stubbins remove that piece of cloth?"

"That's fairly obvious, isn't it? It must have been something, some object, that he thought we could trace to him if we found it. Many of these street people wear ropes around their waist to hold their pants up, their belts having disintegrated long ago. Maybe Stubbins used his rope to kill Edna Pulaski."

"*Was* there a rope around his waist when he got arrested?"

"Well, yes, there was."

"Are you testing it to see if the fibers match the ones on the victim's neck?"

"We are. But the point is a minor one. Even if it turns out this particular rope *wasn't* the murder weapon, that simply means he used something else."

"Did that search the officers made of him come up with anything else?"

"As a matter of fact, it didn't. Obviously, whatever he used to strangle her—assuming it wasn't the rope—he disposed of it before he was arrested. He could have thrown it out the kitchen window, there's an alley in back."

"Have you searched that alley for the weapon?"

"No, we didn't do that actually. It seemed pointless. There's so much junk out there, it's been accumulating for years, how could we ever determine what did or didn't belong to Stubbins? At any rate, it doesn't really matter. I assure you our case is just as strong without the murder weapon."

"Well, we'll thrash all that out in court, won't we?" Ann said. "Now we have to move on to a very important matter—bail for my client."

"Bail?" Grantley's eyebrows lifted slightly. "I'm afraid you'll have to take that up with the district attorney. I don't have the authority to—"

"Come on, Leland. It's your case, you can decide—"

"Excuse me, did I forget to tell you? It's Marvin's case. I'll be giving him as much help as I can, considering my own case-load, but he's put himself personally in charge. He was in his office a moment ago, but I think I saw him leave. He mentioned he was going out to his campaign headquarters to confer with Ed Brock—"

"Wait a minute!" I said. "You're telling us that Marvin McBride got up and went to work before noon—and on a *Sunday* morning!" I couldn't sit still in my seat. This news positively required jumping to my feet. "Next you'll be telling me they've repealed the law of gravity!"

"Well, I'm certainly not telling you *that.*" Grantley smiled gently. "I do expect Marvin back in an hour or so, however. I'll leave a memo for him that you were asking about the bail matter, and I'm sure he'll touch bases with you."

"Tell him I'll be out finding a judge," Ann said. "And that judge will be giving me a writ of habeas corpus. So if Marvin's going to raise some objections, he'd *better* touch bases with me."

With her sweetest smile, she swept out of the room.

FOUR

The clock in the courthouse tower was just striking twelve as Ann and I headed back to the office. Mabel Gibson wasn't there, of course; on Sundays she clucks over her real family, especially her new grandchild, just as on weekdays she does her clucking over Ann, Roger, and me.

Once inside, what I wanted to do was listen to Ann's comments on the incredible news we had just heard—the Miraculous Transfiguration of Marvin McBride. But before I had a chance to say a word, the phone in my cubbyhole started ringing.

I went in there, shut the door, and picked up the receiver. "So where have you been?" said Mom's voice. "I tried you at your house an hour ago. You didn't answer, I was sure you were working."

I knew what she wanted, of course. The murder had been discovered too late for this morning's paper, but it must be all over the TV news by now.

"I saw it on the television," she said. "The eleven o'clock news broadcast. With pictures of the dead body—terrible, terrible, such a little woman! And the assistant district attorney, this Grantley fellow, talked to the television reporter, he said this is a murder investigation like any other one, and the fact that the dead woman was one of society's enemies, and the accused suspect was one of society's dregs, wouldn't stop the DA's office from putting their full resources into the case. Isn't it a coincidence? Only last night the district attorney's election opponent challenges him to take charge of the next murder investigation that comes along—and this morning, a few hours later, one comes along. So is your office defending this fellow they arrested, this bum?"

"We don't like to refer to our clients by such names, Mom. He's an unfortunate victim of a society that turned affluent before it was ready and wasn't able to take all its members along with it. He's not a bum, he's a social problem."

"Thank you very much. So do you know anything already that wasn't on the news?"

I told her everything I knew. I learned a long time ago that it's no use holding out on Mom. If I do she never complains, but suddenly her living room is dark with reproachful looks. They seem to infect the air, the furniture, the very schnecken that she serves with coffee.

When I got to the end of my story, I heard her give a little sigh. "So it isn't much. But after lunch you'll take a look at the scene of the crime, wouldn't you? You'll talk to the dead woman's mother, you'll question some witnesses, you'll have a lot more to report."

"I hope so, Mom. Nothing looks very encouraging so far."

"Absolutely not. Except for one little thing."

"In our client's favor? I'd love to hear it."

"Naturally. According to the assistant district attorney, this Harry Stubbins killed the woman, and then the shock and the liquor he drank knocked him unconscious so he couldn't run away from her room?"

"That's right, Mom. It's a hard line of reasoning to argue with."

"Maybe so," Mom said. "But here's a funny little question. If he killed her, and then he passed out on the floor and didn't wake up till seven in the morning—will you tell me please, how come, when the body was found, the lamps were turned out and the television set was off? A dead woman and an unconscious man couldn't do this. So don't this suggest to you that maybe there *was* a third party who came into the room, like your Stubbins is saying? Maybe this Edna was still alive when Stubbins passed out, and maybe she turned off the television herself so she and this third party could talk? And maybe this third party killed her, and turned out the lamps so her lights wouldn't be seen from the street and nobody would call the police to investigate?"

I couldn't deny it, Mom had made a good point. But it took me only a few seconds to come up with an answer. "Edna Pulaski's mother—the old lady who found Stubbins with the body—*she* must've turned out the lamps and turned off the TV when she got there this morning."

"Not possible," Mom said. "When Stubbins woke up, he saw this old lady screaming in the doorway, isn't this right—and the next second he sees the lamps and the television aren't on? So you're telling me, when this old lady got to the room and found her daughter's body, the first thing she did was she turned off the lamps and the television, and *then* she went to the door and started screaming? All right, even assuming she's got a terrible dislike for wasting electricity, this is a peculiar way to behave."

"Well—maybe Stubbins is lying about the TV and the lamps being on in the first place. After all, we've only got his word for it."

"Why should he tell such a lie? It don't help his case if the dead woman was or wasn't looking at the television, or if the lamps were or weren't lit, when he came into her room. There's no point to such a lie. Things that got no point to them make me nervous, they *ootch* at me, I can't get them out from my mind. All right, we need more facts before we can talk some more. When you go to this Pulaski woman's apartment today, you'll find out a couple of things for me."

"What things, Mom?"

"First, you should find out what was the state of this Pulaski woman's health. Did she have some type condition that maybe she was being treated for?"

"What makes you think she *did?*"

"I don't think she did, I don't think she didn't. I'm asking you should find out."

"All right, what's the second thing?"

"You should find out was she a big drinker? How did she feel about alcoholic liquor?"

"But what does it matter—"

"Never mind matters. Only ask."

God, she gets me furious when she does that! Putting on this big mystery act, like I was some stupid kid and there was no point explaining things to me. And the reason for it is, I *am* a kid, in Mom's eyes. I've never grown older than ten or twelve, as far as she's concerned, even though I've been married and widowed, and I've earned my own living since the age of twenty-one.

One of these days, I told myself, there's going to be a show-down between Mom and me. I'm going to make it clear to her once and for all that I'm a grown man in my fifties and she can't give me orders anymore.

"Okay, I'll find out all that if I can," I said.

"And maybe tonight you and Roger will come over for dinner. You're both looking a little thin lately, I'll make a nice chicken pot pie and fatten you up."

And while she was fattening us up, I thought, she would also be pumping us about the murder.

I hung up. Election day, I thought, is a symbol of freedom and independence. So maybe, by election day, I'd get up the nerve to acquire some of my own.

FIVE

Some days, in this job, you just don't get to eat lunch. It was half an hour past noon already, and I had a feeling this was going to be one of those days. That's why I keep a supply of Hershey bars, with almonds, in my glove compartment. I wolfed one of them down while I was driving to South Arizona Avenue.

Long wide avenues in Mesa Grande tend to be named after either states or people. The ones that are named after people are lined with beautiful old trees and sweep through neighborhoods with big expensive houses on either side. The people they were named after were once distinguished big shots in town; naming an avenue after them was meant to be a compliment. The avenues that got named after states, on the other hand, are the ones that never could have been used to flatter anybody.

Arizona Avenue, one of our longest thoroughfares, is very wide, with an island in the middle to separate northbound from southbound traffic. It passes through the sleazy motel/honkeytonk section at the extreme north and the even sleazier motel/honkeytonk section at the extreme south. In between it touches on some respectable commercial and residential neighborhoods, but none of them is more than modest in appearance or cost. Nobody in our upper crust lives or works on Arizona Avenue.

Edna Pulaski's house, on South Arizona, was two stories

high, the first story long and wide, the second story much smaller, as if it had been stuck on top as an afterthought. The outside of the house was more or less white, with only the tiniest scrub of lawn between its front porch and the street. Sticking up from this lawn was a post with a white piece of board nailed to it. Painted on this board, in large black capital letters, were these words:

Massage Parlor.
Clean Rooms. Expert Masseuses.
Good for Your Health.
E. Pulaski, Prop.

On one side of the house was a small dilapidated-looking motel, with a neon sign that wasn't lit up yet. On the other side of it was a fast food hamburger joint and next to that was a tiny drugstore on whose front window, in whitewash, was the announcement that it was open "all nite." Directly across the street was another motel, just as small and dilapidated-looking, and a fast food fish joint.

This block and the two or three surrounding it would have looked exactly like all the others that stretched along South Arizona Avenue, except for one distinctive feature. Many of the signs mixed strings of Chinese letters (or Korean or Vietnamese letters, I couldn't tell the difference) with the English ones.

A lot of Asians have moved into Mesa Grande in the last thirty-five years or so, first a wave of them from Korea after the war, then from Vietnam after *that* war, and most recently from mainland China. The blocks that intersect South Arizona Avenue to the east and west are pretty much segregated: There's a Chinese enclave, a Vietnamese enclave, even a small one that's Japanese. Which became which was just a fluke, I suppose, depending on who happened to be the first to settle where; once the lines were drawn, they were reinforced by the streams of relations and friends who followed. The different groups get along peaceably with one another, but they keep to themselves. The people who live in the block where Edna Pulaski's house was located are mostly Korean.

Anyway, on this chilly Sunday afternoon, dozens of people from all four Asian groups—and also a lot of whites—were milling around in front of the house and spilling into the street. Some uniformed cops were guarding the entrance, keeping the gawkers from getting too close, and three or four hand-held TV cameras were adding to the congestion. Some of it had even spilled out into the street. You don't see too many classic New York–type traffic jams in Mesa Grande, with wheels screeching, horns honking, exhausts and tempers boiling over. I knew I'd never be able to park on South Arizona, so I swung into a side street and found an empty spot a block and a half away.

Walking back to Edna Pulaski's house, I paused at the alleyway that Harry Stubbins had called home for the last few months. Dark, dirty, and cold—not much different, in other words, from a lot of the other "homes" our city was beginning to acquire. Who said we were the boondocks? Who said we wouldn't some day be right up there with New York, London, and all the other sophisticated cosmopolitan hellholes of the world?

The uniformed patrolman in front of the house was a kid, and not too flexible a thinker. He wanted to keep me out, even when I showed him my identification, because he'd been told to keep people out. Luckily his superior, dressed in plainclothes, came along to see what the fuss was about. It turned out to be Pat Delaney, the big red-faced captain of Homicide, probably one of the few Irish cops west of the Mississippi; the Mesa Grande force is made up mostly of Hispanics and the sons of farm boys from outlying ranch counties.

Delaney and I knew each other, and had cordial feelings toward each other, from a couple of cases in the past. "Didn't expect to run into *you* down here, Pat," I said. "What's the good of being the Big Chief if you have to work routine jobs on Sunday?"

"Routine? Didn't you hear the news? Our esteemed DA is

running this one in person. Seems he got needled a bit at some dinner last night, accused of being an absentee or some such word, and the needle is still sticking up his ass. So we've all been told to give this one the highest priority."

"Yes, I gather the young prime minister was down here this morning, looking for clues."

"The Quiz Kid from Harvard, you mean? I didn't see him myself, but I heard he dropped in and took the Grand Tour. Fortunately, the forensic boys had done their duty before he arrived—dusted for fingerprints, tested for bloodstains, vacuumed for dust and hair, photographed everything, and so forth—so there was no way he could foul up the investigation. Talking about which, I'll show you around myself if you'd like."

He let me into the house and stayed with me as I looked the place over.

Inside the front door was a small anteroom with two corridors branching off from it. The only decoration was a picture on the wall, which looked at first like one of those typical Chinese or Japanese paintings of mountains with a few trees and a waterfall nestling beneath them. Until you looked more closely and saw that those rolling hills were really the curves of a woman's shoulders and breasts, the trees were her legs, and the waterfall was what you generally found in between. Very clever optical illusion. I wondered if there was a factory somewhere that supplied them to Asian-owned massage parlors all over the country.

Delaney gave an ironic grin when he saw me looking at the picture. Then he jerked his thumb toward the corridors. "This is how you get to the rooms. The massage rooms, like. There are two of them off each hallway."

"She had four girls working for her?"

"Right. No big operation, but a nice steady profit, I'd bet. The girls weren't working last night though. We talked to them this morning, and they all had the same story: Their boss came down with the virus or something, so she gave them last night off, they went away around seven."

"They don't live here in the house? Prossies generally do."

"Not these. Pulaski's operation didn't go in for on-campus dorm living. More like a commuter college, you might say."

"Any of the commuters around for me to talk to now?"

"It's Sunday, they didn't come in today. It's only the God-fearing respectable elements in town that sell their merchandise on the Lord's day. I'll give you the names and phone numbers if you want, so you can talk to those girls personally."

We went up the stairs that began in the middle of the first-floor anteroom. On the landing at the top there was only one door, and a uniformed cop was standing in front of it. Delaney led me through it, into the late Pulaski's private apartment. It was very dim; heavy black drapes were shut across both windows.

"We've left it exactly the way we found it when we got here at seven this morning," Delaney said. "Except for the body. You want to see that, you'll have to go down to the coroner's lab."

My eyes were beginning to get adjusted to the dim light. I was in a combination living room–bedroom, which looked pretty much as Harry Stubbins had described it: flimsy lamps with Oriental shades, a couple of chairs, pictures of birds and flowers on the walls, a small statue of Buddha next to the ornate clock on the mantelpiece.

But also, mixed in with the Asian stuff, were items that came as a shock. For instance, on one wall, in a gold frame, was a reproduction of a Norman Rockwell *Saturday Evening Post* cover: a freckled-face redheaded little boy with his mouth grinning around a slice of watermelon. And on another wall was a montage of publicity stills of Elizabeth Taylor, a very young Elizabeth Taylor, in her costumes for four different roles.

What I noticed above all, though, was the bed. A big bed, with dragons carved on the headboard, and bedclothes strewn all over the place. You could still see the indentations in the sheets where the body had been lying. I was struck by the tininess of the shape. It could have been a little child's body.

"Pulaski wasn't very big, was she?" I said.

"When I saw her lying there this morning," Delaney said,

"the first thing I thought to myself was 'God damn it, another kid murder!' Then I saw she was a grown-up woman, only less than five feet tall. In her thirties, maybe older, it's hard to tell with these Oriental women. Like those face cream ads on TV. Anyway, it was a relief. I don't like kid murders."

"Was Harry Stubbins still around when you got here?"

"He was downstairs, they had him in a squad car. The two officers nabbed him just as he was trying to run for it out the front door."

"What got them there?"

"A phone call to the station house. The old lady—the dead woman's mother—found the body and ran out to the street screaming for help. She can't talk any English, so one of the neighbors made the call. The squad car was here in five minutes."

I looked around the room. A pair of sliding doors on one wall pulled aside to reveal Pulaski's closet, a long shallow space packed with clothes on hangers. Next to this was a window. I pulled aside those thick black drapes and lifted the yellow shade behind them. I found myself looking out on the motel next door, with its dead neon sign lined with Chinese letters.

The only other door led to the kitchen, so I walked through it. The kitchen was small, with only one tiny window, looking out to a back alley of dirt and concrete. Most of the space in this kitchen was taken up by a table, a sink, a refrigerator, and a stove. On the stove was a coffeepot, and below it was a cabinet full of pots and pans. Above the stove was another cabinet, which had cans and boxes of food in it. Among them I noticed four different kinds of coffee: Maxwell House regular and decaf, Italian espresso, fancy Viennese.

"She was a big coffee drinker, wasn't she?" I said.

"I guess you have to be," Delaney said, "when you work late hours."

Remembering one of the questions Mom had wanted me to ask, I realized that I hadn't come across any liquor in the apartment. Not even a bottle of wine.

I looked at the sink, which was shiny and clean. No dishwasher, but next to the sink bowl was a drainboard and a wire dishholder. No dishes were in it.

I couldn't think of anything else to look for in Pulaski's apartment, and it was beginning to depress me. These were the wages of sin? It didn't seem to pay as well as it was supposed to. So I had Delaney take me down to the street again.

The crowd in front was as thick as before, though the TV cameras had disappeared. They had to process their film, I guessed, in time for the evening news. I asked Delaney if he saw anybody there who lived in the neighborhood, close to Pulaski's house.

"You won't find out anything we didn't find out already," Delaney said. "None of the neighbors heard anything during the night. And if they did, and if it involved one of the people that lives down here, they wouldn't let us in on it anyway."

Just the same, there were some questions I had to ask, so Delaney picked out a thick-waisted Asian woman, with a gray housedress that matched her hair, and an Asian boy, about fifteen or sixteen, who was peering over a cop's shoulder from behind thick glasses. I introduced myself and said I'd like to talk to them about the victim.

"Oh, very sad," said the woman. "She very nice person, Mrs. Pulaski. Terrible what happened to her."

"You were a friend of hers?"

"Friend? Oh no. She prostitute. You think I have friends who are prostitutes? But we see her every day, my husband and me, in our grocery store. We have small store a block away, we sell vegetables, seasonings, meat, noodles, all kinds of Korea specialties. We do nice business, Chinese and Korea restaurants in town buy from us."

"Mrs. Pulaski was one of your customers too?"

"Oh yes. She buy Korea specialties from us only. She very loyal to neighborhood. She always say, 'I live here, I make my money here, I give my money back to the people here.' "

"Was she generally well liked in the neighborhood?"

"My mom and pop are down on her," said the teenage boy.

"They're always saying she's a disgrace to her people. But most of us around here liked her a lot."

"How much contact did you have with her?"

"I made a lot of deliveries to her from the liquor store."

"She did a lot of drinking?" I came out with this a little sharply, remembering how there hadn't been any liquor, not even empty bottles, anywhere in her apartment.

"Naw, she never touched the stuff. What I brought her was only Cokes and ginger ale and 7-Up, like that."

"And she was a big tipper, was she?"

"About average."

"Then why did you like her so much?"

"She was nice, that's all. She always had a joke or some funny story to tell me. 'Here's a new one I just heard, Tommy,' she'd say. And when I was leaving and told her thank you for the tip, she—she'd always—" The boy's cheeks suddenly turned red, so don't ever tell me that Asians can't blush. "She'd give me a kiss. I don't mean a *real* kiss, like on the mouth or anything. She'd just give me a kind of a quick peck on my cheek, and she'd say something like 'Come back in a couple of years, kid, and we can improve on that one.'"

The boy broke off suddenly and darted a nervous look at the woman who was standing next to him. "Mrs. Sung—you're not going to tell my folks about that, are you?"

Mrs. Sung humphed a little. "I mind my business, other people do same." She turned back to me. "One good thing you say about Mrs. Pulaski. She do bad maybe, but drinking and drugs never. Anybody do drinking and drugs on her premises, she kick them right out. Any girl who work for her she catch her with drinks or drugs, she fire quick. She don't— What she did with a customer, she don't do it if she smell liquor on breath."

"How do you know that?"

"No secret. She tell everybody how she feel about these things. She say she want to advertise it so nobody come to her who won't obey her rules."

"So she was kind of a fastidious type, was she?"

The lady shook her head. "Don't know that word."

The teenage boy spoke up. "It means very neat and tidy, very careful about things."

Mrs. Sung gave a highpitched laugh. "Neat and tidy—*she?* She one big mess. She drop something on floor, she never bother pick it up, just leave it lay. And if you ask how I know, her mother tell me. Her mother don't live with her, she live in house of her own two three block from here, Edna bought it for her. 'Edna is one big mess,' her mother always say. 'She live like pig if I don't clean up after her.' "

I decided my next step was to talk to Edna Pulaski's mother, so I asked Mrs. Sung how to get to her house. She pointed the way for me—it was a few blocks east, off South Arizona—but shook her head gloomily. "She feel very bad now, very much crying. Maybe she won't talk to you. She don't talk English."

"Would you come along with me and translate?"

Mrs. Sung looked tempted for a moment, but respectability won out over curiosity. "So sorry. Can't go into house of prostitute mother. Poor woman, not her fault. But I can't go into house that prostitute bought."

I turned to the boy and asked him if he'd translate for me. He laughed. "Hello and good-bye—that's all the Korean *I* know. My folks are always on my case about it. But to tell you the truth, *they're* forgetting what they know too."

Mrs. Kim's house, off South Arizona Avenue, was even smaller than her daughter's. It was on a block lined with small clean houses, neatly trimmed lawns, but not much in the way of decorations. Nobody in this neighborhood had iron elves or giant plastic frogs on their lawns.

I heard voices coming from inside as I climbed the wooden steps to Mrs. Kim's door. I knocked, but nobody answered. Then I saw that the door wasn't locked; evidently visitors were supposed to simply walk in.

I found myself in a corridor that had half a dozen people in it, which made it feel crowded. All of them seemed to be Asians—Koreans, I supposed, though I couldn't really tell. They were wearing sober dark clothes and talking to one another in soft voices but with great earnestness. I had the only white face in the crowd, and also I was taller than anybody else; I could see them looking at me curiously and suspiciously, but nobody did it for more than a split second, nobody was rude enough to stare.

I made my way as politely as possible into the parlor, which had twice as many people in it. Most of them were in their fifties or older, many a lot older, and only a few of them were men. Across the room I got a glimpse of a very tiny wrinkled old lady in a black housedress. I figured she was the dead woman's mother, because she was sitting in the biggest, most comfortable chair, with a circle of women gathered around her. Even at a distance I could see that her eyes were red with crying.

I didn't think it would do me any good to pull my punches, so I walked straight up to Mrs. Kim and told her I was working for the public defender's office, and I had to find out some things from her in order to prepare Harry Stubbins's defense.

She blinked up at me, as bewildered as if I'd been a visitor from another planet. Which, in a way, I was. But one of the women in the circle stood up and pushed herself between Mrs. Kim and me. "She can't understand English! Why don't you go away!"

This woman was the only one in that circle who didn't seem to be sixty or more. I would have put her in her early twenties, and she was taller than the others, better dressed, wearing lipstick and eye shadow, and talking American English without a trace of an accent.

"I've got a job to do," I said, "I'll go away after I do it. You might explain to Mrs. Kim that the public defender's office is a bona fide law enforcement agency. She has as much of a legal obligation to answer my questions as she did to answer the police's."

I have to make this speech many times during an investigation. People assume, maybe from looking at too much television, that the lawyers who defend crooks are automatically crooks themselves.

"Why do you have to bug her?" said the woman. "Can't you see what she's going through?"

I had no answer to this. Sure I saw what she was going through. But in my job you can't give too much consideration to human feelings. Sometimes there's only one way to find out what you need to know for your client: barge in early and hammer away while people are still too grief-stricken to have their guards up.

So I said to the woman, "Who are you?"

"I'm Madeleine Kim. I'm Mrs. Kim's great-niece."

"Do you speak Korean?" I said. She said her Korean was rusty but she could handle it, and I went on, "Okay, will you translate for us?" And when she opened her mouth to say something hostile: "Look, believe it or not, I'm not enjoying this any more than you are. Let's get it over with as fast as we can."

She tightened her lips but gave a nod. Then she turned to Mrs. Kim and said something that caused the old lady to focus on me with a long hard look, no mistaking the anger in it.

"Mrs. Kim, I'm sorry about your daughter," I said, looking straight into the old lady's face as I talked. I wasn't going to address myself to the interpreter even though I knew the old lady couldn't make anything out of my words. I wanted her to feel that she was conducting this conversation with me, with the law, not with some nice sympathetic intermediary. "But I'm sure you want us to find the person who killed her and punish that person for the crime."

The niece translated, and the old lady said a sentence in a low cracked voice.

"She says the murderer *has* been found. She says you're trying to save him from his punishment."

"That isn't so, Mrs. Kim. All the evidence isn't in yet, things may not be as obvious as they seem. Suppose Harry Stubbins didn't do it. You wouldn't want the *real* murderer to get away, would you?"

Another translation, and the old lady's eyes were as full of anger as before. But a few brief words came out of her, and I knew she was telling me to go ahead and ask my questions.

First I took her through the obvious things that I pretty much knew already. How she came to her daughter's apartment nearly every morning at seven o'clock. How she cleaned up the place as quietly as she could, because her daughter was never awake that early. How her daughter wouldn't do this for herself after she woke up, so there was no other way to keep her from living in mess and filth. How she came yesterday morning, Saturday, as usual, and everything seemed fine, and that was the last time she saw her daughter alive.

She then described how she had arrived this morning, and when she opened the door she saw her daughter lying on the bed. And she saw the man lying on the floor. "The little man with the dirty clothes and the hole in his teeth" was what she called him, according to her niece. And then she ran from the room, frightened that the little man who had killed her daughter would kill her too. She ran down the stairs and out to the street, crying out to people what had happened. The policemen came, and they talked to her, and then she went back to her house.

"And she's been here ever since," said the niece, no longer interpreting, putting in her own two cents instead, "with her relatives and neighbors trying to comfort her. And you don't happen to be helping much!"

I ignored the crack and turned to Mrs. Kim again. "Why did you have to clean up your daughter's place every morning? Why didn't she hire a cleaning woman?"

Mrs. Kim spoke for a while, and the niece said, "Edna wanted to hire somebody, but her mother wouldn't let her. She didn't trust any strange cleaning woman. She could do a better job herself." A sharp laugh came out of the young woman. "Anyway, my great-aunt *is* a cleaning woman. She works for half a dozen people in town; cleaning is what she does for a living."

"Was Edna Pulaski's business doing badly?" I said. "Why did she let her mother do work like that?"

"Business was terrific, from what I heard. My mother told me, she's Edna's first cousin. She doesn't approve, of course. These old Koreans think what you do reflects honor or dishonor on your ancestors. They're big on family honor, that type of thing. But my own opinion is, since prostitutes are victims of a male-dominated society, how can you blame them for—"

"Okay, okay," I said. "But could you ask her my question?"

She turned to Mrs. Kim and translated my question. The old lady answered it in a spate of words, showing more excitement than she had till now. "She says Edna told her plenty of times to stop working, she offered to give her enough money. But my great-aunt wouldn't take it. She said she had an honest job, and she wasn't going to give it up so she could live off—" Madeleine Kim gave a shake of her head. "I don't have to spell it out for you, do I?"

"If that's how Mrs. Kim felt about her daughter's work," I said, "how come she accepted a house from her?"

The question was repeated, and Mrs. Kim looked suddenly stonefaced. Her words were hard and distinct. "She needed a house to live in," said Madeleine Kim. "She couldn't live in Edna's house, under the same roof with— She couldn't live in the streets, she had to accept the house, she had no choice. But she knew it was wrong, she's never been happy about it. And it wasn't a gift. It was a loan. She was paying Edna back, as much as she could afford. Ten dollars a month."

"In other words," I said, "everything wasn't perfect between her and Edna? There was a lot of tension? Did they ever have any arguments, any fights?"

The old lady's answer came, and was duly translated. "Between daughters and mothers the road is never smooth." A sardonic laugh broke out of the niece. "Old Oriental proverb. Charlie Chan."

"If the road was so rough," I said, "why did her daughter let her have a key to her house?"

This time the answer sounded very calm, almost matter-of-fact. "Korean children don't lock their doors to their parents.

The child's house must always be open. She wants to know isn't this true for white people too? Otherwise what kind of people can you be?"

"Fair enough," I said. "Mrs. Kim, is there anybody you can think of who might've wanted to kill your daughter? Anybody who hated her or stood to gain from her death?"

As soon as this was translated, the old lady didn't even pause to think about it. Her answer came in only a few words.

"She says, Edna's life was to give people love, not hate."

I saw no trace of irony on the old lady's face. I saw no expression there at all, in fact. "What about Edna's ex-husband—Pulaski? Was he bitter when the marriage broke up? Is he still living in town?"

This time the old lady took much longer to answer. "She says Edna's husband was a hardworking honest man, and he wanted Edna to give up the life she was leading. That's why the marriage broke up, because she wouldn't listen to him. He wasn't bitter about it. Just sad."

I was about to thank her and go away, but then I remembered the second question Mom had told me to ask; I could almost hear Mom's voice inside my head, insisting.

"Could you tell me something about your daughter's health?" I said. "Was she being treated for any kind of disease or condition, anything like that?"

The old lady gave a frown at this, then she spread her hand over her chest, above her heart. After a while Madeleine Kim said, "She says her daughter had a heart condition, it was diagnosed several years ago. She's got pills that she takes regularly, and now it seems to be under control."

All right, so now I knew. But what the hell did this information *mean?*

I decided I'd just about worn out my welcome. "Okay, Mrs. Kim, thank you for—"

But the old lady wasn't through with me. Suddenly she leaned forward, and her hands, bony and creased with wrinkles, shot forward and clutched at my arm. The grip was as feeble as you might imagine, but still I found I couldn't bring myself to pull away from it. As if I was afraid one of those fingers might break off if I did.

She started talking. The voice rose, got loud, but not excited. She talked for a few seconds, very deliberately and intently, and then, just as suddenly, she let go of my arm and fell back in her chair. The effort seemed to have taken something out of her. She shut her eyes.

"What she says—" Madeleine Kim frowned and creased her forehead. " 'Between me and Edna there wasn't always love and peace. Even so, I hate the man that killed her. He has robbed me of the only joy I could still look forward to in life. For that I'll never forgive him.' "

I nodded and held my hand out to Mrs. Kim. She didn't open her eyes.

Madeleine Kim saw me through the crowd and out the front door. I thanked her for her help and held my hand out to her, and after a moment she shook it. And then her lips curled in a sarcastic grin. "I'll even do you a favor," she said. "Talk to Mr. Chang."

"Who's he?"

"Raymond Chang. He runs the pharmacy on South Arizona, two houses down from Edna's place. Actually he's not Korean, he's Chinese. And he's very old."

"And why should I talk to him?"

"Because the police did, everybody here knows about it."

I thanked her for the suggestion. Then she went back into the house, and I walked to the pharmacy whose "open all nite" sign I had noticed earlier.

The man behind the counter was wearing a white coat and a thin white goatee. He was old all right; his face might have been a piece of parchment dug up by archeologists from some ancient tomb. But he held his shoulders straight, and his voice, though soft, didn't have a quaver in it.

I had no idea what I was trying to find out from him, but I phrased my questions so that he might think I knew.

After telling him who I was, I said, "I understand you talked to the police this morning, Mr. Chang?"

"That is correct. I have told my story several times already. First to the police officer in plainclothes. Then to the assistant district attorney. Mr. Grantley, I believe."

"I know the general outlines of your story, of course," I said. "The police have to keep my office informed of anything they dig up. What you can do is fill me in on the details."

Mr. Chang was brief but complete; in a court of law he'd be the perfect witness. What it boiled down to was, last night Mr. Chang was alone in his pharmacy. A common state of affairs for him, because he kept the place open all night, as advertised, but after dark he was always the only one there; his assistant pharmacist came at ten in the morning, and then Mr. Chang slept till six in the evening. So, at five minutes after midnight—Mr. Chang was very precise about the time, he had carefully checked the clock on the pharmacy wall—he happened to look through the window out to the street.

He saw a man come walking by. Shuffling indecisively would be more accurate. The man paused at the corner, under the street lamp, struggling to light a cigarette in the rain, and Mr. Chang got a clear look at him. He was a small stocky figure in jeans and a leather jacket, with a shock of thick red hair, and Mr. Chang, though he hadn't seen this man in several years, recognized him immediately. It was Ron Pulaski, Edna's ex-husband.

"Which direction was he walking in, Mr. Chang?"

"One moment, let me think. Yes. He was moving from left to right. Moving north."

In other words, away from Edna Pulaski's house. And five minutes after midnight was half an hour or so after Harry Stubbins went out like a light in Edna's bedroom.

Then something occurred to me. "Mr. Chang, you told this story to the assistant district attorney this morning?"

"Yes. We spoke right here in this shop."

"Around what time was that?"

"At eight-thirty perhaps."

"Is that a fact? Just one more question, Mr. Chang. Did you know Edna Pulaski?"

"Oh yes. She was a customer of mine. I made up her heart medicine for her." He mentioned a brand name. "It's a common enough remedy, one of the so-called beta blockers. It stabilizes the heartbeat, reduces the risk of angina attacks."

"Angina was what Mrs. Pulaski suffered from?"

"So her doctor seemed to think."

"What did you think of her, Mr. Chang? What kind of person was she?"

His expression remained amiable and bland, as he thought this over for a moment. "Her intentions were good," he finally answered. "She was like all of us whose intentions are good."

"Meaning?"

"She did terrible things."

As I trudged back to the meter, a couple of blocks away, where my car was parked, my anger started boiling up in me.

All the time Ann and I were talking to Grantley this morning, the little rat was sitting on the testimony of a witness who could've been a big help in our case. And since Marvin McBride had put himself in charge of the case, who could doubt that Grantley was keeping his mouth shut on McBride's orders?

Then it occurred to me that Chief of Detectives Pat Delaney must have known all about this witness too, even while he was being so "honest" and "open" with me. But how could I really get mad at him for it? I would've played it the same way myself, in the old days.

Back in my car, I headed for the nearest corner phone booth and looked up Pulaski in the book. (In Mesa Grande, you can still find phone books in the outdoor phone booths. They haven't all been ripped off by the public yet, though who knows, in a few years we may catch up.) There was Edna and only one other; he called himself Ron, not Ronald. Typical for this section of the world, where perfect strangers address you by your first name the first time they meet you and give you a nickname the second time.

I didn't call the number; the address was ten minutes away, so I drove there, taking a chance he'd be in. Sometimes you waste your time doing that, but the advantage of catching people off guard is worth it.

The state freeway cuts through the middle of Mesa Grande, separating the east side of town, which is growing rapidly, from the west side of town, which has stopped dead on account of the mountains. Pulaski lived in a west side neighborhood that huddles in the shadow of the freeway.

This neighborhood is known as Horoscope Way and consists of half a dozen streets named after the signs of the zodiac. The houses here, put up around the time of World War I by some builder whose wife believed in astrology, are all two stories high, with identical square porches jutting out in front and identical flat slate roofs topping them off. They probably had a nice cozy feeling to them once, when they were surrounded by acres of trees and other greenery, but that was a long time ago. The cozy little houses had turned into shabby dilapidated shanties, a good deal of slate had slid off the roofs, ancient paint was flaking from the porches, and the trees and assorted greenery were long gone. Horoscope Way was now surrounded by auto repair garages and used car lots, and the dominant color had changed from green to sludge gray.

Ron Pulaski's house, at 10 Capricorn Street, was identical in squalidness to all the houses around it. I found Pulaski in a tiny living room, with furniture and a carpet that Goodwill had no doubt been glad to get rid of. He was short and heavyset, had thick red hair and bushy red eyebrows. He hadn't shaved or combed his hair yet, and he was still in his underwear shirt. He was mad as hell at my dropping in without warning, but I gave him my spiel about the legal authority of the public defender's office, and what could he do about it?

With him was a girl, maybe in her late twenties, maybe older, shortish and squat, with long hair that was blonde but not quite to the roots. She was wearing a loose housedress that didn't do much to modify the outlines of her breasts. She introduced herself as Brigitte Martine. "That's not my given name," she said. "That's my stage name. My given name wasn't appropriate, careerwise."

"You're an actress?" I asked. "Are you in a show?"

"Actually I'm waitressing right now. I'm between engagements. I feel it's very important for me not to accept just any role, I have to really believe in it—"

"Nobody's interested," Pulaski said. "He's here to talk business, so why don't you get the hell out?"

"What am I going to do, Ronnie? I don't go on till four."

"Go to a movie. Get some fresh air. How many years is it since you breathed any fresh air?"

She whined and flounced a little more, but she got out.

As soon as I was alone with him, Pulaski offered me a beer. I said I wasn't thirsty, and he shrugged, padded out to the kitchen in his torn bedroom slippers, and padded back with the can in his hand. He took big slurps from it every few minutes, as the interview went on.

He admitted that he'd been walking on his ex-wife's street a little after midnight last night. "That's when I got there," he said, "well, a couple minutes before midnight. But I didn't kill her. I couldn't of. I got the perfect alibi."

"What's that?"

"From nine o'clock till ten minutes of twelve, I was at my weekly bowling. Out at the Sagebrush Alleys, on east Montana. I was with my team, we're the Pulverizin' Plumbers, there's five of us. We were bowling a match against the Slammin' Steamfitters. We did pretty good, beat them five frames to three. From what I hear, the guy who killed Edna got to her place at eleven-thirty—which was just about the time I was making two spares in a row to clinch the last frame."

"You didn't sneak out of your bowling alley for a few minutes maybe?"

"You think I did, talk to the people that was there. There was ten of them between the two teams, more if you include the wives and floozies. I didn't bring mine along though, she's working her shift till eleven. Besides, she gets on my nerves when I'm bowling, with all that jumping up and down and squealing. Anyway, all of them that were there'll tell you I was with them the whole time. I was one of the last ones out the door." Pulaski grinned. "That's a pretty good alibi, wouldn't you say? The DA's office liked it fine."

"They pulled you in for questioning?"

"The hell they did. I went down there on my own steam. Soon as I heard about Edna on the eleven o'clock news. I'm a good citizen, you know what I mean?"

"You talked to the DA?"

"One of his assistants. I was with him for an hour, till around noon. He checked up on my story, called up a lot of names I gave him—I'll give 'em to you too—and all he could do was let me go."

"Why did you go to your ex-wife's street after the bowling match? A cold night—raining—seems like a pretty strange thing to do."

"Who knows? It just come over me. I wanted to take a look at the place, and it's only five or six blocks from the alleys. You're married to somebody a few years, you get curious what's doing with her, you wanna take a look, you know what I'm saying?"

I asked him about his marriage and his divorce.

"I was a dumb kid from East Phillie," Pulaski said. "I just got out of the marines, I had a couple hitches after high school. I ended up here in this town because I had some buddies that came from here, they got discharged the same time as me. I met Edna—okay, I met her at her place, my buddies took me there for a 'massage,' you know what I'm saying? I fell for her hard. She was older than I was, five, six years, but that didn't matter none. The way I saw her, she was like a little girl. She was so—like delicate, you know what I mean? Not exactly the type I'm shacked up with right now, right? Sure, I knew Edna was a hooker, but she told me she was gonna give up all that, on account of she loved me she was gonna turn into a new woman."

70

Pulaski laughed. He was trying for a good-natured, regretful laugh, but it had an edge to it that I don't think he meant me to pick up on. Not bitterness exactly. More like excitement, as if something in this situation was peculiarly stimulating and arousing to him.

"Okay, I told you I was a dumb kid, didn't I? Well, like I said, it lasted a couple years, but the last year and a half was pretty rough. So we decided to call it quits."

"You were pretty mad at her, were you?"

"No, I wasn't mad at her. I don't hold no grudges. People are gonna be what they are, you know? You can't change them. You can't fix them with a wrench, like somebody's toilet. That's what I do for a living, I'm a plumber."

"You have any ideas about who killed your ex-wife? Do you know of any enemies she ever made?"

"She didn't make no enemies," Pulaski said. "She was a good kid. She never held on to her money, she gave it all away. Buying things for people. Guys mostly. There's always slime-balls and assholes that latch on to a woman like Edna."

"If there were a lot of different men in her life, isn't it possible that one of them might've got mad at her for breaking up with him?"

"Maybe so," Pulaski said. "But how're you gonna find out which one it is? You gonna go through the phone book, calling up every guy in town who's over fourteen? About half of them, I'll bet, never even heard of her."

He laughed again. Trying to suggest maybe that his wise-crack had been good-natured.

I told Pulaski I was through with him, and I stood up and started for the door.

Pulaski called after me, "Listen, do you happen to know—how long do they usually go on, these investigations? How long before the cops let you leave town?"

"You're planning to leave town?" I gave him a harder look than before.

"I sure as hell am. I hated this goddamn town for ten years. If I could've gone back to East Phillie a long time ago, I would've. Set myself up in my own plumbing business—if it wasn't for Edna being here. Well, that ain't keeping me here no more."

"And you've got the money to set yourself up now?"

"When did I say that? All I said was, since Edna won't be around no more—"

He broke off and lowered his head.

I could see he wasn't going to do any more talking, so I left.

It was after four, and I had nothing waiting for me back at the office, so I went home.

The first call I made was to Ann, at her house. She told me she had got her bail hearing scheduled for first thing tomorrow morning. Then I told her how McBride had been holding out on us about Ron Pulaski. I expected her to be mad as hell. She didn't disappoint me.

"We'll bring the matter up to Mr. McBride first thing tomorrow," she said. "Maybe we can make the little worm squirm a little."

The next call I made was to Roger. I relayed Mom's dinner invitation to him. He told me she had already called him and invited him herself.

SIX

When I got to Mom's house shortly after six, she had a sad look on her face. Indignation, contempt, triumph, joy were Mom's most frequent looks. Sadness was seldom part of her repertoire. But as soon as she led me into the living room, I understood.

A short fat candle, dripping melted wax into a saucer, was flickering on the mantelpiece. Tomorrow was November 1, of course, Papa's *yahrzeit*—the anniversary, that is, of my late father's death, which Mom was celebrating in the traditional manner. For the last thirty-eight years she lit a candle at sunset on October 31 and kept it lit until sunset on the first of November.

"I was just looking at the album," she said. She sat herself down on the sofa and patted the cushion next to her. "Come."

I'd seen these pictures practically every year for thirty-eight years, but I sat down next to her anyway. It's not such a bad idea to remind yourself every so often what the dead looked like. I don't have an album for my wife Shirley—she's been gone only four or five years; her death was why I gave up my job on the New York Homicide Squad and moved out here to Mesa Grande—but I have a manila envelope at home with loose snapshots in it, and I do pull them out from time to time.

The important thing is not to do it too often or make it last too long.

I was fifteen when Papa died. I have plenty of memories, of

course, but the pictures in Mom's album always seem to contradict them. I don't remember him being such a small man. I don't remember ever seeing that uncomfortable smile on his face—like he was feeling miserable about something but he didn't want people to catch on because they might be offended.

Actually what I remember most clearly about him is the day he took me to the Bronx Zoo when I was thirteen. We stopped at the gorilla cage. I pointed to this huge hairy obese monster that was scratching itself behind the bars and said, "If I ever ran into anything like *him* on the street, I'd sure run the other way fast."

"Sometimes it's not so simple, my boy," Papa answered. "Sometimes they're wearing pants and coats and neckties, and you can't tell them apart from people." He gave a little sigh, which I had heard him give many times before. I'll never forget that sigh.

Two years later, when he had barely turned fifty, he was dead from a heart attack. It wasn't till then that I heard the story of his life: how he'd come to America from some unpronounceable place that kept switching back and forth between Russia and Poland, how he worked for years as a cutter in a ladies' dress factory, how he finally set himself up in a small dress-manufacturing business of his own, how the business went bust toward the end of the depression when I was still a baby, how he went back to working for other people as a cutter.

His life had been a tragedy, I suppose. No less tragic because it was such a common life, because millions of men have suffered the same disappointments. But Mom never talked about it as if it were a tragedy. She went through the album, pointing out this item or that, as if she were going through the life of one of the great men of our age.

"And look at this, it's your papa all dressed up in his best suit, we were on our way to my cousin Reba's wedding, and I had to take a picture with my Kodak camera because I never saw your papa looking so handsome. At the wedding all the girls was falling over each other to dance with him. Even the bridegroom got jealous."

"Did you get jealous, Mom?"

"Me?" She thought it over. "A little bit maybe. But I told myself this was foolishness. Didn't I know what I was letting myself into when I married such a good-looking fellow? Wasn't I ready that he should be catnap to the cats?"

The doorbell rang, and Mom quickly shut up the album. "Roger wouldn't be interested," she said. "Young people don't like to look at old pictures. They don't like to be reminded that old people were young once too."

Roger was looking exhausted, but somehow this also made him look even younger than usual. It's taken me a while to get used to the idea that my chief (and only) assistant investigator sometimes seems to be about twelve years old.

"I'm sorry I'm late," he said. "I've been tramping all over town, half the time I wasn't talking to people at all, just trying to track them down. Doesn't anybody stay home quietly on Sundays anymore? I didn't even get a chance to go back to my house and take a shower."

This was all the encouragement Mom needed. Instantly she was all over him, offering him the use of her bathroom, pushing liquid refreshment on him, urging him to take off his coat and his tie and, if he wished, his shoes. This fussing took up the next fifteen minutes or so, and when she finally had Roger comfortable to her own satisfaction, it was time for dinner.

While we ate the heavenly chicken pot pie that Mom had promised, we talked about the murder.

First Roger reported on what he had done today. He had called up all the local TV stations, and sure enough one of them had shown the old Marx Brothers movie *A Day at the Races* last night. It began at ten-thirty, so it definitely would have been running while Harry Stubbins was in Edna Pulaski's bedroom.

Roger had also managed to get hold of Victor Sanchez, the cop on the beat in Edna's neighborhood, and he confirmed that Harry had been sleeping in that alleyway since the beginning of the summer. Sanchez had kept an eye on him from time to time, but his orders were not to roust any of the bums unless they were making trouble, interfering with people. Harry Stubbins, Sanchez said, was always as good as gold; he got his nightly bottle of cheap wine and curled up in his private living quarters like any respectable householder.

Finally, though I hadn't given him any specific instructions about this, it had occurred to Roger that he might get some valuable information out of the four women who made up Edna Pulaski's "team" at the massage parlor. All of them were Korean, and all of them said that, as far as they knew, Edna had no special man in her life at the moment or any particular enemies from her past. They added, though, that she had always been protective of her privacy. She didn't usually give them the whole night off, like last night, but once or twice a week she would hole herself up in her room, telling them not to come upstairs and disturb her. They always assumed she was up there with some guy, but they didn't get nosy, and they never actually saw who it was. If it *was* anybody.

All four of them seemed to be genuinely broken up about Edna's death. She paid them well, didn't overwork them, was sympathetic when they came down sick, as long as they didn't overdo it, and had high standards when it came to how the customers treated her employees. A certain amount of kinkiness was okay, but not if it involved physical pain or excessive humiliation. "I don't know what I'll do now," said one of the girls, "I don't know if I can go back to working an outside job."

In one direction, though, Roger had made no progress at all. He hadn't been able to find out a thing about Harry Stubbins's past life or any possible connections between him and Edna Pulaski. "The trouble is," Roger said, "these homeless people have cut themselves off so completely from their families, friends, anybody out of their past—it's almost as if they *have* no past."

"Maybe I've got a suggestion for you," Mom said. "The way this Harry Stubbins talks—the long words he uses, how he keeps mentioning things out of poems and so on—he reminds me of this English professor Davey had in college. You remember, Professor Mendenhall from the Shakespeare class, I met him at your college graduation? He had this funny little pointed beard, and he talked like an encyclopedia?"

I remembered him all right, the old prick.

"So isn't it possible," Mom went on, "this Harry Stubbins was at one time in his life a professor in a college? Most likely an English professor because they're the ones that like to quote all the time from the literary classics. And these professors, don't they have a union or some type professional organization that most of them belong to?"

"The American Association of University Professors," Roger said.

"So call them up," Mom said. "Maybe they keep records, they've got a Harry Stubbins in their files from a long time ago."

Roger made a note, and now it was dessert time. Mom brought in one of her chocolate rolls. She didn't make them often, because they were complicated, expensive, and took a lot of time. But they had been Papa's favorite, and she always dished them up in honor of his *yahrzeit*. This was the first time Roger had tasted one, so he was pretty much out of the conversation until he finished it and the second helping Mom heaped onto his plate without asking his permission.

Back in the living room, with coffee cups in our hands, we returned to the murder. I described everything I had done this afternoon: my examination of the scene of the crime, my talks with Delaney and with the people in front of Pulaski's house, my visit to the dead woman's mother, to Mr. Chang the pharmacist, to Ron Pulaski and his girlfriend.

I was tired and irritated, and I let it show now, raising my voice. "You know what's the most frustrating thing about this damned case? I can't get a fix on this dead woman, this Edna Pulaski. The business she was in—it isn't exactly encouraging to sainthood. But the way everybody describes her, you'd think she *was* some kind of saint. The delivery boy from the liquor store, her great-niece, the girls who worked for her, her neighbors—all of them telling us how kind and generous she was. Even Stubbins talks about her as if she was the Whore with the Heart of Gold!"

"*Both* things could be the truth," Mom said.

"How do you figure that?"

"It's a simple question of getting Americanized. Ten years this Pulaski was in this country, so by now she learned how to be a good American businessman, with a personality that's split in half. In your private life, you treat people nice, you give away money, you help poor old men, you pat little dogs and babies on the head. In the rest of your life, though, when profit and loss is concerned, what you do is strictly business."

"What you're saying is, kind and generous as she was, she was doing something on the business side of her life that made somebody kill her?"

"This you didn't hear me say. I got some ideas, but I still need to know a few things. A couple of these things is the answers to the two questions I told you on the phone you should ask."

"I asked them, Mom." And I gave her all the information I had picked up about Edna Pulaski's heart condition and her drinking habits.

Mom didn't say anything at first. She just frowned and pulled at her lower lip.

"That doesn't look so good for our client, does it?" Roger said. "Edna Pulaski's phobia about people who drink, I mean."

"What's bad about that?" I asked.

"Because it's all the more reason why she wouldn't be likely to invite Harry Stubbins into her house for a cup of coffee. An old drunk like that, smelling like a brewery most of the time—wouldn't she be too disgusted to let him in her room? Which means he wasn't there at her invitation."

"This is a reasonable argument," Mom said, looking pleased, as she always looked when one of us subordinates came up with a thought of our own. "Maybe it isn't so bad for your client as you think though. I got a little idea about that."

"Do you really?" I said. "Or are you just saying that because you *don't* have any ideas yet?"

Mom laughed. "They grow up, they move out, right away they get fresh with their parents! My little idea I didn't work out completely, so I wouldn't talk about it yet. On the other hand, this medicine she was taking for her heart condition—this *isn't* such good news for your client."

"In what way?"

"If I'm right, you'll find out tomorrow when you hear about the autopsy and the lab tests. So here's something else you should do for me—first thing tomorrow you should call up this Pulaski fellow, the dead woman's ex-husband, and ask him a question."

"What question?"

"It's something very important. When he woke up yesterday, how did he find out about his ex-wife's murder? He told you he heard about it on the eleven o'clock news, but what you should ask him is, was it the radio news or the television news?"

"What difference does it make? Pulaski didn't kill her. I told you, he has an airtight alibi for the time of the murder."

"That's nice for him," she said. "But do me a favor, ask him this question anyway."

"Why don't you tell me why? I just can't imagine—"

"That's true. You can't. So give me his answer, and I'll do it for you."

"All right, I will." Privately, though, I was saying to myself that there was no hurry about it. Maybe I'd ask Mom's pointless question, maybe I wouldn't. In any case, I'd make up my own mind, I'd trust my own judgment.

Then Mom remembered that McBride was supposed to make a statement to the press about the murder in about fifteen minutes. One of the local stations would be interrupting its regular programming to cover it.

She turned on the TV. We were in time to catch the buildup to McBride's press conference. We saw the crowds milling around Edna Pulaski's house, identified by the TV voice as "the scene of the crime, where murder and massages mingled."

Then we saw McBride at his office desk, looking grim to a room full of reporters. He made one of his feisty-bulldog speeches about how the case had been solved, through the quick action of our splendid police force and the district attorney's office, and how he personally intended to bring this brutal killer to justice, by supervising every aspect of the investigation and carrying straight through to the trial.

"The victim wasn't an exemplary character," McBride said, "she belonged to the lowest element of society. She lived in a squalid neighborhood, she sold sex under the most shocking conditions—ladies and gentlemen, it would make you sick to see the room where she was killed, those Oriental landscapes that turn out to be dirty pictures, garish neon signs with Chinese letters on them flashing through the windows—but all of that is beside the point when it's a question of justice—"

"You're not suggesting, are you, Mr. DA," Joe Horniman broke in from the first row of reporters, "that Asian people have a greater tendency to belong to the lowest element in our town than other groups?"

McBride drew himself up. People are supposed to look taller on TV than they do in real life. For a moment you could have sworn that McBride was a giant. It helped, of course, that he was sitting down. "That's a lie, sir! That's a vicious implication you're throwing around there! Anything I just said about this particular woman was certainly not meant to cast any reflection on the members of our fine law-abiding Ori—Asian community. These people have made an outstanding record in our town. They come here not talking the language, most of them, but they make their kids learn it, they want their kids to get an education, they keep their noses to the grindstone, and a lot of those kids end up beating out our own American kids at school, and going to high-class colleges that our own kids can't get in to—

"The point I'm making is, there are bad apples in every barrel. But we in America, with our God-given sense of fair play and justice, would never hold it against the other apples! What's more, my record on racial and minority issues in this town is well known to everybody. I've made it my personal business to see that plenty of minority policemen, not just O—sians but blacks and Mexicans too, get hired by the police department. Every Christmas I give block parties down there where the Asians live, and also in black neighborhoods, Hispanic neighborhoods—turkey and cranberry sauce, the works, and toys for all the little kids—strictly at my own personal expense! And for the last three years, though it's not generally known, since I'm not the type to blow my own horn, I've attended the Hannakuh dinner at the Jewish synagogue—

"Now if I could get back to the subject at hand, meaning this murder case. And my point is, justice is blind, the law protects every one of us, both the small and the big. Nobody can be allowed to get away with murder, even if society might be better off without the victim. That's why I've put this case under my personal supervision—"

"In other words," Joe Horniman said, "it has nothing to do with your political opponent's recent charges that you never try any cases yourself, you let your assistants do all the work?"

"That question isn't even worth dignifying with an answer," McBride said. "The public record will show that I'm not being any more active in the fight against crime right now than I've ever been. I love this town. I settled here right after I got out of law school, and I made up my mind I would devote myself to the welfare of Mesa Grande. That's what I've always done, that's what I'm doing now, that's why the criminal element will go to any length to defeat me in this coming election. But they're not going to do it, I can tell you that. A week from Tuesday the voters will make their choice—and my prediction is, they'll choose me, they'll give me their mandate to go on prosecuting this vicious killer and all other vicious killers who might come along in the future."

The press conference ended, and the TV station cut to a brief closeup of Doris Dryden, commenting on it. "Actually," she said, "I'm glad to hear that District Attorney McBride is finally taking charge of a case. Now we all have to hope he won't bungle it because he's so out of practice."

Mom turned off the television. She was frowning a little.

Roger was shaking his head and gasping. "But he *does* turn over most of his cases to his assistants! He *knows* he does! How can he have the nerve to look people in the eye and tell such lies?"

"Why not?" I said. "The garbage dump is full of retired politicians who made the mistake of telling the truth. The last thing that most people want to hear is the truth."

"Mrs. Dryden is telling them the truth, and they seem to be liking it. Who knows, there may be a groundswell that'll sweep her into office!"

"And what difference will it make?" I said. "You'll just be exchanging one politician for another. New name, new look, new sex—but the same old tune. You know what the old immigrants used to say, when I was growing up in the Bronx? 'You can't fight City Hall.' They were smart people, they knew what the world is like."

Mom smiled gently and said, "You can't fight City Hall? You know who used to make this foolish remark? A lot of alta cockers who never left the shtetl even after they crossed the Atlantic Ocean. For them City Hall was full of Cossacks, like Russia or Poland used to be. They could never get out of their heads this foolish idea that the people in City Hall weren't human beings too. And this foolishness wasn't good for them, believe me. What it meant was, they could never do anything to get over their problems. Everything was as bad as everything else, so what was the point of lifting a finger—"

And in two seconds flat, Mom and I had plunged into our old political argument.

We kept it up for the next half hour, and then it was time for Roger and me to leave. At the front door, Mom gave us each a hug, but I could see that her heart wasn't in it, a sad preoccupied look was on her face. I asked her what was wrong, and she immediately produced a smile and said, "What should be wrong? Everything's fine."

Then I understood what it was. Mom wanted to get back into the living room and pick up the old photo album again. She was tired of thinking about murders. She wanted to spend the rest of the night with Papa.

SEVEN

I was up an hour earlier than usual on Monday morning. When things get busy in our office—for instance, when a big case comes up at the same time that we're in the middle of a lot of smaller ones—there don't seem to be enough hours in the day.

I gulped down some coffee and a doughnut, while skimming through *The Republican American.* The headlines were taken up with Harry Stubbins's arrest and McBride's press conference. The main story was written by Joe Horniman, but I didn't read past its first paragraph.

I moved to the editorial page and wasn't surprised to find the editor expressing shock and dismay at those surly cynics who were accusing McBride of taking charge of the Pulaski murder case purely out of political opportunism. Our local sheet is just about as conservative as Calvin Coolidge, though a lot more talkative, and McBride's don't-be-soft-on-crime line has always roused its vigilante instincts. It had supported him in his last four campaigns, and just the other day the editor had denounced Doris Dryden as a "bleeding heart liberal" whose election would be an open invitation for the Mafia to take over our town.

I got to the office at eight-fifteen, running into Roger in the elevator. Mabel Gibson, who was always there ahead of everybody no matter how early anybody was, leaned forward and spoke in her low, confidential voice. "She's been in there for heaven *knows* how long. She wants to see the two of you right away."

We went in and found Ann at her desk, in a welter of papers. They looked as if they were spread all over the place, in no particular order, but I knew this was an optical illusion. In her brain every little pile was labeled and filed; mention any particular case to her, and she could instantly pick out all the relevant documents. She had three court appearances scheduled for later today, and she'd go into each one of them fully prepared.

"Okay, let's hear what you've been up to," Ann said. "And make it fast, because you and I, Dave, are seeing McBride in half an hour for the bail hearing."

"You want me to come to court with you?" I was surprised; she didn't usually.

"I wish you would," she said. "I want to buttonhole McBride right afterward and give him hell for holding out on us about the ex-husband. I feel like kicking that snake in the teeth, if snakes *have* teeth, so it's up to you to give me the high sign if I start losing my cool."

We both knew perfectly well that no high sign was going to be needed. I'd been working for Ann for four years, and her cool had yet to be even temporarily misplaced.

So we reported to her in detail on our activities yesterday, then Roger told her he was going to call the American Association of University Professors to find out about Harry Stubbins's background. She complimented him on coming up with this approach. He accepted the compliment and didn't say anything about where the approach had come from.

Then I told Roger he could work at my desk until I came back later this morning. Besides the long-distance calls to those professorial outfits, he had to get in touch with the Sagebrush Alleys, question the people there about Saturday night's bowling match, and also question the members of Ron Pulaski's team and of the team he'd been bowling against.

And once all that was done, he had to finish up a report on one of our other clients. This was a teenage kid; the cops had stopped him for speeding, found cocaine in his glove compartment, and arrested him for possession. The kid was a punk, and guilty as hell, but our contention was that the evidence should be thrown out on the grounds of illegal search.

To tell you the truth, Ann and I have had our disagreements about this sort of thing. Sometimes I catch myself thinking like I'm still on the other side of the fence.

We headed downstairs, and pretty soon we were in the court-room.

The courtroom didn't have many people in it. It was very early, and no trials likely to have fireworks in them were scheduled for the morning. McBride and Grantley were there ahead of us, sitting in the front row of seats. Grantley looked like a yuppie undertaker, as always, and McBride had on a loud sports coat and one of those American flag ties. He was mad about some-thing, spitting out words at Grantley in a low voice. He broke off as we approached. I guess he saw me staring at his tie, because he gave a loud laugh and pointed at it. "My patriotic tie, Dave. What do you think? I had a batch of them made up for me for this campaign. You want me to send you one? Glad to do it, as long as you promise me you'll wear it at every possible opportunity."

He laughed, probably at the expression on my face. Then he stopped laughing, and his angry glare returned. "You want to hear something beautiful? Go on, Leland, tell 'em about the call you got a few minutes ago."

"It came from some young woman," Grantley said, looking very uncomfortable indeed. "A Korean young woman—speak-ing perfect English, however. She introduced herself as Edna Pulaski's niece."

"Oh sure, Madeleine Kim," I said. "She translated for us when I talked to Edna Pulaski's mother."

"The old lady asked her to call me. She had a complaint, and of course she couldn't tell me about it herself. It seems that her daughter, when she was taken to the morgue, was wearing a number of items on her person, and they were taken along with her. This morning, with the autopsy over, the morgue people sent those items back to the old lady, and she says that one of them is missing. A piece of jewelry."

"What piece?"

"The ring her daughter was wearing. On her right hand— with a rather large green stone in it. The old lady says it wasn't worth a great deal of money, it wasn't a real emerald, but she gave it to her daughter as a birthday gift years ago, and it has sentimental value for her. She's furious at the district attorney's office, she blames *us* for losing it. Her niece—great-niece, I suppose—says the old lady is thinking of suing us on account of it."

"Suing us! How do you like that?" McBride lifted a fist to underline his exasperation. "Her darling daughter just got killed, the stiff isn't even in its grave yet, we're working our butts off to bring the killer to justice—and this old biddy is worried about some cheesy piece of cheap jewelry! What kind of people are they, for Christ sake!"

"Did the morgue people itemize those things when they took them off the body?" Ann asked.

"No, there were so few things, and it all looked like cheap junk to them," Grantley said. "Even so, they should've made an inventory, but you know how it is—people get overworked— they foul up. I remember seeing that ring myself, however, when I looked at the body. It definitely went down to the morgue with her, so any number of people might have mislaid it, dropped it somewhere, perhaps stolen it. We're certainly going to check into it—"

"Damn well better!" said McBride. "A thing like this makes the whole law enforcement organization in this city look bad! Goddammit, it's all we need just now, isn't it? With an election coming up—a major murder case—" He huffed and puffed for a while, looking more like one of the little pigs than the big bad wolf.

As soon as he had calmed down, Ann went up to him, smiling her most benevolent smile, giving no indication of her homicidal feelings toward snakes. "Could we have a little chat right after the hearing, Marvin?" she said. "Some points about the case that I didn't get to go over with Leland yesterday."

"I've got a heavy morning, Ann." McBride's voice was hoarser than usual, and I could see his hand shaking a little. For him, I realized, nine in the morning was like the middle of the night. "Call my secretary, maybe I've got a free spot late this afternoon. Or tomorrow."

"Right after the hearing would be better," Ann said. "We won't be here long, will we? Purely routine procedure, I assume. So you should have plenty of time for what we have to discuss."

"You already discussed it—"

"Ron Pulaski." Ann said the name softly and clearly, as if she were pronouncing it for a small child. "Mean anything to you, Marvin?"

Her question was answered by the look on McBride's face and on Grantley's too.

"Okay, okay, I'll give you a few minutes after we're through here. Up in my office."

Ann thanked him sweetly. At this moment, through a door in the corner to the left of the bench, Harry Stubbins was brought in with a uniformed cop holding him by the arm. The shade of red in Harry's cheeks and eyes was as deep as it had been yesterday. The only improvement in his appearance was that somebody had encouraged him to make an effort at shaving the thicket of grayish hair on his chin. The effort had been partially successful. He looked less like a porcupine and more like a goat.

Ann went up to Harry, shook him by the hand, gave him an encouraging smile.

"What's this all about?" Harry blinked at her hard.

"It's a bail hearing," she said.

"You're—you're really going to get me out of here?"

"We're going to try our best."

"Get me out!" He was wetting his lips, and there was desperation in his voice. "You don't have any idea what it's— That's hell, in there. Read plenty of descriptions of hell in my day. None of them comes close to the real thing."

The judge was making his entrance now, so Ann gave Stubbins a pat on the arm and returned to her place.

The hearing wasn't a routine procedure at all. McBride opposed letting the accused out on bail, on the grounds that he was not a reputable member of the community, had no visible means of support, no family, no registered place of residence, and would therefore be likely to flee from the venue of the court if he were released from jail.

Ann argued that the accused's indigence was exactly the reason why he *wouldn't* try to flee; he didn't have the money to get out of town. Furthermore, since the accused obviously was in no position to put up any amount of money for bail, no matter how low it was set, he should be released on his own recognizance—otherwise the court would put itself in the position of discriminating against the accused on account of his poverty-stricken and homeless state.

Furthermore, Ann went on, the district attorney's office was notorious for discriminating against the poor and the homeless, especially if they were elderly. Last month, for example, they asked for ten thousand dollars' bail for an old man who was accused of nothing worse than public exposure.

"And five minutes after you set him loose," McBride said, "he went right out on the street and exposed himself again! That's what's wrong with the system these days! The taxpayers lay out good money so the dregs of society can get some shyster to take their case—"

"Excuse me, Mr. McBride," said Ann, putting on an indignant expression—you had to know her very well to realize how much fun she was having. "Who exactly are you calling a shyster? You're just a little too fond of that word, I think. If I'm not mistaken, I heard you shout it out in open court only a few weeks ago. Right after the jury came in with an acquittal for that Chicano boy you were trying to railroad into prison for drug possession. And if I'm not mistaken the

possessor turned out to be your own stool pigeon who testi-
fied against the boy—"

McBride's voice, which always had a hoarse alcoholized edge
to it, got even hoarser when he raised it in anger. "First of all,
you haven't heard the last of that case! You pulled a quarterback sneak on us, but that kid was guilty as hell, he and my
stoolie were in it together, and you can take my word for it we'll
pin it on him one of these days!"

"Assuming the Supreme Court decides that the law against
double jeopardy is unconstitutional," Ann said.

"We'll get him for something else! I know my Constitution
better than you do, Goddammit!"

The judge broke in, sternly telling them both to stop their
unseemly behavior. But Ann wasn't sorry the shouting match
had taken place. She knew her judges. His Honor Andrew
Phipps, former counsel for the state proverty program, ele-
vated to the bench by a lame-duck Democratic governor
thumbing his nose at his Republican successor, wasn't likely to
take McBride's fulminations lightly. Stubbins was released on
his own recognizance, on condition he checked into the local
Shelter for the Homeless run by the city.

"Oh God, not the shelter! Send me back to jail," Stubbins
muttered to Ann, after the judge had disappeared. "They make
you come in before eight at night—they *frisk* you at the door!
If I'm going to be treated like a common criminal, let me do
it where the food's better and the company's younger."

Ann was gently unmoved, though. I made a call to the
Shelter for the Homeless, and gave Stubbins the address, and
in front of the courthouse I pointed him in the right direction.
To make sure he got there, I reminded him that this was no
time for him to antagonize the public defender.

A few minutes later Ann and I reached Marvin McBride's outer
office. To get to the inner sanctum you had to run the gauntlet
of countless little minions occupying desks and cubbyholes
along the way, and then you found yourself in a small-size
auditorium, where McBride was seated behind a huge desk.

Why is it that short men always like to sit at big desks, even though they look even shorter in contrast?

Grantley was there too, sitting a little to the right of McBride's desk, holding a notebook on his knee.

McBride gave a nod and a growl at us as we took our seats. He was fifty-four years old, about the same age as me, but his bloodshot eyes and the little red veins in his cheeks made him look older.

After the nod and the growl, he went back to what he had been doing, lighting up one of his cheap little cigars. Pretty soon the vile smell would fill his office, and make us all feel sick, but McBride had never been known to care, or even to notice.

"All right," he started in, "what's this all about, Ann? What's that name you mentioned to me?" McBride frowned and seemed to be thinking hard. "Ron Pulaski, was that it? Oh, you mean the dead woman's ex-husband, don't you?"

"That's who I mean all right. Old Mr. Raymond Chang told you about him, didn't he? In case you don't recognize the name, he's the nice old man who owns the pharmacy down the street from the victim's house. Leland talked to him yesterday morning, at which time he said he saw Pulaski in the neighborhood at midnight Saturday night. And Pulaski himself came to see you here yesterday afternoon. Now here's a woman who gets killed, and here's her ex-husband who's in the neighborhood half an hour or so afterward, and you don't think you owe it to the defendant to tell his attorney about it?"

McBride gave a grunt. "You're wrong about one thing. I never talked to Pulaski, yesterday or any other time. Leland talked to him. Isn't that right, Leland? Gave me a complete report afterward, of course."

"Of course," said Ann. "You're personally in charge of the case. If a shady maneuver gets pulled, like trying to cover up a witness who might help the defense, you have to take full responsibility."

"Now that's not fair." Grantley looked up from his notebook, his smile a little tight at the edges. "Very well—I see why you and Dave might jump to the worst possible conclusion. I see that there's room for misunderstanding and misinterpretation here. I don't blame you for what you're thinking, believe me I don't. I'd probably be thinking the same thing in your place. But I assure you—I give you my solemn word—there's no foundation whatsoever to your suspicions."

"It's nice to have your solemn word," Ann said, "but even nicer would be an explanation of why we had to dig up this pertinent information for ourselves?"

"Because it *isn't* pertinent, that's why. Pulaski did come to see me in the afternoon, I talked to him for an hour, but I finally let him go. I couldn't hold him, for the simple reason that there's conclusive proof he didn't commit the murder. If you know as much as you do, you must also know that he's got an airtight alibi. That's why he got in touch with me. He wanted to admit that he *was* in his ex-wife's neighborhood at midnight or thereabouts on Saturday, but he came there directly from his weekly bowling match. Ten or fifteen people who knew him well were at that match with him, and we've talked to most of them, and they all swear Pulaski got there before nine-thirty and didn't leave till the match broke up just a few minutes before midnight.

"Granted, it would've been physically possible for him, or somebody else, to kill her after midnight—we have the autopsy report now, I'll tell you all about it in a moment—but your client's own statement makes that unlikely. Your client claims that some unknown person entered Edna Pulaski's room at eleven thirty-five, just as he—your client, that is—was losing consciousness. Now that person has failed to come forward, which suggests one of two things about him—or her. Either this was the murderer—in which case the ex-husband Pulaski can't be guilty—or this is a figment of your client's imagination. Needless to say, the second alternative is what we favor in this office.

"And either way," McBride put in, "there was no reason for us to let you know about Pulaski. Like Leland just said, he isn't relevant."

"Maybe the unknown visitor wasn't the murderer," Ann said, "but is afraid to come forward on account of the publicity."

"So Pulaski came in and killed her *after* that visitor left?" McBride laughed. "You're putting an awful lot of people into that room at midnight on a cold rainy night! Come on, Ann, admit it, we've got good reason for thinking that Pulaski is in the clear. For Christ sake, you *know* I wouldn't hold out on you. I've got a legal obligation to keep the defense informed at all times of every pertinent fact that comes into my possession. I take that obligation very seriously. That's the way I operate. Have I ever operated any other way?"

The question was so fantastic as to make both of us speechless for a moment. A dozen times since I've been on the job we've caught McBride out trying to suppress evidence that was favorable to our clients. Every time it's happened we've let him know about it, and every time he's been forced to give one of his sheepish grins and apologize. So what the hell could he mean by asking that question? Was he making some kind of cynical joke? Or—and this is the possibility that boggles the mind!—did he really *believe* in his own protestation of innocence? Could a man be such a natural-born liar that he gets to believing his own lies?

A stupid question, I realized. This is practically the definition of a politician.

"Of course you couldn't do anything underhanded, Marvin," Ann said. "It's just because I know you couldn't that I fully expect you to tell me everything you've learned this morning from the coroner's autopsy and from your various lab reports. There's no chance you'd even *think* of leaving out any of that information—is there?"

McBride grunted. "You got that stuff for them, Leland?"

"Absolutely." Grantley flipped open his notebook and read from it. " 'Time of death, as determined by the contents of the stomach, etcetera—somewhere between ten-thirty and one A.M.' So you see Stubbins could well have killed her before he passed out on her floor.

"Report from the fingerprint people. The room was loaded with prints, of course. Plenty of Edna's, her mother's, the girls who worked for her, plenty of your client's. And about two dozen unidentified prints, some comparatively new, some pretty faded and probably unidentifiable. Customers of hers from the recent past, no doubt. We'll try them out on the FBI fingerprint bank, but most of them, I'd guess, won't have any record."

"How about Ron Pulaski?" I asked. "Any of *his* prints in her room?"

"I thought of that," Grantley said, "so I had Pulaski's prints taken when he came to my office yesterday. Results negative. No prints of his showed up in her room.

"Now for the test results from the lab. Let me see—yes, well, at first glance this item *might* appear to confirm *one* part of your client's story. The coffee cup had traces in it of a common drug, known as a beta blocker. It's the Pulaski woman's heart medicine, she was taking one pill at every meal for angina pectoris. It's supposed to regularize the heartbeat, but one of its most common side effects is to cause drowsiness, fainting, in large enough doses unconsciousness. Stubbins had enough of the stuff in him to make up three or four doses. More than enough to knock him out."

"Well, there you are," Ann said.

"I'm truly sorry, Ann, but if you think about it for a moment, it really strengthens *our* case, not yours. You were asking yesterday why Stubbins didn't get out of her house right away after he killed her, why he fell asleep in her room and stayed there until the next morning when the old lady found him? Well, this lab report answers that question, doesn't it? Edna Pulaski was preparing to take her heart medicine when Stubbins broke in. She'd put the pills in her coffee, but she hadn't drunk it yet. After the murder, Stubbins swallowed down that coffee— needing something to steady his nerves, I imagine—and the drug knocked him out. He was just unlucky."

So the report on Edna Pulaski's medicine definitely *wasn't* good news for our client, I thought. Chalk up another to Mom.

"If Edna Pulaski was planning to take her medicine in that coffee," Ann said, "how come she put in three times her usual dose?"

McBride spoke up. "Happens all the time, doesn't it? People get confused, they forget how many pills they've taken, done it plenty of times myself."

"What about the murder weapon, the cloth that was used to strangle her? You said you found some fibers around her bruises?"

"They were cotton," said Grantley, "but the lab can't determine the color or what kind of object they came from."

"You compared those fibers to the rope Stubbins was wearing around his waist?"

Grantley cleared his throat slightly. "They didn't come from that rope, as a matter of fact. Of course, that's not at all inconsistent with our contention that he used some other weapon and threw it out the window."

"Did the Pulaski woman have any kind of record?" I said. "Did you ever arrest her? She *was* breaking the law, wasn't she?"

"It isn't easy, nailing these prossies," said McBride. "You need witnesses, and the johns—their clients—don't usually want to come forward. Actually, the Pulaski woman did come to our notice once. Six or seven months ago the cops arrested her, one of those roundups they make every so often. They brought her in on a vice charge, and she was questioned by some of my lower-echelon people, and then I talked to her myself for a few minutes. But her lawyer got her out on bail, and the charge had to be dropped on account of the witness changed his mind and refused to testify. When I heard about this murder yesterday, I didn't remember the name. It was only when I got to looking over my records this morning that I recognized who she was."

Then he got to his feet, rubbing his hands together. "So we're all busy people, better break this off, pleasant as it is to talk to you both. Everything all straightened out between us, sweetie?" he said, coming around the desk to Ann. "Just a little misunderstanding, right? No offense meant, no offense taken."

He took her by the shoulders and gave her a big loud kiss on the cheek. She tried to hide her reaction, but I heard her gag a little, and saw her eyes roll up, the way your eyes do when you're disgusted. No doubt about it this time—whatever had put McBride on the wagon Saturday night, he was definitely off it again.

EIGHT

When Ann and I got back to the office, toward eleven-thirty, Mabel Gibson greeted me with the news that my mother had been trying to get me for the last hour. I went into my room, shut the door, and dialed Mom's number.

"It just came to me," Mom said. "All of sudden into my head it popped. What was bothering me last night."

"You told me nothing was bothering you."

"Naturally. Did I want you worrying? You're a good boy, you always believe what I tell you. So I'll meet you at lunch, you'll hear something positively amazing."

"About the Pulaski murder?"

"What other murders have you got? Bring Roger with you too—someplace near your office."

"We could meet downstairs in the courthouse cafeteria."

"No, this wouldn't be good. Too many big ears belonging to lawyers. You know the little Chinese place two blocks away from you? What's it called—it's something like New York City?"

"New Wok City, is that the place you mean?"

"Exactly. I knew it was a name I had good feelings about. Could you and Roger be there in ten minutes maybe, fifteen top? Otherwise we'll have to wait for a table."

"I guess we could manage that, Mom. Give me some hint what—"

But she hung up the phone. So I went out to the waiting

room to look for Roger, and found him making long-distance calls through our switchboard.

"Are you hungry enough to eat an early lunch?" I said. Unnecessary question. At Roger's age you're always hungry enough, even if you just finished a five-course meal.

We walked the two blocks to the New Wok City. It was bitter cold out, and my nose and ears were red and stinging by the time we got inside. The place was small and bare—only a few paper lanterns and some dragon drawings on the walls to give it a more or less Chinese atmosphere. (Actually it had been an Italian place until six months ago, and a Hungarian place six months before that, and it still had the same waiters.) Mom was already seated at one of the tables. Tapping on the cloth with her spoon, looking as if she could hardly contain herself.

She did though. Her sense of drama was stronger than her impatience. She told us to order our food, and she waited for her tea, and she took a few sips of it. Then she asked us to tell her in detail exactly what both of us had been doing this morning.

First Roger described the results of the long-distance calls he had been making. "The American Association of University Professors," he said, "are very friendly, obliging people. They dug up Harry Stubbins—or at least, there was *a* Harry Stubbins who was a dues-paying member until five years ago. Then he dropped out of sight completely. He was an associate professor of English at the University of Michigan in Ann Arbor, and they've given me the name of his department chairman. He's out for lunch just now, I've left a message for him at his office. Also, I managed to talk to three or four of the guys who were bowling with Ron Pulaski on Saturday night. So far they confirm his story, but I've got a lot more to go."

Then it was my turn to give a play-by-play account of my morning. As soon as I was finished Mom asked me sharply when I was planning to put that question to Ron Pulaski— whether he'd heard the news of Edna's death on radio or television. I suppressed my annoyance as best I could, and answered stiffly that I just hadn't had the time yet but I would get around to it shortly.

Finally Mom came out with what was on her mind. "All along I had the feeling there's something about this murder that was right in front of my eyes only I wasn't seeing it. Until this morning early I suddenly saw it."

"So what *was* it, Mom?"

"Two facts you picked up in the last two days. Two diffcrent facts, but now you should put them together, you should look at them side by side, you'll see there's one thing only they could mean. First fact: Talking to people at this Pulaski's house, you found out what I asked you to, that she didn't like drinking. She wouldn't let her massage girls do any of it. She wouldn't stand for it in her customers even. A customer comes to her, he's got liquor on his breath, she kicks him right out of the bed.

"Second fact: What I pointed out to you yesterday, and you agreed I was right. At the dinner Saturday night District Attorney McBride didn't do any drinking. Not a drop of alcohol he took, not even a sip wine or beer. Only water.

"So isn't it possible, this first fact is the explanation for the second fact?

"Why wasn't McBride drinking last night? Because he had after dinner a date with Edna Pulaski, and he didn't want on his breath the smell of liquor, so she wouldn't kick him out of bed."

It was a little hard for me to catch my breath after this. "You're saying that Marvin McBride and Edna Pulaski—"

"A little bit of old-fashioned hanky panky, like there's been between men and women for a million years already. Why should it come to you like such a shock?"

But Roger and I were still in the grip of that shock, so Mom sat back and went on talking. "Almost I could feel sympathy with this McBride. At that dinner he's a man who's being pulled in two opposite directions, like a tug of war. In one direction is that delicious wine, everybody around him is drinking it, it's practically begging him to drink it too. In the other direction is this delicious woman, waiting for him in her apartment, lying on the bed with her clothes off. Which direction is going to pull him harder? It's a simple case of Uncle Moe all over again, only with Moe it was eating not drinking."

"I don't know what you're talking about," I said. "Who was Uncle Moe?"

"Your papa's uncle, your great-uncle. He was the rich one, and you couldn't get around it, he was a man that enjoyed his food. Thick juicy steaks, with so much gravy on them the meat looked like it was drowning. Chocolate eclairs, the type you stick your fork in them and the cream squirts all over the table. All his life Moe eats and eats. The doctors tell him he wouldn't do his health any good with so much food, but Moe goes on eating. And getting fat!

"And the other thing I should tell you from Moe, he loves his wife, your great-aunt Millie. They got married when they were both young kiddies. Moe wasn't older than twenty, he didn't weigh more than a hundred eighty-five. And Millie was younger even, and she *never* weighed more than a hundred ten. And they're married forty years, and Moe is swelling up bigger every day, and one day Millie says to him, 'Moe, you got to lose some weight!'

"And Moe says, 'Why? Are you listening to those doctors? They told me I'd be dead in five years I didn't stop eating, and that was thirty years ago, and most of *them* are dead.'

"And Millie says, 'It isn't the doctors. It's when you climb up on top of me, Moe. You're too heavy already. You sink down on me, it's like the whole ceiling is coming down, I can't breathe, I feel like every bone in my body is breaking. I'm telling you, Moe, you lose a few pounds, like maybe fifty or a hundred, or else you don't climb on top of me no more!'

"So maybe you can imagine it, what a blow this was for Moe. He hoped there was some easy way out. Like Millie should climb on top of *him*. But this didn't work neither. He was too round, his stomach stuck up too high, she felt like she was climbing on top of a wave in the ocean, and she kept sliding off before either one of them could do anything. So finally Moe knew what he was up against. It was do without the thick steaks or do without Millie. One or the other.

"Such a terrible decision to make. Back and forth he went, fighting it out inside himself. For weeks he wasn't getting any sleep, there was bags under his eyes, everybody felt sorry for him what he was going through."

"How did everybody find out?" I said.

"Millie told them, naturally. It wasn't easy by her either. She needed sympathy. A woman can't keep her troubles in a bottle inside herself, like a man can do. So the whole family gave a big sigh from relief when Moe finally made his decision. And this—the point I'm getting at—is exactly what your McBride went through last night at the dinner. A bottle wine or a good time in the bed with Edna Pulaski? He decided on the bed."

Finally I was getting over the shock Mom had given me. "The evidence seems a little thin to me," I said. "Maybe McBride *is* having an affair with someone, that wouldn't surprise me a bit. And maybe that's why he wasn't drinking Saturday night. But the fact that Edna Pulaski didn't like men who drank could be nothing but a simple coincidence."

"Naturally. So let's throw in a third fact. What happens right after the murder is discovered? What amazing thing happens, like a miracle, you said it yourself, Davey? McBride suddenly gets up early in the morning—a Sunday morning yet—and breaks the habits from his lifetime by going to work. He announces he's taking charge personally of this murder case. So why?"

"Because Doris Dryden shamed him into it. She challenged him, at Saturday night's dinner, to take over the first murder case that came along, and he accepted the challenge. When a murder case *did* come along, he had no choice, he had to put up a show. Once the election is over, he'll drop this case and let Grantley handle it."

"If this is true, isn't the show he's putting up a little bit too realistic so far? He was down in his office by nine o'clock Sunday morning. This early he didn't have to be. He could wait till noon before he made his announcement. And this morning too, also at nine o'clock, he's in court personally to argue against the bail. He was drinking last night—Ann Swenson smelled it on his breath—but he *still* got up and went to court. To me this don't sound like being ashamed he shouldn't accept a challenge. To me this sounds like he really *wants* to handle this case. He don't want to let go any part of it. He wants to keep his eyes on every development, every clue, every new piece information. And again I'm asking why."

"Because he's personally involved in it somehow!" Roger suddenly spoke up. "And he's afraid some embarrassing facts might come out!"

"What else?" said Mom, with a nod of satisfaction. She curled some noodles around her chopsticks, shoved them into her mouth, and washed them down with a swig of tea. Then she went on, "So let me throw at you fact number four. We all saw McBride on the television last night, talking to the reporters. You remember one of the things he said to them? He said what a terrible room Edna Pulaski got killed in—'with the neon sign, with the Chinese letters on it, flashing on and off through the windows.' Those were the words he used, more or less. But when did McBride ever get a chance to see that room? He didn't go down to look at it on Sunday morning, like his assistant Grantley did. And even if Grantley described it to him, he couldn't describe any neon sign with Chinese letters flashing on and off through the windows. Because in broad daylight the sign was turned off, there wasn't any flashing. In other words, is it crazy to imagine that McBride *does* know that room—because he's been having an affair with the woman that lived in it?

"And if you add to this that McBride admits he actually met this Edna Pulaski—six or seven months ago, when she was arrested."

"But he talked to her for only a few minutes—"

"He *said* it was only a few minutes. Whatever it was, how much time would he need to decide he wanted to pursue the acquaintanceship? He called her up that night maybe, that's when the affair got started maybe."

"Mom, Mom, don't go so fast! Are you saying that McBride—Marvin McBride, our district attorney—is the one who *killed* that woman?"

"I'm not saying, I'm not *not* saying. But I'll point out a few more facts you should think about. For instance, the story Edna Pulaski told to Harry Stubbins—that she's got a boyfriend who's been trying to dump her, which gets her mad at him, she's threatening to tell the whole world about him. This fits very nice with McBride, you wouldn't agree? Just before the election—for McBride this would be the worst time for such a thing to happen. Can you come up with a better motive for killing somebody?

"And here's another fact you should also throw into the pot. To strangle somebody with a necktie, you have to pull it pretty tight. I couldn't be so easy to untie it again and tear it off somebody's neck. So why did this murderer go to such a lot of trouble to take this necktie away with him? Neckties are neckties, most of them aren't such personal individual items—but this one was! This one the murderer couldn't afford to leave behind. Maybe because it was a red-white-and-blue tie with little American flags on it, right away everybody would recognize it was McBride's."

"But he was wearing that tie when Ann and I met him at his office the next morning. If he'd used it to kill her the night before, it couldn't have been in any condition—"

"You said he had a whole batch of those ties specially made up for him. So the one he was wearing on Sunday wasn't the one he killed her with on Saturday. That one he got rid of the same night."

"My God, Mom, you *are* accusing McBride of the murder!"

"No, no, always you want to leap before you walk, Davey. What I'm telling you is, there's reasons to do a little more investigating, to look at him close and find out some things. Like where was he when the murder happened? The dinner from the Women's League of Voters broke up at eleven—plenty of time for McBride to get to Edna Pulaski's house at eleven-thirty-five. Did he do this, or did he go someplace else—

has he got maybe an alibi? You take my advice, you'll ask him about all this, you'll repeat to him my theory. Even if he denies it, the *way* he denies it could tell you something."

I promised her I'd pass her suggestion on to Ann, and a few minutes later it was time for Roger and me to get back to work. I paid the check, and we went out to the street. Mom's little red Japanese car was parked right in front of the restaurant. She stepped into it, but before she could go tootling off Roger went up to the window.

"My curiosity is killing me. Which way did he decide?"

Mom lifted her eyebrows at him. "Which way did who decide what?"

"Your uncle Moe, I mean. Did he give up eating or did he give up sleeping with his wife?"

Mom beamed. It's always gratifying to her when the audience takes an interest in one of her stories. "He cut down on the eating and lost sixty pounds in a month, and he and Millie had some wonderful nights in the bed."

"I'm glad the story had a happy ending," Roger said.

Mom shrugged. "Only partly. At Moe's age, in his weakened physical condition, the strain and exertion was too much for him. He had a stroke on the third night, and he died."

NINE

When we got back from lunch Roger returned to the switchboard, and I went straight in to Ann and told her my astounding deduction about McBride's having an affair with Edna Pulaski—and the possibility that he was the murderer. (Well, Mom's deduction, of course, but her modesty will never let me reveal that to the world. Roger is the only other person who's in on the secret.)

Then I had the supreme pleasure of seeing Ann's mouth fall open and her eyes widen. It takes a lot to produce a reaction like that in her.

"So what do you think?" I said. "Is our crime-fighting DA going to turn out to be a love-nest killer?"

Ann started shaking her head, her cool coming back to her. "I can believe the love nest part all right. But somehow I can't see him actually killing somebody in cold blood. First, he wouldn't have the guts. Second, he'd probably make a mess of it and end up with a scratched face and a live victim. Still, even if he didn't do the killing, this theory of yours *does* account for how eager he is to pin it on Harry Stubbins. Blame it all on an old bum who broke in to rob her, and nobody has to poke into the details of her private life."

"So what do we do now?" I said.

Ann thought it over a few seconds, and her jaw set grimly. "What've we got to lose by trying this out on the little son of a bitch? Just to see what happens."

She called McBride's office, and asked his secretary if he could see us on a matter of great importance. She said he wasn't in, he had gone downtown to his campaign headquarters with Mr. Brock. Ann hung up and looked at me a moment and then gave a little grin. "Why not? Carrying the war into enemy territory, bearding the lion in his den—all the military experts recommend it, don't they?"

We got our coats and went to the outer office, where Roger was bubbling over with news. "I just talked to that professor in Michigan," he said. "He was chairman of the English department when Harry Stubbins was teaching there. He gave me a lot of interesting dope."

And Roger told us the sad story of Harry Stubbins. Thirty years ago he had gotten out of graduate school at Berkeley, an up-and-coming young scholar from California, an expert on Romantic poetry. He had taught at a couple of lesser places and ended up as a tenured associate professor at Ann Arbor. He had published a couple of books and a lot of articles in learned journals. He had also acquired a wife and two young daughters. Life couldn't have been more beautiful.

Seven years ago, when the daughters were in their teens, an icy road three blocks from his house had brought an end to all that beauty. His wife was driving back from grocery shopping, and the daughters were with her in the car. A beer truck, coming at them down a long hill, had gone into a skid on the ice, and in five minutes Harry Stubbins had lost his whole family.

That was when he started drinking. Well, actually—his chairman told Roger—Harry had been a fairly heavy drinker for many years, but it had never been a problem for him to keep his thirst under control. After the death of his wife and children, the control ended, and two years later the university fired him. It's not easy to fire a tenured professor. Incompetence, surliness, lechery, even failure to show up at your classes won't do it. His chairman didn't specify what Stubbins had actually done, but it must have been way beyond the pale.

After that Stubbins sold his house and left Ann Arbor, and

the chairman lost track of him. Nobody else in the department seemed to have kept in touch with him either. There was a rumor that he had gone back to the town where his wife had been born and grew up—some town in the mountains out west somewhere—but that rumor was never confirmed.

"All right, life isn't fair," Ann said after a moment. "If we're desperate enough, I suppose we can use some of this in court, it might squeeze some sympathy out of the jury. But just between us, I'd prefer a few hard facts. For instance"—her face lighted up—"a nice plausible alternative murderer." Then she gave a brisk nod, rubbed her hands together, and said, "Come on, Dave, we've got a lion to beard."

Ann and I used my car to drive out to the Richelieu Hotel, where McBride's campaign headquarters were located—the Richelieu did a nice business at election time. McBride's campaign headquarters took up a couple of suites on the second floor and must have been costing a pretty penny. One of the suites was filled with desks and people chattering on the phone and pounding typewriters. Most of these people looked to be in their sixties or even older.

The connecting suite was less hectic, just one secretary in the outer room. The walls were covered with posters that showed McBride glaring out at you and stabbing his finger at you. Over his head was his slogan, in black belligerent letters: VOTE FOR MCBRIDE! HE'S ON YOUR SIDE!

The secretary told us McBride was in conference and would see people only by appointment, but Ann insisted she let him know we were there. A few seconds letter, rather miffed, she told us to go right in.

McBride, as usual, was sitting behind a big desk, looking small. He jumped up as soon as we came in and bustled up to us. He gave Ann a big hug and me a vigorous handshake.

Ed Brock, his face and his bald pate scrubbed bright like a fat baby's, gave us a couple of amiable how-are-yous from one of the chairs. Brock didn't get up, though, and nobody expected him to.

Ann got right down to business. "Something's come up in the Pulaski murder, Marvin. We thought we'd better discuss it with you, before we decided what to do about it."

Her solemn tone of voice didn't seem to perturb him in the least. "Sit down, make yourselves comfortable." He settled back in his desk chair, picked up the smoldering cigar from his ashtray, and waved it at us. "Let's hear what's up."

Ann and I sat. "I think we'd better talk in private," she said.

"Why should we? Ed is like my double, my second self—right, Ed?"

Ed nodded slowly, smiling, but his eyes were fixed intently on Ann's face.

"Even so." Ann said, "I may be telling you some things now—well, maybe you wouldn't want your second self to hear them. You might as well know, what we have to say doesn't concern my client alone. It also concerns you personally. And the private nature of this information—"

"How private can it be, for Christ sake?" McBride said. "I don't have any deep dark secrets. Okay, I'll come clean, I snore whenever I sleep on my back. Otherwise"—he grinned and took a big puff from his cigar—"my hands are white as snow. Everything on the up-and-up. Strictly kosher, like the ki—like our Jewish friends say."

Ann looked steadily into his grin. "If Ed were ever subpoenaed, he'd have to testify to this conversation."

"In my entire life," Ed said, "nobody's ever obliged me to tell anything I didn't want to tell. Not anybody. Not even my late sainted wife." He hitched forward a little in his chair. "What's this about being subpoenaed? In what context? How could my testimony possibly be required in the Stubbins trial?"

"If it turned out," Ann said quietly, "that Marvin had some personal knowledge in the case. If it turned out, for instance, that he had an intimate connection with the dead woman that was relevant to the circumstances of her death."

McBride's grin disappeared. "What the hell are you getting at? I told you everything about my involvement with that Pulaski broa—dame—woman! I talked to her for a few minutes six or seven months ago, when we brought her in for questioning. I never saw her before or since in my life."

Ann sighed. "That's really a lie, isn't it, Marvin?"

His face got redder. "Goddammit, if any *man* called me a liar to my face—"

"Just a minute, Marvin." Ed Brock spoke softly, but McBride ground his teeth together and shut up. "I assume"—Ed turned to Ann—"you've got some grounds for these rather provocative insinuations?"

Ann sighed again, then she went through Mom's line of reasoning step by step—the steps, that is, leading to the conclusion that McBride had been having an affair with Edna Pulaski. She didn't mention, as yet, the steps leading to the conclusion that McBride might have killed her.

When she stopped talking, Ed Brock's head was lowered, and his huge hand was shading the upper part of his face; no way to see what his expression was.

McBride chomped at his cigar for a while, and then he removed it and looked up at us. "That's not evidence, for Christ sake. You couldn't come out with any of that in court, the judge would kick you out on your ass. And if you went to the newspapers with it, if you were crazy enough to make any public statements about it, I could sue you for every cent you've got."

"Oh, I doubt that," Ann said. "If we were really pressured into it, I have a feeling we could come up with some facts here and there that'll tie the two of you together."

"You couldn't, because the two of us never *were* together. But even if we *had* been, even if I *was* having an affair, don't you think I'd be damn careful about leaving a trail? What kind of a moron do you think I am?"

"We're pretty good diggers, Marvin," Ann said. "And nobody can think of *everything*. For instance, did you always meet her in her house? Didn't you ever take her out—to a restaurant, for instance, or to the movies?"

"You think I'm a total basket case? If I was having an affair—which I wasn't—would I go anyplace where people could see us together?"

"What about money?" Ann said. "Assuming there *was* something between you and Edna Pulaski, wouldn't you have given her money from time to time? Are you sure you never signed your name to any checks that you made out to her?"

"I'd have to be out of my mind. Any money I'd ever give her would be cash. And if I ever gave her presents, flowers or a bottle of perfume, say, you'd better believe I'd always bring them to her in person, I'd never have the store send them. And it would never be anything fancy or expensive. Any relationship of that type that *I* ever got into, money wouldn't enter into it, believe me. Women are attracted to me because they're attracted to me." Onto his face came a self-congratulating simper that made my stomach turn a little. "You'd be surprised how attractive I can be, when I put my mind to it." The simper spread into a grin. "Besides, Ed would never let me do anything with a woman that could be traced back to me. If I started to make a wrong move, he'd always catch it in time."

McBride laughed and leaned back in his chair. He couldn't have looked more relaxed. Then, suddenly, he produced a grin that was practically boyish. Like a naughty kid caught out in one of his pranks. "Okay, why not? Strictly off the record, Ann, you double-cross me on this and I'll deny every word of it—"

"Marvin, I wouldn't advise you—" Ed Brock started in, but McBride laughed and rode right over his words.

"Don't be such a worrier, Ed, you'll make yourself bald before your time!" Brock settled back in his chair and put his hand over his eyes again.

McBride turned back to Ann. "Okay, I'll put you out of your misery. You're absolutely right about Edna and me. You worked it out very neatly, women are getting too damn smart these days. I was telling the truth when I said I didn't know Edna until early this year, when the cops pulled her in on that raid. There wasn't enough evidence to go ahead with a prosecution against her, but I talked with her for a while, and I got the feeling maybe we could get something going between us.

You know how you get that feeling sometimes? It's something about the way somebody looks at you or the tone in her voice, you can't put your finger on exactly why, but the feeling always turns out to be right. And I was thinking, it might be kind of interesting and unusual, a healthy change, I never *did* have any of that Oriental pussy before. You read a lot about it, all the amazing things they can do, those geisha girls—"

"That's Japanese," I said. "Edna Pulaski was Korean."

"Whatever." McBride made a gesture, pushing aside my hair-splitting. "So a couple nights later I called her up, and sure enough she *had* been thinking what I was thinking. So I started seeing her on a regular basis. She always got rid of the girls that worked for her first, told them she was coming down with the bug or something and had to close shop. Because she knew I had a public position to keep up, there couldn't be any ugly rumors, I had my duty to my constituents. Anyway, for the last six months I've been seeing her one night a week. That's the best I could manage. Fact is, I'm a busy guy most nights, what with political dinners, public functions, Bar Association and Chamber of Commerce— you name it, I have to put on my fancy dress and be there. Anyway, in a situation like this, it isn't a good idea to see the woman too often. She could start to get ideas about how serious you are. Anyway, that's my experience."

"How much experience do you have?" I put in. "How many other little lapses have you gone in for in the last few years?"

McBride looked at me, friendly, without taking offense. "Not all that many, Dave. A man gets to my age, your marriage isn't doing too well, for years your wife won't satisfy your natural desires and finally she throws you out—well, I'm a normal healthy guy, I never claimed I was the type to be a monk. Anyway, I never have more than one of them going at a time!" He emphasized that with a firm nod: a definite point of honor with him. "More than that would be greedy, right? Even if I didn't have enough sense myself to go easy, Ed would never stand for it."

"Wait a second, wait a second!" Ann turned to Ed sharply.

"You knew what was going on between Marvin and Edna Pulaski?"

Ed spread his hands. "In a way."

"What do you mean, in a way? You either knew something or you didn't?"

"In the world of logic that might be the case," Ed said. "It's different in the world of politics. Let's say that Marvin never actually told me what was going on, because as his campaign manager I would certainly never condone such immoral behavior. I would have advised him to bring an end to it right away, and if he refused to do so I should have been obliged to resign from his campaign. Therefore he never *did* tell me anything. If I became aware of anything, that could only be a guess on my part, an abstract speculation, and if I gave him advice on what to do—and what to avoid doing, what precautions to take, et cetera—it was strictly abstract advice, designed to apply to general situations and not to any that actually existed."

"It doesn't bother your conscience any," Ann said, "that you've been conniving at a coverup, letting him go on prosecuting a case when he himself was personally involved?"

Ed leaned forward in his chair, with a more earnest expression on his face. "My dear Ann, why should my conscience enter into this at all? You have to look at these things in context. This is politics we're talking about, not life. When you're in politics, you have to get elected. That's the whole basis of our democratic system. Whether you're tricky Dick Nixon or Saint Franklin Delano Roosevelt, you can't do a bit of good for yourself, or for your city or country or what-have-you, if the people throw you out at the polls. High ideals are useless, unless you're in office to do something about them."

He sat back again, spreading his hands. "I'm not trying to excuse Marvin's little lapse, I'm just trying to make you aware of certain realities that all of us in politics have to be aware of all the time. We may not *like* those realities, but we can't afford to pretend they don't exist. If Marvin allowed his relationship with that woman to be made public, there's an excellent chance he would lose this coming election. I don't think he

---

112

should lose. I believe he's the better candidate. No doubt I'm biased, but that's what I believe. Therefore, on the principle that a man of integrity should stand up for his beliefs, I would really be violating my conscience, wouldn't I, if I *didn't*—what was your phrase?—'connive at the coverup'?"

"Terrific!" McBride clapped his hands together. "Couldn't have put it better myself! That's exactly how I feel about it. If that business with Edna happened to come out, the DA's office might be turned over to that liberal feminist wimp. *Then* what happens to this town? My God, they've been trying to get me for years—you don't expect me to just roll over and let them do it!"

"Who's 'they'?" I said.

"They, they! The criminal element, who else! The ones who've been laying for me ever since I first took on this job. At considerable personal and financial sacrifice, incidentally, because of my commitment to this community—I've got the right to defend myself, damn it! This is America, a man can't be discriminated against on any grounds, neither race, creed, nor color, nor previous condition of servitude, nor—"

Realizing he was getting a little mixed up, McBride dissolved into spluttering, wheezed, and blew his nose. One good thing came out of this gesture; he had to put his cigar down. In his agitation he forgot about it, so it lay in the ashtray and pretty soon it went out.

"That's all very well," Ann said, "but I've got a client to defend, and I can't overlook anything that might strengthen my case."

"Just a moment, Ann." Ed Brock leaned forward again. "If Marvin's relationship with the Pulaski woman came out, I grant you it might be embarrassing to him. But what difference could it possibly make to the murder case? How could it possibly? Unless you intend to suggest that *Marvin* had something to do with . . ."

He let his voice trail off, but his eyes didn't leave Ann's face.

And now, finally, McBride caught on too. "My God, you're

saying *I* killed her?'' His voice rose to a roar, and his face got redder than the fire in his cigar.

"I understand why you're upset," Ann said. "But looking at the matter objectively—which of course you can't do—there *are* some fairly suggestive points. For instance, what Edna Pulaski told Harry Stubbins—that she had a boyfriend who wanted to break off their affair, that she threatened to tell the newspapers about it—"

"That's all a lie! I *never* told Edna I was going to dump her! Why should I? We were getting along fine, one night a week, it couldn't have been friendlier. What did I want to throw that away for? And even if I did, why would I take the chance of antagonizing her just before the election? Why wouldn't I wait another couple of weeks until the election was in the bag? Your client's lying through his teeth about that! For Christ sake, are you going to take the word of a miserable old drunk over *mine?*''

"There are other suggestive points too," Ann said. And she trotted out Mom's point about McBride's "patriotic" necktie.

"That's supposed to be evidence?" McBride practically screamed. "I'm wearing that tie right now! Look, here it is, same tie I wore at the dinner Saturday night! Take it to the lab, get it tested, if you find anything to connect it with that strangling—"

"How do we *know* it's the same tie?" Ann said. "You've got dozens of identical ones, you told us that yourself."

"And this town is full of guys who wear neckties, for Christ sake! Any one of *them* could've done this killing!"

"But very few of them have the motive and the opportunity—"

"What opportunity?"

"The dinner Saturday night was over by eleven, and Edna Pulaski's murderer didn't get to her house till after eleven-thirty, according to Stubbins—"

"Stubbins again! Terrific witness you've got there!"

"He's got no reason to make up that time, Marvin. It doesn't help *his* case any to say the murderer came in at eleven-thirty-five. But it does fit nicely with your own—"

"Look, I wasn't *near* her house on Saturday night!"

"Where *did* you go then? You could put an end to this whole line of inquiry if you happen to have been with somebody at eleven-thirty."

"After that dinner, I went home. If you can call it home. I've got this one-room dump on the North End. Nellie's got the house—naturally, she needs it for the kid. Anyway, I dropped Ed off at *his* place first, in my car, and then I went straight home and I went to bed."

"Can you prove that?" I said.

"How the hell am I supposed to prove it? You go to bed alone, you haven't got any witnesses. From now on I'll take a broad to bed with me *every* night, that way I'll always have an alibi for everything." He gave a violent shake of his head. "Ann, Dave, for Christ sake—Ed—you *can't* believe I killed her?" McBride was holding out his arms, and there was real feeling in his voice.

Ann met his gaze steadily. *"Did* you kill her?"

"I didn't, Goddammit! I never touched that Pulaski woman. I'm telling you the God's truth. I swear it, on my mother's grave!"

That did it. For a moment there he had almost had me convinced that he wasn't acting, that he was innocent and felt genuinely wronged. But then I recovered my wits and laughed at myself. Except maybe when he was in the throes of a particularly bad hangover, there was *never* a time when McBride wasn't acting.

"Excuse me, Marvin," I said, "but your mother is alive, isn't she? Didn't you tell me once that she's living in a home for the aged in the south of the state?"

McBride puffed at his cigar, and the boyish grin reappeared. "Good thinking, Dave. You're right, my dear old mother has a lot of years to go, I hope. I was just using what you might call a figure of speech."

He broke off abruptly, and his good humor disappeared

fast. "Wait a minute, why am I answering all these questions about where I was and who I was with? Why am I having this conversation with you? You haven't got a damn thing on me. You're trying to smear me. I'm on to the waste and inefficiency in your office so you're trying to get my opponent elected. I think it's about time you got the hell out of this office, because in another minute I'm liable to lose my temper!"

We took him at his word and got out of there.

I drove Ann back to the courthouse—she had an appearance to make in connection with an entirely different case—but I didn't get out of the car. I had a lot to think about.

McBride's affair with Edna Pulaski did give him a motive for murder, I thought. And it gave the same motive to Ed Brock, whose interest in protecting McBride's reputation before the election must be pretty much as strong as McBride's own—and who, incidentally, lived alone and had been let off at his house a little after eleven on the night of the murder.

But it also occurred to me now that the affair between McBride and Edna created a *different* kind of motive for somebody else. For McBride's wife who, even though she had dumped him, might not look so kindly on somebody else he was sleeping with.

Obviously the time had come for me to talk to Mrs. McBride. And since it was after three o'clock, and school was out, I might be able to talk to his daughter too.

As usual, I didn't call beforehand.

They were living, as McBride had told us, in the same house where he had lived for most of his married life. It was located a few blocks away from the Richelieu Hotel, one of the best sections of town. Full of impressive mansions, some of them must've sold for a million or more, but McBride definitely didn't have one of those. His house was the smallest I saw in the neighborhood. It had just one story and there was an infinitesimal lawn in front. In the old days, when these estates were even bigger, it had probably been somebody's servants quarters.

The door was opened for me by a dark thin girl, about sixteen. She had no makeup on her face, her hair was faded and stringy, touches of acne were imperfectly covered up by some kind of lotion. Behind thick glasses, her expression was tight and anxious.

I told her who I was and reeled off my usual spiel about the public defender having as much right to question witnesses as the police. She looked at me in a dull scared way, and finally she stepped aside to let me into the foyer. "I'll tell Mommy you're here," she said, and turned away to the archway just behind her. I figured she was McBride's daughter, but she made no attempt to introduce herself.

A moment later she was back. "She says come in." She showed me into the living room, which was full of overstuffed furniture that looked old. Secondhand old, not antique. McBride's money, it occurred to me, had gone into the address and the neighborhood, not into space or luxury.

On the sofa was a middle-aged woman, plump, plainly dressed, wispy gray hair, watery blue eyes. The first impression she gave was of mildness and bewilderment. She didn't stand up, but she held out her hand, and when I went over to shake it she told me she was Nellie McBride, and she introduced her daughter, Laurel.

"I'm sorry to bother you, Mrs. McBride," I said. "I'm investigating the death of Edna Pulaski for the public defender's office. Our client, Harry Stubbins, is being held for the crime by your ex—your—"

"My husband," Mrs. McBride said, in the flat twang that belongs to the southern end of our state. "We haven't been through any divorce yet. I'm not sure we'll ever do that." Then, without putting any noticeable emotion into her voice, she added, "I'm not sure it'd be right. When two people have been joined together in the eyes of God—" her voice trailed off. Then she said, "I don't know why you're coming to *me*. I don't know as how I've got any information you could use. I never even met this woman that got killed."

"Mrs. McBride—" I gave a glance at her daughter. "Do you think I could talk to you in private?"

A shadow came over her face. "Well, yes, sure. Laurel, honey, how'd you like to go upstairs and do your homework before dinner?"

Laurel hesitated, as if she meant to disobey her mother's orders. But the hesitation didn't last more than a split second. Then she was moving toward the living-room archway.

"Can I ask one question before Laurel leaves?" I said. "This last Saturday night—were the two of you here in this house together?"

Laurel's chin turned in her mother's direction. Her eyes blinked through her glasses, as if she was looking for instructions.

In a steady voice, still without any emotion in it, Mrs. McBride said, "I was home, right here, all night Saturday. I had one of my headaches, I get these headaches, so I went to bed early. Fixed my Ovaltine and put a sleeping pill in it, I do that when my headache gets really bad. Took it up to the bedroom with me, and it put me right to sleep."

"And Laurel was with you all this time?"

Laurel opened her mouth, but stopped herself from saying anything. Another quick glance at her mother, and I saw Mrs. McBride gave the slightest of nods. Then Laurel spoke, in a very low voice, which had in it a muted version of her mother's nasal twang. "I wasn't home Saturday night. I mean, not till late. I'm in this play at high school—we're doing this musical, *Peter Pan*. I don't have a very big part, I'm just one of the Indians. But I have to be there all through rehearsals anyway."

"And you were at rehearsal Saturday night?"

"It went real late. I didn't get home till after one. Mommy was asleep, I looked into her room but I didn't wake her up."

"What school do you go to?"

"Laurel goes to General Wagner High," said Mrs. McBride. "That's the public high school in this neighborhood. She's real interested in drama and acting in shows and all, and they've got a real good program there. Laurel's got a beautiful singing voice—"

"Mommy!" The girl's voice was filled with pure agony. I understood her feelings completely, so I changed the subject. "You and Laurel are all alone in this house, Mrs. McBride? No live-in help of any kind?"

"There's our cleaning woman, she comes in twice a week. Otherwise we take care of the place ourselves. I got along without any help for plenty of years, I guess I still know how." A pause, and then another flat emotionless afterthought. "The house seemed kind of big and empty when Marvin first moved out. But I guess we're used to it now."

"How long has he been gone?"

"Almost a year. As of next Thanksgiving."

"Since you're not divorced, does he keep any of his things here? Clothes, personal articles?"

"He don't keep anything here. I made him take away every bit of that stuff. There's not even a button left."

Her voice didn't quaver or tighten, but now, for the first time, I saw a glint of emotion on her face.

I turned to Laurel. "When you see your father, I suppose you go to his apartment?"

"Laurel don't see her father." Mrs. McBride's voice couldn't have been quieter and steadier.

"I don't want to see Daddy," Laurel said, her voice trembling. "He didn't want to go on living with us. He didn't care about us. So I don't care about—" She broke off suddenly and moved to the archway. "I'll do my homework now!"

She darted out of the room. She didn't give me a good-bye nod.

Mrs. McBride gave a little sigh. "Poor little baby—Marvin's leaving us hurt her a lot. She's at what d'you call it, an *impres*-sionable age. You can see how shy and withdrawn she is. She's got no social life at all, that poor baby. I keep telling her, at her age she ought to have a half a dozen boys calling her up, hanging around the house. Right now it don't look like she'll *ever* find herself a boyfriend."

"Do you blame her father for that, Mrs. McBride?"

She fixed her eyes steadily on my face. "Understand me now—I'm not saying anything against him. You can't make me. A wife is loyal to her husband, even if they're not living together. You don't wash your dirty clothes in public. That's how I was brought up."

"Did you know about his relationship with Edna Pulaski?"

She said nothing for a long time, though her eyes never moved away from my face. Finally she said, "I guess I knew there was somebody. Marvin's not the type to go for long without somebody. I never had any idea who it was though— till a week ago."

"What happened a week ago?"

"A friend of mine—a woman who's in my church—saw him going into this house one night. This house on South Arizona. She and her husband were driving by, and they saw Marvin going through the front door. This massage parlor—that's what they call those houses, don't they? There was a sign in front, it had this woman's name on it. My friend told me about it the next day."

"Were you curious to find out more about the woman who lived in that house? Did you call her up on the phone, go to see her maybe?"

"I put it out of my head. Marvin's life is now his own business."

"Did you know Edna Pulaski was Korean?"

"I figured she'd be some kind of Oriental. In spite of the name. On account of that neighborhood is full of them."

"And how did you feel about this affair? Did you resent it? Were you jealous or angry at him?"

Her voice got a little louder and sharper. "Didn't I tell you—I'm not saying anything bad about Marvin. I'm not saying anything against my husband."

"You still love him, Mrs. McBride?"

For the first time a kind of smile twitched at her thin pale lips. "I loved him the first time I ever set eyes on him. We were in high school together. Marvin was the smartest, most up-and-coming boy in the class. I know what you're thinking, but you should've seen the *rest* of them. That little town—sand and mud and hogs. But he was bound and determined to go on to college and make himself into a lawyer, and since I was lucky enough to attract his favor—well, I was bound and determined I'd help him. We got married right after graduation, and I went to the state university with him. I didn't go as any student, I was never much good at reading books and such. I went there to keep house for him, and see to it he knuckled down to his studies and didn't get tangled up with distracting influences."

"There *were* such influences?"

"I kept him from getting tangled up with them. Same thing when he went to law school, at the University of Northern Michigan. Maybe it isn't the best law school in the country, and Marvin didn't graduate at the top of his class, more like the lower middle. I knew he wasn't ever going to be on the Supreme Court or anything like that, but he had his law degree, that was the important thing, and he had this natural ability to stand up in front of a crowd of people and talk louder and faster than any of them. So I could see he had a chance to make it in politics.

"And that's sure how it worked out. You can say, I guess, being district attorney in Mesa Grande don't amount to much. He isn't exactly any big fish in a big pond. But he's got second best. He's a big fish in a little pond—maybe even a middle-size pond—and it's not bad being the wife of that kind of fish. A lot better, let me tell you, than if I'da stayed home with the sand and the hogs."

She came to a stop. Then in a quieter, more thoughtful voice, "Do I still love him—?" She broke off, looking at me again, no expression on her face. "I guess we better break this up now. Like I told you—you're not going to hear me say one word that's bad—"

TEN

It was after five when I got back to the courthouse. Ann wasn't out of court yet, and Roger was at the switchboard, talking to various members of the Pulverizin' Plumbers bowling team. He stopped for a moment to report to me that, with most of them now accounted for, nobody had failed to confirm Ron Pulaski's alibi for the time of the murder. Then I went into my office and put in a call to Mom.

She sounded harried. "You have to talk to me quick," she said. "I'm going out for dinner in a couple hours, and I didn't take my bath and get dressed yet."

"What's the dinner, Mom?"

"It's only a friend of mine. We're going to a restaurant and afterward to a movie. The new one with Arnold the Schwartze. You know who I mean? This big German fellow that's got so many muscles you think he buys them cut rate in the store."

"I didn't know you went in for that sort of movie. All that violence, people fighting and getting bloody."

"To tell you the truth," Mom answered, "I personally prefer the old Bette Davis type pictures. I like it when she's this nasty woman, she does everybody dirt, she steals everybody's boyfriend, she wears beautiful clothes on her, and at the end she gets religion and sacrifices herself for the man she loves. Five handkerchiefs at least I have to bring to the theater. But movies like those they don't make anymore. And my friend who's taking me out tonight, he's crazy for this Schwartze fellow. He's younger than me, so naturally his taste isn't so old-fashioned."

"Younger than you?" I couldn't keep the uneasiness out of my voice.

"Five years. He's going on seventy." Mom's tone of voice was perfectly casual. No way to figure out if she was putting me on.

"Who is this guy anyway?" I said.

"Only a man. At the YMCA I met him. We see each other every week at the swimming pool. Finally he asked me I should go out with him."

"The YMCA? He isn't Jewish?"

"Who says so? The YMCA is open to everybody that pays the membership fee. Am *I* a Christian? For that matter, am I young, am I a man?" She gave a laugh. "Since when do you care about such things, if people are Jewish already? It never bothered you when you were growing up. All the shiksas you went out with, and if I mentioned it to you what did I get? 'Mom, you're so narrow-minded!' And what about the women you're going out with here in this town? Did you bring one to meet me *yet* that knows what a circumcision looks like?"

"I *married* a Jewish woman, didn't I?" But I broke off, losing heart for the argument. I didn't feel like talking about Shirley. Not to Mom anyway, who had never liked her and made no bones about showing it. "Besides, the women I've gone out with aren't the point. The point is—" But I couldn't go on. The point was, no matter how far away *I* strayed from the old values and traditions, I expected my mother to uphold them. If I said this out loud, though, she'd give one of her sarcastic hoots and I'd feel like an idiot.

"Excuse me, but time is flying," Mom said. "Are you planning to tell me what happened with the case since we had lunch—or are you planning *not* to tell me?"

So I went through it with Mom in detail, Roger's information about Harry Stubbins, his confirmation of Ron Pulaski's alibi, the confrontation Ann and I had with McBride at his campaign headquarters, my talk with Mrs. McBride and her daughter. I could imagine Mom nodding and pulling at her lower lip. When I came to a stop, she said, "It's funny. Very funny."

"What's funny?"

"Believe me, I wish I knew. It's a little something that's inside my head, only it won't come out." She broke off with a little sigh. "I'm getting old, this is the problem."

The "little something" must have been pretty annoying, because otherwise Mom never starts talking about getting old.

But a moment later she snapped out of it, and her voice was brisk and businesslike again. "Enough wasting time on things we couldn't help yet. How about you should pay a little attention to a couple things you *could* help?"

"What are they, Mom?"

"The first thing is, call up the high school that this little girl, McBride's daughter, goes to. Find out if she was really at a play rehearsal till late Saturday night."

"Laurel McBride is a sixteen-year-old kid," I said. "You don't actually think she—"

"Call the school, then I'll know what I think. Second thing— you should do please what you didn't do today, you didn't talk to the Pulaski girl's ex-husband and ask him the question I told you to ask."

"I just didn't have any time for that."

"No time."

I heard Mom heaving one of her deepest sighs. "All right, all right, now I have to hang up, but tomorrow you'll ring me up maybe, when you've got a few more answers."

I made a noncommittal noise and hung up the phone. But inside my head I was telling myself: Enough already, a man your age is too old to be intimidated by his mother. When in the course of human events—

I looked up and saw Roger standing in my doorway. I supposed he had heard pretty much everything Mom had said to me. When she talks on the phone, she always shouts at the top of her voice; it's as if she doesn't really believe this invention will work.

"Would you like *me* to take care of that, Dave?" Roger said.

"I could drop in on Ron Pulaski first thing tomorrow morning—"

"Why would you do that?"

"To ask that question. Did he find out about the murder from the radio news or the television news?"

"What's the difference?"

"Well, I don't know. I heard your mother saying it's important—"

"I'll decide what's important in this investigation, okay? Who's in charge anyway?"

His face got red, and he went scurrying out the doorway.

ELEVEN

The next morning, Tuesday, I started to the office shortly before nine. My head was aching just a little, after a heavy night with this woman I was going out with; she worked as a legal paraprofessional with one of the judges in town, and her staid and formal manner on the job would never prepare you for the way she could cut loose after hours.

It was pretty cold out, and the heater in my car wasn't operating too well. I turned on the radio. Some country music, with all the instruments and the singer sounding as if their noses were stopped up, twanged away at me, irritating me enough to keep my mind off my goose pimples. I was just turning into the downtown section, seven or eight blocks from the courthouse, when I saw something through the windshield that made me pull up quickly next to a parking meter.

Our client, Harry Stubbins, was standing on the corner. He had his hat—or the dilapidated hunk of cloth that passed for a hat—in his hand, and he was holding it out at passersby.

I got out of the car and went up to him. "What're you doing here? You're supposed to be at the Shelter for the Homeless! You heard the judge—"

"My dear fellow—" The words were slurred, but they came rolling out of Stubbins with a definite reverberation to them. I couldn't tell whether or not he was drunk. Maybe he couldn't tell the difference himself any more. "—you don't suppose they make you huddle in their depressing barn all day long?

Matter of fact, they kick you out of there shortly after you've had your breakfast, won't let you back in till dinnertime."

"That's all right then. They did give you some breakfast before they let you loose today."

"Ample portions of coffee, juice, and griddle cakes, made from the finest shoe leather. Kind of nourishment that sticks to the ribs. Truth is, I'm wondering if it'll ever get *un*stuck."

"You shouldn't be out on the street begging though. It's against the law."

"Is it?" His bloodshot eyes blinked up at me in amazement. "Very odd law. You'd think they'd *want* a man to ply his trade, earn an honest living. With laws like that, they could drive a man into a life of crime. Good God, I might become a *stockbroker!*" He gave one of his thin hacking laughs. "Not to worry, however, my dear fellow. Been doing this sort of thing in this town for years, nobody ever arrested me for it yet. Authorities have much bigger game to stalk. All those drug dealers and rapists and serial killers we're always reading about."

"Still, you don't want them to run you in while you're out on bond. It would embarrass the judge, and he could blame the public defender for it at some future date. Here, let me give you a couple of bucks so you can have lunch."

"*Much* too early for my lunch."

"I'm expecting you to hold onto it till the time comes. Meanwhile, I'll deposit you in a nice warm place."

He gave a deep sigh. "No such place, not for wicked old derelicts like myself. Used to sneak into the movie theaters in weather like this. But the movies don't open till two in the afternoon."

"You don't have to sneak into the place I've got in mind. It's free and open to the public. Come on, get into the car."

He scrambled in. I admit it made me nervous to have him there; I had just had the seat covers cleaned. But I swallowed my qualms, like a good Samaritan, and we started west.

On the way I said, "We're making some progress on your case. Ann may have some news for you soon."

"Ah yes, many thanks." He burrowed down into the seat, as

if he planned to hibernate there for the rest of the winter. "My old father always said to me, 'Make sure you've got a good lawyer, everything else will take care of itself.' "

"Your old father? Where was that? Where *did* you grow up anyway?"

One round bloodshot eye rolled up at me from the pile of rags that enveloped him. "Thought we agreed about that. No probing into the dead dark past. You don't stick your nose into *my* history, I won't stick mine into *yours.*"

I hesitated, then I decided there was really nothing to lose. "You should feel pretty much at home in this place we're going to. It's the public library."

He didn't say anything. The bloodshot eye was still fixed on me.

"After all, literature *is* your line of work, isn't it, Professor Stubbins?"

For another moment the eye glittered, and then it rolled up and disappeared from view. After a moment a noise came from deep within the pile of rags. A soft whimpering noise.

"What'd I do to you?" The noise finally turned into words. "Did I hurt you? Why'd you steal from me?"

"What did I steal from you?"

"Privacy. Sacred right of privacy. Protected by the Constitution. Why'd you take it away from me?"

"We're not taking anything away from you. We're trying to keep them from taking *everything* away from you. We have to know who you are if we're going to help you."

He said nothing to that. The whimpering noise started again.

"Is this really how you want it?" I said. "Your kind of privacy—it's nothing but wallowing in self-pity!"

"Self-pity!" The word came spitting out of him, and at the same time his head popped up from the pile of rags. His eyes were gleaming, and they seemed to be perfectly focused. "Any idea how *tired* we are of hearing that word?"

"We?"

" 'Self-pity'—the all-purpose anesthetic. Not for us, for *you.* Sure cure for feeling somebody else's pain."

"We want to help you get rid of your pain!"

"Who asked you?" His voice got louder. "What do you know about it anyway? Did you ever lose everything?"

He showed me a contorted face, blazing up into mine.

"Yes," I said. I started to say more, to explain what I meant, but suddenly the words wouldn't come out of me. I remembered those first few months, after Shirley died. I remembered being alone in that apartment, sitting there night after night. Maybe, if I'd had a bottle to keep me company— Maybe, if I hadn't been brought up by a Jewish mother who looked down her nose at drinking— Who was I, or anybody else, to give another human being grades on how he handled his despair?

"Okay, okay, I'm sorry," I said quickly, and thank God we got to the public library just then, and I was able to bundle the old man out of my car and into the front entrance.

I was still a little shaky when I got to the office. Roger even asked me if I was feeling all right. I ignored the question and told him to call up Laurel McBride's high school and find out about her Saturday night play rehearsal. He gave me a look of astonishment. "She's a sixteen-year-old kid! You don't really think—"

He was saying pretty much what I had said to Mom over the phone yesterday. So I gave him the same treatment Mom had given me. "Call the school, then I'll know what I think."

Then we were interrupted by Ann buzzing for me in her office.

"I just got a call from Doris Dryden," she said. "She's got some information for us about the murder. She wants to talk to me right now."

"She couldn't talk over the phone?"

"Her information is too 'sensitive,' she says. That's the word she used. 'Phones can be tapped,' she said. So I'm going down to her campaign headquarters, and I'd like you to come with me."

Dryden was running her campaign from her own apartment, a condominium in a nice little building close to downtown.

In the last few years, I should explain, Mesa Grande has discovered the condominium. Half a dozen new apartment houses have sprung up; they're constructed mostly of red brick, and what you buy are picture windows, built-in air conditioning, landscaped driveways and parking lots, and terrific views of the mountains, if you happen to be located on the expensive side of the building. Rumor has it that these apartments sell for pretty stiff prices, anyway by Mesa Grande standards.

Dryden must be doing pretty well for herself, I thought, as Ann and I drove up to her building. At the front entrance, after I had parked the car, we came up against another luxury that few apartment houses in Mesa Grande have: a doorman. He was tall, black, and dignified in his gold braid and epaulettes. He gave us a fishy look as he asked *whom* we had come to see. Then he rang her from his lobby switchboard, and his fishy look relaxed somewhat after she told him to send us up.

Her living room had half a dozen people in it, sitting on folding metal chairs at makeshift desks, pounding away at typewriters or barking into phones. Whatever Doris ordinarily had on her walls—reproductions of slick hard-edged abstract art, judging from the style of her furniture—it was all covered up now by campaign posters. They featured her own face, in various sizes and with various expressions: earnestness, happiness, grim determination, sympathetic concern. All of these faces illustrated her slogan, in big black letters: VOTE FOR DRYDEN: GIVE COMPETENCY AND COMPASSION A CHANCE.

She was looking over the shoulder of one of the typists, a smooth-cheeked college boy who, it seemed to me, couldn't be older than fourteen. (On the whole her campaign workers seemed to be about one-third the age of McBride's.) She saw Ann and me, patted the boy on the shoulder encouragingly, and waved at us to follow her. We went into a small room with a desk, a couple of chairs, and three phones in it. From the bed-sofa shoved against one of the walls, I figured this had been some kind of guest bedroom before she turned it into an office.

She shut the door behind her, blocking out some of the noise, then she told us to take a seat and flopped behind the desk with a long weary sigh. "What a zoo! It isn't usually this hectic, but we've been fielding a lot of calls on account of McBride's press conference the other day. You have to hand it to the old swindler, don't you? He's a total loss at enforcing the law, but when it comes to conning the public he's P. T. Barnum and Ronald Reagan rolled into one. All he's done with this murder case is make a big noise, but he's already got half the world convinced he's won some kind of big victory over me."

"Don't you think," Ann asked, "that the people who are taken in by his noise would've voted for him even *without* this murder?"

"Maybe you're right. Still, it's worrying." She sighed. "It's a great game, but sometimes it tires you out, I have to admit that. The other night, after that dinner, I got back here around eleven-fifteen—which isn't that late for me ordinarily—and I unplugged my phone and collapsed on my bed, without even taking off my clothes, and I didn't wake up till ten Sunday morning. Who ever thought that little fart would be such a drain on my energy!"

She shook away her sigh and laughed again. "Did you happen to hear the latest McBride fuck-up story? Last month, in that swindling case that involved the City Procurement Department, he made the unprecedented decision to cross-examine one of the witnesses himself, instead of leaving it to Grantley. He studied this fellow's deposition the night before—it was one of the accountants for the clothing firm that was swindling the city—and began throwing hard angry questions at him, lots of fist-shaking and finger-pointing, you know what McBride can be like when he's suffering from the delusion that he's Perry Mason. Well, something was obviously going wrong. The witness kept saying things like 'I don't know' and 'That's really not my area of responsibility' and 'I never heard of anybody by that name.' Until Grantley suddenly noticed that McBride—

get this one please!—was cross-examining the wrong witness! The deposition he'd read was from an entirely different case, and the questions he was throwing at this swindling accountant all had to do with marijuana use. Grantley grabbed hold of McBride before anybody else in court could realize what was wrong, and practically had to pull him down into his seat, then he asked for an adjournment and explained the matter to our intrepid but confused DA—who got so flustered, he turned the whole thing over to Grantley and rushed out for a well-deserved martini."

Ann had been joining in on Dryden's laughter, and barely managed to get out her words. "Come on, Doris, he didn't *really*—"

"I swear to you he did. They hushed it up at the time, of course, but—" Her laughter kept her from talking for a while longer, but finally she put on a serious face and said, "Enough, enough. Nobody enjoys this screw-McBride game more than I do, but I better get down to why I asked you to drop in this morning."

"Something about this murder case, wasn't it?"

"Absolutely. What I'm about to tell you is going to surprise the hell out of you. Maybe you won't believe it, but I've got evidence that it's absolutely true."

"What's the big surprise?" Ann asked.

"Do you know why McBride is working so hard to pin this rap on your client? Because he wants to get this case out of the public eye as fast as he can—because he's afraid of what might come out. Namely, that he, McBride himself, has been having an affair with this Pulaski woman for the last six months."

I didn't need any cue from Ann that I was supposed to keep a straight face at this.

"You say you've got evidence of this?"

"Incontrovertible evidence."

"What is it?"

"A photograph. A beautiful candid snapshot showing McBride stretched out in Edna Pulaski's bed, fast asleep and naked as the day he was born."

"And Edna's stretched out next to him?"

"Well, no, he's alone. But the bed is definitely hers—here, I'll show you." She reached into the top drawer and pulled out a brown manila envelope. From inside it she took a small snapshot and handed it to Ann across the desk. "See the fancy carvings on the head of the bed—dragons kind of twining around each other? See the landscape painting on the wall over the bed—Oriental-style landscape, isn't that right? Won't be hard to prove where this picture was taken."

Everything she mentioned was there all right. The bed was definitely Edna Pulaski's—I recognized it right away—and in the center of it was McBride, with his eyes shut and a cherubic smile on his face. *Still Life with Politician.*

"How did you get this picture?"

Dryden laughed. "Sorry, Ann, that's a trade secret. Reporters aren't the only ones who have to protect their sources. Hold on to it, keep it as a souvenir. I've got plenty of copies. And before you leave here today, I'll give you the negative—I've got copies of that too—and you can have it examined by experts, make sure it's not faked, not doctored in any way."

Another long pause. Then Dryden gave a quiet little snicker. "Don't overwhelm me with your excitement and enthusiasm, for God's sake!"

"All right," Ann said after a moment, "I'll take the negative. If there's any legitimate way to use it at Harry Stubbins's trial, I'll be glad to—"

"Hold it, hold your horses!" Dryden stopped smiling. "That trial could be months from now. It won't do me a bit of good if you come out with this snapshot *then.* The whole point is to get this information before the public as soon as possible— tomorrow or Thursday at the latest—so it can have some influence on the election."

"All right then, make it public now. Call a press conference, show this snapshot to the media people—"

"You still don't get it, do you? *I* can't bring this before the public. I'm his opponent. If the public knows this picture came from *me,* they'd automatically suspect it of being a phony.

Besides, I'm supposed to be running a smear-free campaign, I've made a point of saying that I'm taking the high road.''

"Send it to the newspaper and the TV stations anonymously—"

"That's out too. No self-respecting editor—not even the editor of *our* local rag—is going to print something like this without knowing exactly where it comes from. No, there's only one way to handle this. Everybody trusts the public defender's office. Your reputation for honesty and integrity couldn't be higher. *You* have to call the press conference, Ann, and release this photograph.''

"On what grounds? Unless the connection between McBride and Edna Pulaski turns out to be relevant to my case—and that's something I can't know until much further down the line—I'm certainly not going to cast slurs on a man's reputation, expose the secrets of his private life—"

"Why not?" Dryden laughed again, but I didn't hear much mirth in her voice this time. "How do you feel about the job Marvin McBride's done as district attorney? You agree with me, don't you, that the man is a joke?''

"I certainly have plenty of reservations about—"

"Exactly. Anybody in this community who has any sense at all shares those reservations. All right, so now you've got your chance to do something practical about this situation. Here's the negative, you know what to do with it.''

Dryden reached into the manila envelope again. Ann lifted her hand and shook her head. "Don't bother, Doris.''

Slowly Dryden pulled her hand out again. "That's your final answer, is it?''

Ann got to her feet, and so did I. But before we could turn away from her desk, Dryden stood up too. "One more point I'd like to make.''

We waited patiently. I suppose we both pretty much knew what was coming.

"You don't take me up on this offer, I think you'll be very sorry.''

Ann managed to keep her voice steady. "What do you mean by that exactly?"

"What I mean is, when I get elected—and take my word for it, I *will* get elected—the first move I'll make, as the new district attorney, is to recommend to the City Council that they fire you and replace you with an efficient and responsible public defender."

"It seems to me," I said, "that I've heard you mention, in plenty of speeches, what a good job Ann's been doing. You've said it in public, it's on the record."

"So the public will find out I'm flexible, I'm not afraid to admit when I've been wrong. I'll discover I was wrong about Ann all these years. My close observation of the public defender's record has now convinced me that the city can do a lot better. And since the electorate and I will be in the middle of our honeymoon just then—I'll be the new broom, the great reformer, the breath of fresh air, the marines to the rescue— the council will listen to my recommendation."

"It won't bother you that it's a lie?"

"That'll bother me a hell of a lot less than if I lose this election. To keep that from happening, I guarantee you there's *nothing* I won't do." She lifted her chin. I doubt if McBride, even by his high standards, would have found any shortage of balls.

After a moment Ann said, very quietly, "A kinder gentler district attorney's office. Didn't we hear you say that a little while ago?"

"And I meant it too. I'm an idealist, and I always will be. What's eating you is that I take my ideals seriously. I'm willing to face up to the fact that those ideals are riding on this election. Either this town will go on the way it's been going, with justice in the hands of a lazy drunken clown, or the people will finally get some honest, vigorous, enlightened law enforcement. That goal is bigger than you, Ann, or any other individual, including myself. Kinder and gentler is for after elections. All right, I'm asking you one more time. Do you call a press conference and release this snapshot?"

She waited a beat, then her chin came down from its perch. She was smiling again and her tone of voice couldn't have been friendlier. "Well, it's been nice talking to you. No hard feelings, I hope. We all fight for what we believe, don't we, in our own way?"

We left her bedroom-office and made our way through the living room, trying not to bump into her little army of shining, newly scrubbed college idealists.

On the way back to the courthouse, I was careful not to talk too much. I knew how Ann was feeling. Her budget increase meant a lot to her, and she'd been pinning her hopes on Dryden's goodwill if she succeeded in driving McBride out of office. No doubt she'd get over the disappointment. She was a realist and a philosopher. But even the most philosophical animal has to be allowed to lick its wounds for a while.

Personally I wasn't feeling any wounds. What we had just learned about Dryden didn't come as any surprise to me. She was a politician, wasn't she? She simply confirmed what I had known all along—there's no choosing between them.

I did decide, though, that I wouldn't tell Roger about Dryden's little attempt at bribery and intimidation. When he talked about her, his eyes still filled with stars. What was the point of replacing them with cataracts?

The moment we stepped through our front door, Mabel Gibson was giving us a hoarse whisper: "Mr. Ed Brock on the line."

I went into Ann's office with her, and she picked up the phone. She confined herself to a couple of yeses and one "give us fifteen minutes," then she hung up and turned back to me. "He wants us to meet him right away. At the Marriott-Chinook. He claims it's an urgent matter."

So we left Roger to hold the fort—he was waiting for the drama teacher at General Wagner High to respond to his message—and drove down in my car to the Marriott-Chinook, a ten-story hotel in the center of downtown that is the Richelieu's only serious competition. If you're looking for fun and games, you go to the Richelieu; if you're in town to do business, you go to the Marriott-Chinook. It has its twin in every fair-size city in America, and the same slicked-up, weatherbeaten traveling-salesman types hang out in its lobby, coffeeshop, and bars. Ed Brock had told us to meet him in Room 216, which turned out to be a perfectly ordinary hotel room, not even one of the de luxe suites. Ed beamed at us from a big easy chair, looking more than ever like a clean-shaven, slightly mischievous Santa Claus. He didn't get to his feet—a process that would have involved major physical dislocations—but he was always careful about his manners, so he held out his huge hand and shook ours. "Nice to see you, Ann, damned nice of you to come down here like this, Dave."

There was only one other person in the room with Ed, his honor the Mayor of Mesa Grande, Willard A. Butterfield. He was a pudgy little man with thick, black-rimmed glasses and thick black hair that everyone in town knew to be a toupee; only by this time we were so used to seeing it on his head that he would have looked unnatural to us without it. He owned the biggest cut-rate appliance store in town, Butterfield's Bargain Basement, and dabbled successfully in real estate.

Ann gave him a sharp look as soon as she caught sight of him, sitting at a table that was set up in the corner of the room. This table was covered by a white tablecloth, and on it were plates, cups, a pot of coffee, and a platter with three or four cinnamon buns on it. "How are you, Willard?" Ann said. "Ed didn't warn us this was some kind of high-level official meeting."

"Who says it's official?" the mayor put in, his gravelly voice sounding tight and angry. "Nobody's allowed to take any notes. Everybody promises this is off the record. You say anything about it afterward, I'll deny it on a stack of Bibles."

"Don't get in an uproar, Willard," Ed said. "Ann and Dave understand perfectly, I'm sure. This is just an informal get-together among friends."

"Meaning by that," Ann said, "people who happen to be in on a deal together?"

Ed laughed and said, "Can you think of a *better* basis for friendship?"

For the next few minutes we all exchanged amenities about the beautiful weather, more like spring than November, have a cinnamon roll, let me pour you some coffee, all we've got is the caffeinated stuff but we could call room service. . . . You never came straight to the point when you had dealings with Ed. He would've been offended, I think, if he hadn't been allowed to go through every step of the ritual.

Finally he was ready to come out and say what was on his mind. "Ann—Dave—you're probably asking yourself by now why we're all here."

"Actually," Ann said, "I was asking myself whose room is this anyway?"

"It's a room the city keeps in this hotel, full time," said the Mayor. "For informal meetings, no more than three or four people."

"Is that a fact?" Ann said. "I've never noticed it on the city budget."

"It's there," said the mayor, sounding a little aggrieved. "You'll find it under 'miscellaneous.' "

"Getting back to the thread of what I was telling you," Ed said. "In a nutshell, I'm worried about the election. That's not a statement too many people have ever heard me make. I'm not usually the one who paces the floor and breaks out in a sweat. There's very little I haven't seen in this world, and consequently my expectations are low. My tendency is to sit back and assume things will turn out badly, and if they don't I'm content to be pleasantly surprised. But at this particular phase of the game, I have to admit it, our situation is precarious, and I'm worried."

"I can understand why *you're* worried," I said. "But what's his Honor doing here? *He* isn't running for election."

"I'm here," said the mayor, "because Marvin McBride is an old and dear friend as well as a valued ally in the fight to get the best for Mesa Grande, the city we both love."

Translation into English: The real estate interests, who had the mayor in their pocket, wanted McBride in office because they knew he wouldn't go out of his way to make trouble when real estate activities and illegal activities moved a little too close to each other.

"All right, Ed, what are Dave and I doing here?" Ann asked. "What've we got to do with Marvin's election? Send him out to kiss babies, and let us get back to work."

"Exactly what we're hoping you'll do," Ed said. "The problem is—not to mince words with you—you're the ones who've *got* us worried."

"Really? I have a feeling we ought to be flattered. *How* have we done this to you?"

"That not very pleasant meeting we had with you yesterday afternoon. Frankly, it's been on my mind ever since, you gave me something of a sleepless night. I decided we'd better get together this morning, just to clear the air. We'd better discuss those hints you dropped about Marvin's alleged involvement with the Pulaski woman—"

"I didn't think of them as hints exactly. I thought I came right out and said what I meant. I was also under the impression I heard Marvin admit they were true."

"Well, as far as that goes"—Ed's smile grew broader and friendlier—"I'm not sure *I* heard quite what *you* heard. Language can be awfully ambiguous. So often it's really a matter of interpretation. . . . Well, in any event, what's been worrying me is, if you happened to allow your version of what was said to come to the attention of the wrong parties—elements in town that might be hostile to Marvin and might be interested in twisting his words for their own ulterior purposes—"

"What elements are you referring to, Ed? Doris Dryden? Joe Horniman? The TV news people?"

"Among others, among others. The point I'm trying to get across—I have a sense that Marvin didn't make his full position on this matter entirely clear to you yesterday. There was a certain agitation in the atmosphere, a certain emotionalism. Now that we've all had a chance to sleep on it, sweet reason can reassert itself, I hope. We can see *your* point of view, and you

139

can see *our* point of view, and I feel sure an arrangement can be worked out to everybody's satisfaction. What is politics after all? The game of give-and-take, you scratch my back and I'll scratch yours."

"Just a minute, Ed," the mayor put in. "I don't consider my political career some kind of game. I consider I'm performing an important duty on behalf of my fellow citizens."

"Naturally, naturally." Ed nodded. "You're a man of integrity, Willard, completely sincere and truthful. As I was saying—"

"What *were* you saying?" Ann broke in. "If you're offering us some kind of proposition, I wish you'd come out with it, so we could all go home before the end of the week."

Ed laughed. It was a matter of principle with him to laugh at everybody's jokes, even if they were at his expense. Then he turned to the mayor. "You tell her, Willard. That matter we talked about earlier."

The mayor had grown very white, and had to wet his lips a few times before he could talk. "I know the public defender's office is planning to ask the City Council for a higher budget in the next fiscal year. You need another investigator, more office space, maybe even a second trial lawyer. I'm sympathetic, very sympathetic, with your needs. I intend to ask the council to give you what you want—and as you know, a majority of the members tend to go along with my views about what's best for the city. You can write your own ticket—within reason, of course—providing the district attorney doesn't raise any objections."

"There won't be any objections," said Ed, "if the present district attorney remains in office. On the other hand, if he loses this election, you can't expect us to exert any influence over a *new* district attorney, can you? And incidentally, if you don't see fit to cooperate in this matter and Marvin gets elected *anyway*—" Ed gave a sad shrug. "Well, if you demonstrate that you don't have the city's best interests at heart, what attitude would you expect a conscientious public servant to take toward you?"

Ann said nothing for a while. I was probably the only person in the room who could read the signs that she was close to an explosion. When she spoke, her voice was as quiet as ever. "I'm going to tell you just one thing, gentlemen. We haven't decided yet if we're going to use that information you refer to. We haven't evaluated its potential effectiveness in court. But one thing I can promise you—our decision will be determined by what's best. And I mean for our client, *not* for the city. If that means bringing out certain facts that might be embarrassing to Marvin McBride—or to any other fat cat in town—I give you my solemn word we'll bring them out anyway."

"See here," the mayor began, but Ann didn't let him get the rest of it out.

"If I have to listen to one more word on the matter," Ann said, "I'm calling up *The Republican American* and every TV and radio station in the area, and scheduling a press conference for this afternoon."

"Oh, come now, Ann," Ed said, "you don't seriously believe you could *prove* any of your innuendoes against—"

"Who cares? I'll present my theories to the media—less than a week before election day—and we'll see what the public makes of them. My offhand guess is that our office's reputation for integrity will persuade a lot of voters *not* to pull down Marvin's lever. And incidentally, I'll also have something to say about attempted bribery and intimidation—"

The mayor stood up, pushing away from the card table. "I'm getting out of here," he said. "I was never here in the first place. I don't know anything about anything anybody said. I was twenty miles away, and my wife and kids will swear to it." Then he stamped across the room and practically hurled himself through the door.

In the long silence that followed, Ed gazed at the door thoughtfully, then at the floor and the ceiling, and finally focused once more on Ann. He produced a brief but heartfelt sigh. "I *am* sorry our talk couldn't have been more productive. So few people nowadays—even the most intelligent people—understand the art of negotiation. Confrontation, confrontation, confrontation, that's all anybody seems to be interested in. Ah well. Thank you so much for coming anyway.

"No, no, don't wait for me. I'll be staying here for a bit, it would be a shame to let these lovely cinnamon rolls go to waste."

He was reaching out for one as Ann and I left the room.

TWELVE

It was nearly one o'clock when Ann and I got back to the office. My stomach was letting me know I hadn't eaten lunch yet, but I ignored it and holed up behind my desk so I could think about the case. I didn't get very far. I was interrupted by my phone ringing. It was Mom.

"I been calling regular the last two hours," she said. "You were eating a long lunch?"

"As a matter of fact, I haven't *had* my lunch yet."

"You don't eat lunch till one o'clock? You'll ruin your digestion!"

"If you've been calling me regularly for the last two hours, then *you* haven't had your lunch yet either. Did you get home so late from your date last night that you just woke up?"

Mom ignored the nose I was poking into her private life—just as I always ignored hers. "At my age who's got a digestion to ruin?" she said. "Now the reason I'm calling you—" I'm sitting around here with nothing to do for the next hour, so I thought maybe, so it shouldn't be a total loss, I could pass the time using my brains. If you tell me the latest developments, what you and Roger are doing with your murder case all morning, this could give me something to use my brains on."

I told her what I had been doing this morning—my meetings with Harry Stubbins and Doris Dryden and Ed Brock (and the things Roger had dug up so far about Ron Pulaski's alibi).

"I think that's all of it," I ended up. "Does any of it mean anything to you? Any great new revelations to give us?"

"Revelations don't come until you work for them. If you're not willing to work, you take the consequences."

"Are you saying *I'm* not willing to work? My God, I've been knocking myself out—"

"If this is so, tell me please about this question I keep telling you to ask the dead woman's ex-husband. About the news broadcast, you remember? You didn't say yet what he answered."

I found myself picking at my desk blotter. "As a matter of fact, I didn't get around to seeing him today. It's been one thing after another—"

"You didn't get around?" I could imagine Mom shutting her eyes and lifting her face, as if she was making some communication to God.

"I'm sorry, Mom. It was just an oversight."

"An oversight yet! You know what can happen from such oversights? Adam didn't notice that Eve had a taste for fruit. Richard Nixon didn't notice that he made a lot of tapes that gave away his shady dealings. My cousin Oscar didn't notice that he put his girlfriend's brassiere in his wife's laundry hamper."

"All right, all right—even though Pulaski has an airtight alibi, and there's no way he could have any connection to this murder, I'll call him up and ask him that question."

I put down the phone, and for a second or two I asked myself why I was giving her such a hard time on this one point. After all, I had answered all her *other* questions, done everything *else* she had told me to do. Was it necessary for me somehow to have one little battlefield on which I held out against her, refused to follow her orders, clung to the illusion of independence?

THIRTEEN

Just as I was picking up the phone to call Pulaski there was a knock on my door. I yelled come in, and Roger did.

"Anything to report on that McBride kid?" I said.

"I was just coming in to tell you," he said. "It's really a big surprise. At least it is to me. I tracked down the drama teacher at General Wagner High. He says there *was* a rehearsal of *Peter Pan* on Saturday night, and Laurel McBride was there, but it didn't break up nearly as late as she said. It broke up around eleven, this drama teacher never keeps the kids later than that. You know, I never would've picked that kid to be a liar!"

"It's a talent," I said, "that's distributed equally among all ages, sexes, races, and religious preferences. Did this teacher have any idea where Laurel went when she left the rehearsal?"

"He assumed she was going home. She doesn't have a car, she usually gets a lift from one of the kids who does. By the time this teacher left the school himself, they were all gone. He gave me some names, other kids who were at the rehearsal. I'll try to track them down, find out if anybody saw Laurel leave, and when and who with."

"Sounds promising," I said. "Did you have your lunch yet?"

"No, I didn't. I wanted to be sure I was in when this drama teacher called back."

"All right, I'll order something for you. Get on the phone to that school and see if you can talk to any of those kids. Mabel!" I yelled into the outer office. "Call up the deli, will you, ask them to send me up two hamburgers, rare, and two Cokes. No, wait a second, we've got a growing boy here. Make that *three* hamburgers."

Mabel Gibson, muttering about the case of ulcers Roger and I were giving ourselves—"and *she's* just as bad, *she* didn't have a decent hot lunch today either!"—nevertheless called the deli for me. And I went to my desk to catch up on work I should have done days ago. Harry Stubbins, after all, wasn't the only alleged criminal our office was defending that week.

A few hamburgers later, around two-thirty, Roger came in to report the latest dope on Laurel McBride. He looked even more puzzled and disturbed than ever.

"I managed to dig up one of the kids who was at that rehearsal with Laurel McBride Saturday night," he said. "According to him, she usually gets a lift home with one of the other kids—sometimes he drives her himself. But when he offered to on Saturday night, she said no, she had other plans. She didn't tell him what they were, but she was still standing in front of the school when he drove away. That was around a quarter after eleven, he says. Oh, and he also says the same thing had happened before—three or four times in the last few months she's turned down a lift at eleven or so, saying she had other plans."

I had no idea what this meant, if anything. But I had no time to digest the matter, because just then my phone rang, and one of my back cases took me out of the office. Out to the zoo, in fact, to look at a giraffe up close—but that's definitely a different story.

Kicking around in the back of my mind was the thought that I still hadn't called Ron Pulaski and asked him Mom's question. Okay, okay, I'd get around to it as soon as I had a free moment.

When I got back in half an hour, everybody was gone except Mabel Gibson. She told me that Ann was in court and that Roger had left about fifteen minutes ago, without saying where he was going. "He moved pretty fast though," she added.

Then my phone rang. It was Roger, and his voice was high;

it always lifted half an octave when he was really agitated about something.

"Dave, you have to get here right away! It's urgent!"

"Where are you?"

"Down here—Capricorn Street—Ron Pulaski's house."

I said I'd get there as fast as I could, and hung up the phone without asking him what he was doing there. I had a pretty good idea what the answer was.

Ten minutes later I pulled up to the sidewalk, where Roger was standing and waiting for me. His face was sludge-gray, fitting in nicely with the surroundings.

"Come on in quick," he said, grabbing me by the arm as I stepped out of the car. "Before somebody sees us."

Looking to right and left, he drew me up the porch and through the open front door, then quickly shut the door behind him. We were in the small narrow living room, with its threadbare furniture and its even more threadbare carpet.

Lying face up near the sofa was Ron Pulaski. One glance told me he was dead. He was wearing jeans and a sleeveless striped shirt. His legs were crumpled under him, his eyes were bulging up at the ceiling. His thick-lipped mouth was wide open, and his tongue was sticking out. His hands clutched at his own throat, his red hair was a mess.

I took a look at his neck. He had been strangled all right, and whatever had strangled him had left ugly red bruises, but once again the murderer had removed it. There was no evidence that Pulaski had put up much of a fight. It looked as if somebody had come up behind him, maybe while he was sitting in a chair, whipped out the weapon, and applied enough pressure to knock him out in the first few seconds.

"Did you call the cops yet?" I said to Roger.

He shook his head. "I thought you'd better take a look first. There's another room, a little bedroom, I used the phone from there."

"How did you get into the house?" I said.

"I rang the bell, there was no answer. So I tried the door, and it was open, just a crack. I thought I ought to see what was up."

"Okay, call the cops now, will you," I said.

He hurried off to the bedroom. While he was gone, I moved around the room, peering at the floor, looking for anything that might mean something to me. I didn't find a thing.

Then I knelt down by the body and touched my finger quickly to one wrist. It felt cool but still fairly flexible. Rigor mortis hadn't set in yet, though it would pretty soon. My guess was that he'd been dead for an hour or two, probably not much longer. I noticed a smell, so I took a big sniff just to make sure. Pulaski's face was reeking of alcohol.

Could he have knocked himself out with drinking, I wondered, before his murderer got to him? If he was more or less dead to the world already, then anybody, even somebody who didn't have much strength, might have been able to finish the job. Roger came back into the room. "They'll be here in ten minutes, maybe sooner."

"Okay," I said. "So tell me quick—what brought you down here?"

"I—" Roger had the guilty look and the confused manner of a kid caught in the bathroom with his father's copy of *Playboy*. "I finished my work. It was still only three o'clock, and I was thinking—about that question your mother said we ought to ask Pulaski. I was thinking, since I had nothing else to do, maybe I'd go down to see him, and ask him—" His voice got louder. "I'm sorry, Dave. I know you told me not to. But it seemed to me, if your mother thought it was important—"

"It's okay, it's okay," I said. "You did the right thing. It's too bad you got here too late."

As soon as these words were out of me I felt the dull sour ache in my stomach. If I *had* asked Ron Pulaski Mom's question, maybe he wouldn't be lying on the floor with his tongue sticking out. Maybe the dead man could've told us something, and we'd know who killed Edna Pulaski. And maybe, because of my stupid obstinacy—because I'd been so hung up on asserting my independence from Mom—we'd never find out the truth now.

I gave my head a hard shake. This was no time for a guilt trip, I had to get out of there before the cops came.

"What're you doing here? Where's Ronnie?"

Standing in the front doorway was Pulaski's girlfriend, that chunky little blonde who called herself Brigitte Martine. She was holding a paper grocery bag in her arms. I was sure I had closed the door behind me. She must have had a key.

I started toward her, but suddenly she saw the body. A scream broke out of her, and she was running across the room, dropping the bag of groceries without even knowing she was doing it. A couple of soup cans and a pineapple went rolling across the carpet.

"Ronnie! Oh, God, Ronnie!"

She fell to her knees, reaching for him. I went up behind her and pulled her back. "The police are on their way," I said. "They wouldn't want you to touch anything."

"Oh, God, oh, God!" Her screaming voice had turned into a wailing voice. Then she looked up at us, and her eyes got wide. "Don't hurt me, please don't—"

I tried to reassure her, as fast as I could. The fear faded from her eyes as she recognized us, and tears took over. They started down her face, while she sobbed out "Ronnie! Ronnie!" over and over again.

No use in my going away now that she'd seen me there, I thought. So I might as well get a head start on the cops.

"When did you see him alive last?" I asked her, very sharp and authoritative. It always works with people who are in a state of shock. Make them think you have a right to ask questions, and they'll automatically answer you.

"I've been gone two hours," she said. "He sent me out to the supermarket. He said I shouldn't come back for two hours."

"Do you know who he was expecting to meet here?"

"I don't know. He never told me things. He was drinking a lot, he was doing it to celebrate, he said. He started at lunch, he took the day off from his job. He was on the couch when I left."

"Did he ever talk to you about his ex-wife's death? Did he ever say he knew who did it, anything like that?"

"No, he never— He was there Saturday night, on the street outside her house. But he never went in, he didn't get there till after she was killed. He was at his bowling match, he told the cops all about it."

"He went to the DA's office around eleven on Sunday, right? After he found out about the murder? Did he hear about it from the radio or the TV?"

"The TV, what else? We don't even have a radio."

"So what did he do then?"

"As soon as the news was over, he jumped up and said he was going out to talk to the cops, to that assistant DA that was in charge of the case. I didn't go with him. I was still in bed. I sleep late on Sundays, it's my day off."

"Where do you work?"

"At the Neapolitan Grotto, that's this new Italian place downtown."

"Did he tell you *why* he was going to the police?"

"He never told me nothing. All I know was, he didn't get back till after twelve. And he was looking pretty happy. He kept saying the same thing, 'I saw, baby, I saw.' That's what he always called me, he called me baby. 'Wasn't supposed to be there,' he said. 'I told him, that little prick the assistant DA. Wouldn't the cops like to know *what* I saw! Maybe I'll tell them, maybe I won't. All depends on that little prick assistant DA. He don't come through, I know someplace else I can go. There's big money for what I saw.' "

"What did he mean by that? Was he trying to sell information to the authorities?"

"I don't know, I don't know. He never told me nothing. I asked him what he meant, and he just laughed. 'It ain't every day you see what I saw!" he said. And the last couple days, in between talking big, he's been singing! 'Philadelphia, here I come!' He sang that a hundred times today. 'Right back where I started from!' He had a lousy singing voice, but *he* couldn't hear how he sounded."

"Now let me make sure about one of the things he said to you? If the DA's office didn't come through with enough, he'd go someplace else—was that it?"

"Yeah, that's what he said. Someplace else."

"And you've got no idea what place he was talking about?"

"Like I said, he never told me nothing."

She was cut off by the sound of a siren, loud enough so that it couldn't be more than a block away.

I went up to Roger quickly and spoke in a low voice. "We came down here together. And the first thing we did was call the cops."

Roger gave a nod, asking for no explanations. The kid was learning.

Then we heard the police car pulling up to the curb, and a few moments later big feet and uniforms were clumping through the front door.

It was nearly five-thirty when Roger and I got back to the office. Ann was at her desk, finished with her afternoon in court. Mabel Gibson was getting ready to leave for the day, piling all sorts of things—knitting, a paperback book, the uneaten half of a sandwich—into the huge tote that she carried with her at all times.

I went into Ann's office and told her about Pulaski's murder. She frowned and shook her head. There was a lot for us to think about. How was the death of Ron Pulaski connected, if it was, with his ex-wife's, and was there any way to use it to help our client? Where *was* our client at the time Pulaski got killed? Would he have an alibi for this one?

First of all, though, Ann had a curse or two for Leland Grantley, because he hadn't told us all the details of his conversation with Ron Pulaski. In fact, she decided to give him a piece of her mind right away.

She got on the phone, while I stood right behind her and listened. She tracked him down to his home, and a moment later he was on the line.

"Leland, you're a slimy bastard," Ann began.

I heard him laughing a little, but Ann plowed right on, confronting him with the information that Ron Pulaski's girl-friend had given us. "So let's have a straight answer from you for once. When you questioned Pulaski the day after the murder, did he or didn't he tell you he had some incriminating information? Did he or didn't he offer to sell it to you?"

"It's not quite so simple. Yes, in a way, the man did make certain implications—"

"Which you very conveniently forgot to report to his defense counsel."

"In my opinion, there was nothing *to* report. Pulaski implied he had a story that he would tell to the authorities if we made it worth his while. I told him he'd have to follow our usual procedure—give us the information, and then we'd decide if it was worth paying for. He wouldn't go along with that, which convinced me he was lying. He had no information, he was just trying to gouge a few dollars out of us. I told him in no uncertain terms that I wasn't interested. I discussed it afterward with Marvin, of course, and the reason we didn't pass all this on to you—frankly, we felt it would be a waste of your time."

"Whatever you felt, it was highly unethical of you not to report the conversation to me. And the way you handled the matter was also pretty damned irresponsible. By refusing to take him seriously, you probably forced him to make his proposition to the murderer. And that's probably why *he* got killed. Well, one good thing has come out of this, at least from our point of view. This pretty much puts Harry Stubbins in the clear."

"How do you arrive at *that* conclusion?"

"Harry's not exactly the type to be a blackmail victim, is he? He hasn't *got* anything for any self-respecting blackmailer to screw out of him. You and Marvin think that over, okay?"

And then, before hanging up, she couldn't resist one last potshot. "Incidentally, Leland, I heard this crazy rumor about the swindling case that Marvin and you handled last year. It can't be true, can it, that Marvin read the wrong deposition and cross-examined the wrong witness?"

A definite chill came into Grantley's voice. "I have no idea what you're talking about. At any rate, no harm was done, we got a conviction, if you remember. Now I really must put an end to this conversation. I'm working at home this afternoon, and any minute now I'm expecting a call from my wife in Rhode Island—"

As she put down the phone, I could see that Ann was feeling a lot more positive about life already.

No way I could join in with her on that though. I still had a large helping of humble pie to eat. I went to my desk and dialed Mom's number and asked her if I could drop by for a few minutes after dinner. She said yes—which didn't exactly fill me with elation. Even with Mom's coffee to wash it down, that humble pie wasn't going to taste very good.

FOURTEEN

The door opened, and Mom's big welcoming smile switched off instantly.

"What's the matter? You're sick! Come in, come in, lie down on the couch, I'll get you a nice cup tea. What've you got, is it this bug that's going around?"

I let her lead me into the living room, but the tea and the couch I refused. "There's nothing wrong with me, Mom, not physically. I'm ashamed of myself, that's all."

Mom lowered her hand from my forehead and heaved a deep sigh of relief. "That's all it is, ashamed of yourself? Thank God! A little shame never hurt anybody. It's good for you, if you don't overdo it. So sit, tell me."

But I couldn't sit, I had to pace up and down while I got it off my chest. "I was stupid and stubborn. It's just possible that a man is dead on account of me. Maybe he'd still be alive if only I'd listened to you, if I'd got to him sooner and asked him that question you told me to ask. I apologize to you, Mom. Not that my apology does *him* any good."

Then I poured it all out, ending up with "So go ahead and tell me what a pigheaded idiot I am. You've got every right. Whatever you tell me, I deserve it." And I dropped onto the couch, breathing hard. Beating yourself is a tiring activity.

Mom was in her chair, looking across at me. I couldn't see anything like gloating or self-satisfaction on her face. The expression I saw was nothing but gentle worry. "Davey," she said, "nobody died on account of you. This Pulaski fellow, isn't it obvious why he got killed?"

"He knew something about the murder, I suppose. He saw something when he was hanging around his wife's house on Saturday night, and he tried to sell the information to the assistant DA. When Grantley wouldn't pay for it, he went to the murderer. I suppose they made a deal, because his girlfriend says he was singing about Philadelphia. He told me, when I questioned him, how he hated this town and always wanted to go back to East Phillie and open his own plumbing business. I suppose he thought he was about to get the capital to swing it."

"Exactly. Blackmail is what he was up to. It's a dangerous business, people get killed at it all the time. Is it your responsibility this fellow was a lowlife?"

"Maybe if I'd questioned him seriously—"

"Maybe, maybe, life is full of maybes. If we worried about all of them we'd put ourself into an early grave."

Mom was up from her chair, coming over to me. "All you did was, you decided to do something without running to your mother." Now she was on the couch next to me, holding onto my hands. "Why not? You're a grown-up man. You did plenty things before against my advice, and they turned out fine. Like becoming a policeman, for instance. I told you don't do it, I told you be a doctor or a lawyer. You went ahead and did it anyway, and thank God you did! As a doctor or a lawyer, you'd be miserable. Also not so good at the job. So this time what you did *didn't* turn out fine, so all right, who's perfect?" Mom gave me a kiss on the cheek. Then she was up again and bustling out to the kitchen. "Now you'll have some tea, and I wouldn't take no for an answer."

I would have preferred coffee, but this was no time to argue with her. In a few minutes tea and schnecken—Mom's quicker, cheaper, and more efficient substitutes for psychoanalysis—made their appearance.

And I have to admit it, they began to do the trick. Slowly but

155

surely I was feeling good again. The tea was tasting delicious. The old punch had returned to Mom's schnecken.

"So tell me," she said, sitting down on the couch next to me, "you don't have the answers yet to those two questions I mentioned to you—am I right?"

"You're wrong. I *do* have the answers." I told her what Roger had told me about Laurel McBride and her play rehearsal. And then I told her what Pulaski's girlfriend had told me, that he had found out about the murder from the TV.

"What is it, Mom?" I broke off suddenly. "Are you all right?"

At first she seemed to be having a fit or something. She had one hand over her forehead and was waving the other in the air, and little yelping noises were bursting out of her. But then I realized she was expressing joy and satisfaction.

"You've got the answer, Mom? You know who killed Edna Pulaski?"

"When did I say so? All right, *most* of the answer I got. But there's one more piece I need—one little piece to finish the picture."

"How can I help you get it?"

"You couldn't. Nobody can get it for me. What I have to do now is tickle my brains a little so maybe they'll come to life. And it wouldn't hurt to do some praying too. Darling, I'm going to be very rude. I'm asking you to go home."

I got out of there, excited and puzzled and frustrated as hell. I went home and looked at "L.A. Law" on the TV, and thought how nice it would be if real life was like that.

FIFTEEN

Wednesday was one of those days that you can look back on years later, and you suddenly find yourself groaning, just as if you were still living through it.

It began as merely a mild disaster. *The Republican American,* which I read with my soft-boiled eggs and coffee, devoted the upper half of its front page to the murder of Ron Pulaski. Joe Horniman, writing the lead story, wasn't above using phrases like "epidemic of homicide" and "serial killer" to spice things up for his readers. I could imagine Joe chuckling to himself as he dipped into his file of clichés, compiled after years of labor in the vineyards of journalism.

The paper's coverage of the murder reached its high point in the featured editorial, which had stern words for "permissive judges" who granted bail to "known sociopaths," thus sending them out into the world to slaughter yet more of their fellow citizens. Harry Stubbins's name wasn't mentioned, and the editor was careful to say that his remarks were not intended "to prejudice the case against any specific accused persons, who of course, on the great principle of American justice, are entitled to be presumed innocent until found guilty by a jury of their peers." It sure gives you a warm secure feeling to know that *The Republican American* is standing up for American justice.

I spent most of the morning at my desk—writing reports and filling out forms, what else?—when the day started sliding even further downhill. Ann called Roger and me into her office, her face a shade of greenish white that told me something awful was up.

"Just got a call from the homeless shelter," she said. "My friend who runs the place says our client made a disturbance a few hours ago, yelling and taking swings at people—none of which connected, thank God—and after breakfast ran off into the streets somewhere. The other inmates say he smuggled in a bottle of cheap wine, he's been taking swigs of it all morning, and the drunker he got the more he's been throwing around wild threats."

"Threats against who?" I asked.

"Against Marvin McBride. 'Our vicious, pernicious, malicious, and lubricious district attorney,' that's what Harry keeps calling him. The idea seems to have planted itself in his head that McBride is out to get him, is deliberately railroading him for Edna Pulaski's murder, and is now trying to pin Ron Pulaski's murder on him too."

"Why does he think McBride is doing all this to him?"

"He didn't exactly make that clear. The best those other men could figure out was, McBride hates his guts because he's McBride's long-lost twin brother, his exact double who's two minutes older, and McBride is afraid he'll come back to claim his rightful inheritance. They say he kept yelling about *The Man in the Iron Mask* and *The Prince and the Pauper*. And here's the part that's got me really worried—the last thing he yelled before he ran off was 'I've got no choice! Have to get him before he gets me!' "

The upshot of our client's disappearance was that Roger and I had to put the rest of our work on hold while we went out to look for him. The hope was to find him before he had a chance to do something crazy that he'd never recover from. It wouldn't be easy. All we could do was move from one street corner and alley to the next, from one bar to the next, in the neighborhoods where he was most likely to hang out.

And the job was complicated by the fact that Ann, after a lot of soul-searching, decided she had to call up McBride and tell him what was happening. I didn't think there was much chance that Stubbins would actually carry out his threats, bust into McBride's office or charge up to him in a restaurant or anything like that; more likely Stubbins would spend the day drinking himself into a sodden mess, then slink back to the shelter with all the fight pounded out of him. Still, as long as he was on the loose, it seemed only fair that McBride should be warned to keep his eyes open.

So Ann called him at his office, and of course, since it wasn't lunchtime yet, he hadn't come in. She talked to Grantley, who said he'd pass the warning on as soon as McBride arrived. In the meantime—and I guess we knew this was inevitable—Grantley felt he had to alert the police.

"I don't suppose," Grantley said, "the man could conceivably get hold of some kind of lethal weapon, could he?"

"A gun, something like that?" Ann said. "I very much doubt if he owns one. And where would he get the money to buy one?"

"The reason why I ask," Grantley said, "you know about the rally tonight, don't you?"

"What rally?"

"Marvin is holding a big rally—for his election campaign—eight o'clock tonight, in Manitou Park, right in the center of town. In fact, he didn't come to the office at all yesterday, he stayed home to write his speech. The park will be full of people, I expect, so if Stubbins isn't apprehended before then—well, it wouldn't be difficult for him to keep himself concealed in the crowd, and when Marvin appears on the platform—all alone, up above everybody—a very exposed position, if a man happened to have a gun."

"I'd be surprised if Harry Stubbins even knows how to *fire* a gun," Ann said. "And by tonight he'll hardly be in any condition to aim one." But she was frowning just the same. "I don't suppose you could persuade Marvin to call off this rally? Until we find Stubbins, I mean?

"No, I don't suppose you could. In his whole life Marvin never voluntarily gave up an opportunity to make a fool of himself in front of a crowd. Well, thanks anyway, Leland. We'll just have to hope for the best."

Roger and I went on looking for Stubbins all that afternoon. Roger took the north side of the city, and I took the south side, and we each made a quick odyssey of sleaze, until at sundown we met in the middle. No sign of the old man, though occasionally we talked to a bartender or a barfly who claimed to have seen him "a little while ago."

At six o'clock we reported to Ann by phone, and she told us to give up the search. If Stubbins was going to come up out of the ground, she decided, the most likely place would be at McBride's political rally tonight. We agreed to meet at Manitou Park at seven-thirty, which would give us half an hour to comb the area before the rally began.

I went home, heated up a TV dinner—chicken fricassee with rice, which always ended up either undercooked or soggy—and made a quick call to Mom. Just to keep her posted on the latest developments and to find out if that "final piece" had clicked into place for her yet.

It hadn't. She told me to take care of myself. "I don't like the idea you should be in the park at night with a man who's got a gun," she said.

"He *hasn't* got a gun," I said, "and there's going to be hundreds of people out there with me, not to mention a dozen uniformed cops."

But to tell the truth, I didn't much like the idea myself.

The closest parking space I could find was three blocks away from Manitou Park. Very unusual for a Wednesday night in Mesa Grande. It looked as if McBride was drawing a big crowd for his rally.

I stepped through the front gate to the park, as arranged, and looked around for Ann and Roger. At first I couldn't spot them, on account of all the people.

Manitou Park is the smallest and oldest park in Mesa Grande. Occupying only one square block in the middle of the downtown area, it was laid out over a hundred years ago by General William Henry Harrison Wagner himself. In the center of it is a statue of him, wearing his Civil War uniform and sitting on his horse. (He fought for the North eventually, though for a year or so, until he decided who the winner was going to be, he considered offers from both sides.) During the day the park is the playground of very young swingers—children on swings, that is—and elderly horseshoe pitchers. As soon as the sun goes down, the drunks, the homeless bench people, and the buyers and sellers of dope move in. Every once in a while our local police swoop down and haul in these antisocial types, but most of the time business, pleasure, and mere survival go on undisturbed, behind the thick hedges that grow along the park's tall iron fence.

Tonight, though—Wednesday night, less than a week before election—Manitou Park had been taken over by the forces of democracy. Three or four patrol cars were parked on the curbs next to both its gates, and several uniformed policemen were strolling around its shady walks. Folding chairs—brought in and set up, I felt sure, by Sanitation Department workers earning overtime from the taxpayers—filled the large cleared space in front of General Wagner's statue. Spotlights and lamps circled the edges, shining into the crowd and especially the speakers platform. Heavy cables and wires were attached to loudspeakers, which were in turn attached to strategic trees; these arrangements, I guessed, had been implemented by the city Gas and Electric Department.

To the general's right was a stone platform that had been built five or six years ago; jazz, folk, and rock concerts were held on Thursday nights during the summer, and the sweet smell of pot mingled with the music in the evening air. Streamers were strung now from the posts of this platform, balloons were tied to the chairs that sat on it, and a huge McBride for the American Way banner was stretched between two trees above it.

It was only a little after seven-thirty, but a sizable audience had already gathered. Some of them had buttons in their lapels that read MCWIN WITH MCBRIDE! Some of them were waving small pennants with WE'RE STARVIN FOR MARVIN on them. I also caught a glimpse of one or two dissidents in the crowd: buttons that read DORIS IS FOR US! and COMPETENCY AND COMPASSION.

Most of the crowd seemed to be there, though, for the fun of it rather than out of political conviction. In spite of the uniformed cops all over the place, I saw a lot of bottles that obviously didn't contain Coca-Cola and a lot of suspiciously skinny, mangy-looking cigarettes.

Then I saw Ann, and Roger was with her.

"We're meeting Marvin behind the platform in twenty minutes," she said as I moved up to her. "That gives us some time to look through the crowd."

We did, each taking a different section of it, but I didn't see anybody that looked vaguely like Harry Stubbins.

The three of us met up again at five minutes to eight. Ann and Roger hadn't been any more successful than I. So we went around the raised platform to a small stone structure, looking something like a shed. This was the "dressing room," where performers or speakers holed away until it was time for them to make their entrance.

A uniformed policeman stood outside the door, and inside were Ed Brock and Marvin, sitting at a table, and Grantley standing behind them. Marvin had a sheaf of papers in his hand, no doubt filled with purple platitudes about softness on crime and the scourge of drugs that threatened Our Young People. I noticed immediately that he was wearing his red, white, and blue necktie, with its pattern of little American flags.

"So that old drunk thinks he's going to take a potshot at *me*, does he?" Marvin said. "Well, he's got another think coming!"

I pointed out that there was very little chance of potshots, since there was absolutely no reason to believe Stubbins had a gun.

"You won't be foolhardy though, will you, Marvin?" Ed said. "If any disturbance starts up in the crowd, I hope you'll duck down fast."

McBride laughed. "Duck! I never ducked out of a fight in my

life! I'll stand right up there and tell him to shoot at me! I'd just like to see him try it!"

Laughing again, he turned to Ann. "See what an upstanding, exemplary, honest type you're defending these days, sweetie? 'Homeless,' everybody calls them. And we're all supposed to cry our eyes out over them. 'Gutless!' that's more like it, if you ask my opinion. When I was growing up, we pulled them in for vagrancy and threw them in the tank until they dried out. Now we send them to psychiatrists, and pray over them, and make speeches about them. In New York City—did you know?—they put them up in luxury hotels!"

Then, for a moment, McBride wasn't smiling any more, and his voice got tighter. "God, if there's anybody I really hate in this world, it's these drunken old bums!"

He grunted, then he looked at his watch. "So I guess you haven't dug him out of his hole yet, have you? What about the cops, Leland?"

"Pat Delaney is in charge, he's here personally. He told me he'd let us know right away if they caught Stubbins."

"Pat came down himself to keep the son of a bitch away from me? I feel honored. It never occurred to me Pat had so much affection for me he'd give up an evening to keep me in one piece."

McBride laughed, then he looked at his watch again, and in practically the same motion he jumped to his feet. "Sorry, fellows, it's game time, the team has to get out on the field. Come on, Ed, it's five after eight, we don't want to keep the fans waiting." He squeezed his hands together, which somehow came through as a gesture of tremendous elation. "Suddenly I'm feeling terrific! I holed myself up for the whole afternoon yesterday, working on this masterpiece—believe me, it's going to kill the people!"

And he swept past us, through the door, with Ed Brock bustling behind him as fast as his bulk could carry him. A few seconds later we heard the roar of the crowd.

* * *

163

My original idea was to describe that political rally in detail—the people cheering and heckling, the signs and pennants being waved, the TV cameras set up on all sides, the flashbulbs going off. Above all, McBride's speech, full of inflated rhetoric, wild promises that nobody expected him to keep (least of all himself), scornful abuse heaped on "them"—it had a good chance of being one of his greatest performances, because he was on a real high that night. Every minute his face got redder, his gestures wider, his voice hoarser and more feverish. He was hotter than the crowd he was trying to heat up.

I've decided against this, though. Everybody knows what a political rally is like. It's not much different in Mesa Grande from anywhere else in the country, except that here there tends to be a higher percentage of cowboy hats in the crowd. Not worn by cowboys, by the way. There are very few cowboys left in our section of the country. The hats are carried by all the fanciest haberdashery stores, and they aren't cheap. Anyway, as Roger pointed out while we all stood and watched McBride, with Ed Brock and Grantley sitting behind him, "It looks like a B-picture version of *Citizen Kane.*"

McBride began with the barefoot farmboy and Great University stuff, then switched to leading the crowd in a chant of his own invention, "Hard on Crime, Soft on People." Roger was watching in disgust, but also he couldn't take his eyes away. When you're young, it's still possible to be fascinated by the lunacy; you're seeing it for the first time.

As the McBride juggernaut rolled on, I looked around the crowd for Stubbins. I still didn't see him, but the way people were squeezed together it wouldn't have been hard to miss him.

And then, suddenly, he was there. He rose up from the center of the crowd. Like one of those old Esther Williams movies, one of those water ballets where the girls are swimming around in the form of a flower, and out of the middle of the flower Esther comes popping up. Not much resemblance between Harry Stubbins and Esther Williams though. With his scrawny arms and neck, his pasty complexion and his red eyes, he looked more like a ghost. In a torn flopping ragged over-coat, instead of a clean white sheet.

"Murderer!" the ghost called out, in a hoarse cracking voice. "You're a murderer!"

"Who's that, who's that?"

McBride, standing on the platform, clutching the micro-phone, swiveled his head around, trying to locate the source of the disturbance. His jaw shoved forward and his eyes bulging, he looked even more like an angry bulldog than usual.

"Trying to kill me!" Stubbins went on croaking at him. "Trying to send me to the gas chamber! Murderer, murderer!"

McBride's head stopped swiveling as he got Stubbins into focus, and his eyes bulged even wider with shock.

Though I was seven or eight yards away, with a lot of the crowd in between, Stubbins's voice, thick from alcohol, was still loud enough to carry to where I was standing. "What're you doing up there? Sounding off up there—big crimefighter, are you? Everybody knows what you are! Drunkard, whoremonger, cheat!"

I started to push my way toward him. I could see Roger, off to my left, doing the same thing. And I could see some of the cops, on the edges of the crowd, trying to make their move too. One of them was Pat Delaney.

Stubbins shot out a skinny arm, stabbing a finger in McBride's direction. "You're *me!*" he cried. "We're one and the same person! *Hypocrite lecteur, mon semblable, mon frère!*"

I feel pretty sure that McBride didn't understand a word of the French, but he must have caught the general idea, because he turned as red as Stubbins and made a little backward jump. This seemed to infuriate Stubbins. His croak turned into a shrill screech: "Don't run away from me! Long-lost brother you tried to hide from the world! Should be up there with you—"

By this time Delaney and another cop, in uniform, had broken through and were getting closer to Stubbins. But they were a little too late. Suddenly Stubbins was moving forward, plunging through the crowd in the direction of the platform, shouting as he went, "Let them see us together! Let them see by this image, which is thine own, how utterly thou hast murdered thyself!"

"Stop him!" McBride's voice was as loud and shrill as Stubbins's. "Don't let that nut up here! Where are the cops, for Christ sake?"

The crowd seemed to give way before Stubbins like water, and the next thing I knew he was scrambling up the platform, fantastically strong and agile considering what a wreck he was. And at the same time he was reaching into the pocket of his ragged overcoat, trying to pull something out.

"My God"—a piglike squeal from McBride—"he's got a gun!" He started backing away from Stubbins, waving his hands in front of his face. "Don't shoot! For Christ sake, don't shoot!"

Stubbins's hand came out of his pocket, but I couldn't see any gun come out with it. "Judas!" he was shouting. "Want to crucify your brother, do you? Ought to get the going rate! Here's your thirty pieces of silver!"

A splattering of small objects sprayed out of Stubbins's hand and made clanging clattering sounds on the floor of the platform. Most of them were coins, also I saw some buttons and nails. As they hit the floor, Pat Delaney and the uniformed cop finally made it to the platform, jumped up, and grabbed Stubbins by the arms. The energy seemed to go out of him all at once, he went limp between them, hanging like a popped balloon. And McBride was standing still, blinking, looking as if he was hypnotized.

Then I heard Delaney's voice. He had bent down to the floor, and now he was straightening up, holding something in his hand. "Hey, we been looking for this!" I heard him say. "It's that ring—"

Getting closer, I saw what he had in his hand—a gold ring, with a large green stone in it. What else could it be except Edna Pulaski's ring, the one that had been stolen from her effects when her body was taken to the morgue?

A wail broke out of Stubbins. "Somebody gave it to me—I

was begging on the street yesterday, somebody put it in my cap—I swear it, I swear it!"

McBride gave himself a shake, blinked, came out of his hypnotic trance. His voice was a little shaky at first, but it gained strength as he went on: "Arrest him!" He waved at Pat Delaney. "Do your duty, Captain! Arrest that man—put him behind bars—"

Leland Grantley, his hand on McBride's arm, spoke in a low urgent voice. "He's free on bond, Marvin, you can't really—"

"Son of a bitch, he's violated his bond! Disorderly conduct—making threats of violence—possession of stolen property—suspicion of committing a second murder! For Christ sake, arrest him, take him away, get him out of here!"

I saw Delaney heave a sigh, then Stubbins was hustled away, and Ann and Roger and I followed. We saw him being put into a squad car, with Delaney sitting next to him, and Ann had just time to assure him we'd meet him shortly at the jail. "Don't say anything to anybody till we get there!" she called out to him as the squad car pulled away.

Behind us we heard the voice of McBride. All his confidence was back, and his voice, as he harangued the crowd, couldn't have been more full of triumph. "Yes, Goddammit, I *am* a fighter against crime! I'm *proud* that people call me that! I'm the best damn crimefighter who's ever held office in this fair city—which the good people of Mesa Grande know is the gospel truth, which is why they've returned me to office four times in a row already! And they'll be returning me a fifth time, so I'm giving fair warning here and now to the bums, the thieves, the druggies, the killers—you don't stand a chance in this town! That's my pledge to the people of Mesa Grande—vote McBride in, kick the vermin out!"

I could hear the crowd going wild with delight. Because they believed he was a knight in shining armor, or because he was putting on a great show? It didn't matter, he'd get their votes anyway. And a lot of other votes too, I thought, seeing that on the outskirts of the crowd the TV cameras were grinding away.

These days the difference between entertainment and politics is getting harder and harder to notice.

We were at the jail till after ten that night. We stood by while Stubbins got booked, with Grantley and Pat Delaney in attendance.

After the booking, we talked to Stubbins for a while, though it wasn't easy. The drunkenness had gone out of him, but what was left was pure exhaustion. When we asked him questions, it took him a long time to answer them, and then the most he was able to squeeze out were monosyllables.

All we really found out from him was that he didn't have any idea who had given him Edna Pulaski's ring. When people dropped things in his hat, he never bothered to lift his head and see who they were. "You don't want to do that," he said. "You could find yourself looking them in the eye."

SIXTEEN

Just before I left the jail building, close to ten-thirty, I gave Mom a call. I knew she'd still be up, waiting to hear from me, because she'd been anxious about my mission to Manitou Park. Also she undoubtedly wanted to hear everything about these latest developments.

Mom told me she'd been watching the television news reports about McBride's rally. "But the cameras weren't close enough I could see what was happening up on the stage. Some kind of fight, wasn't it? And this crazy old man—this was your client?"

I filled her in on all the details, everything that had happened at McBride's rally. There was a long pause after I finished, and then she said, "It's interesting, isn't it?"

I knew that flat noncommital tone of voice very well. "What does that mean, Mom? You tickled your brains, you've found your last little piece, you're ready to clear up the case?"

"It means I couldn't get to sleep yet. If you aren't too tired, why don't you come over here, I'll give you a cup coffee, and we'll talk a little."

"That definitely means you've got the answer, doesn't it?"

"In half an hour I'll see you," Mom said. "Do you think you could invite Roger? If he isn't too tired either."

In exactly half an hour, at a little after eleven, Mom opened the door for us. She had coffee and schnecken all laid out on her kitchen table, following her usual principle that our stomachs have to be full before she can start filling our brains.

Tonight I was too curious to stick by the rules. "Never mind the coffee," I said. "Tell us what's up. Our tongues are hanging out from the suspense."

"Put them back in, they could bump into something." Mom went ahead and poured coffee. Then she returned to her chair, took a couple of sips, leaned forward, and told us who the murderer was and how she knew.

Obviously she was right.

"But the problem is," she went on, "you couldn't prove this yet. First you have to clear away the lies, you have to make the liars start telling the truth. Does your boss, Ann Swenson, still have that snapshot Doris Dryden gave her—the picture of McBride lying in the Pulaski woman's bed?"

"I think she does."

"Good, good. So here's my suggestion what you should do. First thing tomorrow morning . . ."

SEVENTEEN

As soon as I got to the office Thursday morning, I filled Ann in on everything Mom had told me the night before.

At first Ann was as skeptical as I had been, but I could see her turning into a true believer as each logical brick was added to the house Mom had built. Ann also agreed that we didn't have quite enough yet to bring our theory in front of a jury. So I outlined the strategy that Mom had suggested, and Ann agreed to follow it.

The big moment had to wait until early evening, after working hours, because otherwise our key player wouldn't be free. But we were able to spend the rest of Thursday morning setting everything up. We had to make sure that the room we wanted would be available; then we had to do a little fast talking to Captain Pat Delaney of the Homicide Squad; finally we had to issue our invitation, in such a way that the guest of honor wouldn't turn us down.

As anticipated, he put up a lot of resistance at first. The fact is, Marvin McBride likes to go home at six o'clock and get started on the evening's serious drinking. "An informal discussion!" He hooted at Ann through the phone. "What the hell does that mean? What's to discuss? We've got your client exactly where we want him!"

"There are a few aspects of this case that we'd like to put before you, Marvin. We'd like to get your input on them, knock around some ideas with you, maybe come up with some mutually agreeable approach—"

"We'll do our approaching in front of a jury!"

"But you never can tell what a friendly frank talk might lead to. Maybe even a plea bargain."

"Who needs a plea bargain? I told you what I feel about this lazy good-for-nothing old lush. He's not going to wriggle out of this, he's not going to get away with some nice easy vacation for a few years. The bastard's getting the gas!"

"You're a hard man, Marvin. Let me just try out one more argument on you that might soften your heart. If this case goes to trial in front of a jury, I can't guarantee I won't be forced to bring in certain evidence—about certain intimate relation-ships that the murder victim had with certain public figures, for instance—"

"You better not try it! Didn't we warn you already—"

"And I'm taking the warning very seriously. That's why I'm suggesting we have this nice easygoing, informal talk session. The public defender's office will put its cards on the table, and get your reactions to them, and maybe the whole matter can be settled quickly, without any unpleasant publicity."

There was a long silence. Then McBride spoke, in a some-what less strident voice. "You're saying you might be interested in pleading your client guilty?"

"Well, that's certainly a possibility."

"He doesn't get the gas, he saves his neck, but he goes away for life. I'm not settling for anything less than—"

"Let's not get ahead of ourselves, Marvin. Let's see what develops after we have our talk."

A few more moments of silence, during which I could imag-ine McBride puffing furiously at his cigar. Then he said, "All right, I guess it won't hurt to talk. Come up to my office at six."

"Sorry, but we can't have this meeting in your office."

"Why the hell not? I've got a lot more space here than you've got."

"Don't I know it." Ann's laugh had a little edge to it. "But the fact is, Mr. Stubbins has to be present at this meeting too. And he doesn't feel comfortable in your office. It scares him. In the event that we *do* reach some sort of plea-bargaining

172

stage, he'll be a lot more likely to cooperate if he isn't in a state of panic."

"All right, we'll meet in your office."

"No, actually we can't do that either. As you've correctly pointed out, we don't have nearly enough room here. Suppose we meet in the interrogation room, down in the basement of this building."

"That hole! I don't see why—"

"Think of it as neutral ground, all right? See you at six, Marvin. Try not to be late."

"I'm bringing Ed Brock with me."

"Why not? As I've said, it's going to be completely informal. Ed may have a lot to contribute. And oh yes, I'd appreciate it if you called the jail and gave orders for our client to be delivered there too."

Ann hung up the phone, wearing a satisfied grin.

We had known perfectly well that McBride would insist on being propped up by Ed. How could the dummy do his talking without his ventriloquist?

Actually it suited us perfectly.

EIGHTEEN

A little before six Ann and Roger and I got into the elevator. It stopped two floors below us, and McBride and Ed Brock got on. McBride gave a grunt, and we rode down to the basement in silence. Then we started along the long corridor to the interrogation room.

Ann was in front, McBride followed with Ed by his side, and Roger and I brought up the rear. It was a little bit like a condemned man marching to his execution, flanked by guards, the chaplain in front of him reading from the Bible. Maybe the resemblance struck McBride too. I could see small beads of moisture forming on the back of his neck.

The interrogation room is located halfway between the boiler and the machinery that runs the elevators. Ordinarily assistant DAs and their investigators use it for confidential talks with suspects or defendants who aren't important enough to rate the palatial upstairs setting. Most of Ann's clients fall into that category, so the two of us had seen a lot of this room. Our guess was that McBride had never been down here. The people *he* deigned to question were never that low.

We reached the door of the interrogation room. Three uniformed cops were stationed outside of it. They saluted, and one of them opened the gray door. McBride gave them a quick nervous look. "What's this bunch doing here?"

"One of them brought our client from the jail," Ann said. "The other two are extra security."

"Who decided we needed extra security? You never checked that with *me*, did you?"

"You were in court this afternoon, Marvin—"

Quickly Ann led us into the room, low-ceilinged, no windows, no decorations on the walls, only a wooden table and some wooden chairs. Dim light came from a ceiling fixture, and if you listened hard you could hear the ventilation system humming.

The first person we saw was our client, Harry Stubbins. He was sitting—more accurately, he was huddled up—in the chair nearest the door. He looked even more wretched than when he was on the street; his jailers hadn't made him shave or clean himself up, his clothes were as rumpled as ever, and his eyes were red in the center and black around the edges. His hands, linked at the wrists by handcuffs, were shaking softly, and I had no trouble figuring out why. The poor slob needed a drink.

Farther into the room, also seated, was Leland Grantley, wearing his grayest suit, complete with vest and sober tie. McBride frowned when he saw him. "What're you doing here, Leland?"

"Ann asked me to come. She said—some arrests might have to be made."

"Arrests!" McBride's eyes started blinking. "What arrests? *I'm* the one that makes the arrests around here! And why the hell didn't you tell me you were going to be here?"

"Well, as a matter of fact, Ann asked me to keep it to myself—"

"Ann asked you? Who the hell do you think you're working for anyway?"

"You've always said we should cooperate with the defense attorneys, Marvin, because it doesn't look good if we— Well, if I made the wrong decision, I apologize. But as you're always telling me, I have to call the plays as I see them. No football team can be run with two quarterbacks."

"Don't give me quarterbacks! You never even knew what a football *was* until you came to work for me! What's going on here, for Christ sake?" McBride's eyes were shifting back and

175

forth between Ann and Grantley. Then, suddenly, they stopped shifting. "I'm getting out of here! This meeting is over! When they start going behind my back, to my own assistant—"

He was stamping to the door, just as we had expected he would. We had thought up several methods for stopping him, but as it turned out, we didn't have to put any of them into operation. Ed Brock, moving amazingly fast for his bulk, stood in McBride's way. "I'd reconsider if I were you, Marvin."

"Ed, they got no right! Bringing in uniformed cops without even consulting me! Am I the DA, or am I some punk off the streets—"

"Listen to me. Will you please listen?"

The two men faced each other. Finally McBride lowered his eyes.

"Now what on earth have you got to lose by hearing Ann out?" Ed said, smiling, using his most soothing voice. "You know the principle you and I have always lived by—negotiation is better than confrontation. If Ann wants to share some of her ideas about the case—and if this process might lead eventually to the avoidance of a messy and expensive public fight—well, good heavens, Marvin, nobody's going to hold it against you if you at least listen. Everybody will appreciate your generosity and flexibility—don't you agree?"

McBride's shoulders lifted and dropped. He said something under his breath and started back to his chair.

"Suppose we get started," Ann said, moving into the chair behind the table, casually putting herself in the center of the room.

"Wait a second," McBride said, reaching into the inside pocket of his sports jacket. "I need a cigar."

"I'm sorry, Marvin," Ann said. "There's no smoking down here. It's strictly against the law."

McBride looked up at her, a sudden flash of panic in his eyes. Then he sank into his chair.

Since I was closest to it, I shut the door to the interrogation room.

* * *

McBride sat across the table from Ann. Grantley sat a little farther away, and Roger and I stood near the door, trying to be as inconspicuous as possible.

As Ann started talking, McBride hardly took his eyes off her. He had cross-examined plenty of witnesses in his day, but this must have been the first time he was ever on the receiving end.

"I don't want to bore you, Marvin," Ann said, "but in order to be clear about where our thinking has been taking us, I'll have to go over some old ground. Specifically some of those deductions I was making the other day about your relationship with the dead woman."

A dark cloud came over McBride's face. "Like I told you the other day for the record, for public consumption—I *had* no relationship with the dead woman. I deny it, and you can't prove it."

"Even so," Ann said, "let me repeat my original reasons for believing there *was* such a relationship. Because that will lay the foundation for some further observations."

Then, one by one, Ann went through the points she had made two days ago at McBride's campaign headquarters, the points I had taken from Mom and passed on: McBride's admission that he had met Edna Pulaski six months ago when she was arrested, his not drinking anything at the League of Women Voters dinner, Edna Pulaski's dislike of men who drank, McBride's giveaway remark about the neon signs flashing through Edna's windows.

Her words produced a big reaction in the audience. Stubbins suddenly raised his head and quavered out, "Knew it, knew it all along—liar and hypocrite—"

And Leland Grantley, his mouth open, was staring at McBride with wide eyes. Every Puritan bone in his body seemed to be shocked by what he had heard. "Marvin—if you were having an *affair* with that woman, how could you *prosecute* this case? You should have disqualified yourself. You've told me so often that absolute integrity and impartiality is the hallmark of—"

"Oh, shut up!" McBride spit out at him. "If I want lessons

in integrity, I won't go to some sanctimonious Harvard asshole, for Christ sake!"

Grantley shuddered back, as if he'd been hit in the face. But McBride, with his chin in the air, was already including all the rest of us in his outburst. "How many times do I have to keep saying this—there's absolutely no proof I was having any affair with that woman!"

"You're sure of that, are you?" Ann said quietly. Then she turned to me. "Dave, show it to him, will you?"

From the pocket of my jacket, I took out the snapshot Doris Dryden had given Ann—McBride lying nude and asleep in Edna Pulaski's bed—and held it out to him.

McBride looked down at it, and I could see his face turn a sick shade of white. "Where the hell did you get that? Give it to me!" He made a snatch at it, but I was too fast for him.

"Don't be childish, Marvin," Ann said. "Do you suppose we haven't got copies? Show it to Ed and Leland, Dave."

I did so. Ed frowned at it hard, and I knew the wheels were turning in his head, but he showed no expression on his face.

"That picture's a fake!" McBride was saying. "It's a lie! I want to know what goddamned liar took it!"

Ann told him, just the way Mom had figured it out and explained it to Roger and me the night before. . . .

"What started me wondering," Mom said, "was this remark that Doris Dryden made to you after the women voters dinner. You remember, you met her in the lobby, and she told you McBride's wife kicked him out of the bed years ago, even before she kicked him out of the house. I asked myself, when I heard about this, 'How can she know such a thing, such an intimate fact that's strictly private between a husband and a wife?' She made it up, I decided. She don't like this McBride, she's running against him in the election, so she makes up stories about him so he'll look like a fool. If this is the truth, Doris Dryden don't come out looking like such a nice person, but so what? I put the incident out of my mind. There wasn't any murder yet, so why should I give to it any significance?

"Until you repeated to me, Davey, your conversation with

McBride when he said to you for years his wife wouldn't satisfy his natural desires. Which makes it sound like this story is true, his wife *did* kick him out of the bed years ago. In other words, Doris Dryden wasn't lying—which puts into my mind all of a sudden a very important question: How did she find this out? Only two people could know such a private thing—McBride and his wife. She's the type of woman who can't stand the world should know her private affairs, and his pride is hurt by what she did to him. Is it likely either of them is going to tell it to Doris Dryden?

"And then I'm getting a little idea. There *is* somebody McBride could tell such things to. His lover—the woman he's sleeping with instead of his wife—Edna Pulaski. In the privacy of lying in bed with a woman, sometimes a man isn't so careful about keeping confidential matters to himself."

"But, Mom, that doesn't tell us how Doris Dryden found out about it."

"Edna Pulaski told her—what other explanation makes sense? She's a businesswoman, this Pulaski. Her business is going to bed with men. Any profit she can make out of this, she's happy to make. You're going to bed once a week with a politician, he's telling you intimate secrets about himself, so what's wrong with passing them on to one of his rival politicians and making a little extra money on the side?"

"You think Edna Pulaski was a spy for Dryden?"

"This is my thought. The idea came to her maybe when Doris Dryden made the announcement she was running against McBride in the election. A perfect opportunity already! Edna Pulaski got in touch with Dryden and they worked out a deal. So anyway, as soon as I was willing to consider this possibility, other things came along to show me I was right. For instance, Doris Dryden tells you she knows all about McBride's affair with Edna Pulaski. How should she know? McBride was careful, he didn't leave any trails behind him. So who told Doris Dryden about it? It could only be one of the guilty parties—and we're pretty sure, aren't we, which one it *wasn't*?

"And what finally makes it positive is this photograph.

179

McBride with his clothes off is lying fast asleep in Edna Pulaski's bed. Who took this picture? Somebody sneaked in from the outside and took it, and ran away again? An idiot wouldn't believe this. Only one person could take such a picture—Edna Pulaski herself. Which explains, incidentally, why she isn't lying in the bed next to McBride. . . ."

"I don't believe it!" McBride broke in on Ann, shaking his head violently. "She could never do such a thing to me! She was crazy about me!"

He turned to look at Ed, at Grantley, at Ann—as if he expected somebody to reassure him, to tell him how impossible it was. Nobody said anything. Nobody was able to meet his eye.

He sank back in his chair without making another sound. There was still a grin on his face, but all the cockiness had oozed out of it, it was a hideous imitation of itself. And he looked as if he had suddenly shrunk in his clothes. He had become as small and huddled-up as Harry Stubbins.

"So you see how it is, Marvin, don't you?" Ann went on. "If I show the jury this picture—if they believe you were having an affair with Edna Pulaski—that might be enough to raise real doubts in their mind. About the murder, I mean. How could they find Harry guilty with you looking like such a promising alternative?"

McBride didn't look up, and the words came out of him in a kind of groan. "I didn't kill Edna. I wasn't in her room that night. Okay, okay, I *was* having an affair with her, I admitted that to you a long time ago, but I swear I didn't kill her."

"You can't prove that, Marvin. You don't have any alibi for the time of the murder."

"I was home in bed. I don't have to prove that. You have to prove I wasn't."

"True enough, if you're on trial. But not if you're a witness for the defense. I won't hesitate to call you, you know. And I won't have to make an airtight case against you, all I'll have to do is convince the jury that you *might* be guilty, that you're just as likely a suspect as my client is."

McBride glared up at her, and I could see a nasty word forming on his lips. But he forced it down, and let out a long sigh. "I was hoping I wouldn't have to say this. But—on the night of the murder I've got an alibi."

"Is that so?" Ann settled back in her chair.

"After I left the dinner and dropped Ed off at his place, I—well, I didn't go home. Okay, I had a date. I met her around eleven-thirty, and we were together for an hour and a half after that. And we weren't anywhere close to Edna's place."

"Who is she?" Ann said. "Will she swear to this?"

"Sorry, I'm not saying who she is."

"If you expect us to believe in this alibi of yours—"

"I'm not telling you who she is!" McBride's chin lifted and quivered, and his voice got stronger. "She'd be in a lot of trouble if it ever got known that she was seeing me. I'm a gentleman, for Christ sake. A gentleman doesn't get a lady in trouble."

"If there *is* such a lady," Ann said with a laugh. "Honestly, do you think anybody's going to swallow this story of yours? Chivalry's been dead a long time, Marvin, and nobody in their right mind ever suspected *you* of being Sir Galahad. I promise you, if you don't produce this mysterious girlfriend of yours, I won't hesitate to build my case around you."

"Do whatever you want to do! Wild horses couldn't drag that name out of me! Wild horses!" And McBride glared around, as if he heard those horses in the corridor, pawing the ground and champing at the bit.

Ann watched him a moment, and then she smiled. It was the first friendly smile she had given him all evening. "You know what, Marvin? I'm beginning to think there might be some hope for you, after all. Maybe you don't deserve to be drummed out of the human race just yet. All right, I'll put you out of your misery. We *know* who was with you on Saturday night. So let *me* tell *you.* . . ."

Mom had laid it all out for us last night, of course, neat and clear.

"He was with his daughter, this Laurel girl, who else? She

tells her mother she's at a play rehearsal till one in the morning. Actually the rehearsal is over by eleven. She also won't take a lift in the car with her friend, she tells him she's being picked up by somebody. And three or four times before, this same thing happened. So who could this be, this somebody who picks her up so late at night and she don't dare tell her mother about him?"

"Why couldn't it be a boyfriend?" I said. "Some kid her mother wouldn't approve of?"

"*Why* wouldn't her mother approve of him? Her mother was saying to you she only wished the girl went out with boys more often. Why such secrecy, when she could bring him home for dinner and her mother would jump up and down from pleasure?"

"An older man then? A married man maybe, so he has to see her in secret?"

"Maybe so. Only he's picking her up so late at night—for a married man it's harder, not easier, to make dates with his floozies after bedtime. He can't give the excuse, at such an hour, that he has to work late at the office. And look at this girl, look how you're describing her to me. Does she sound like some type vamp that older men are losing their heads over? She's skinny, she's got pimples, she wears thick glasses, she's generally a mess—like most girls her age.

"And one more thing. This date don't last very long, does it? From eleven-thirty to one, this is a pretty short time for any serious hanky-panky.

"Still, it *could* be a secret boyfriend, it's possible, but it came over me there's somebody a lot more possible it could be. A man that she could be dying to see, and he could be dying to see her, only they have to keep it a secret because her mother would have fits if she found out. A man that was busy till eleven on the night he picked her up, and he's often busy till late at night because he has so many social functions to go to. A man that wouldn't want her to smell liquor on his breath. Her own father, who else?

"What they did together, who knows? They went maybe to an

all-night cafeteria and had a couple hamburgers. They talked. She told him what she was doing and how she was feeling, and he told her the same. Father-daughter type talk. But he don't want to tell you about it, even though this gives him an alibi, because he's trying to protect his little girl, his baby. In fact, this is maybe the biggest clue of all. If people are saying that McBride is a murderer, and if there's a woman he was with that night who can give him an alibi—is he going to keep her name to himself if she's only one of his girlfriends? In the past did he ever show such respect for his girlfriends? She has to be somebody he has a *different* kind of feeling about, a feeling that with him goes deeper.

"So give him a little credit already. He isn't such a nice man, he's a cheater and a liar, but for once in his life he's telling a lie to help somebody *else.* . . ."

"All right, all right," McBride said, letting out his breath, looking very tired. "I was with Laurel, we went to Denny's, we talked for an hour. She had a hamburger and I had an order of french fries. You go there and talk to the waitress, maybe she'll remember us."

"Was this the only time she sneaked out to be with you?" Ann asked the question in the softest, kindliest way she could.

McBride shook his head. "We did it plenty of times before. Whenever she had to stay late at school. What's wrong with that, for Christ sake? I love that kid—and she loves me, believe it or not! She couldn't see me out in the open, because she didn't want to hurt her mother. And I damn well wasn't going to expose her to one of her mother's scenes. Believe me, that bitch knows how to stage a scene."

Then, suddenly, McBride's voice sounded different from how I had ever heard it sound before. He was actually pleading with us. "Look, this doesn't have to come out, does it? If that bitch ever finds out, Laurel's life won't be worth living. . . ."

His voice trailed off. He lowered his head.

Ann said quietly, "This conference is strictly off the record. I see no reason why anything we say here should go any further."

After that we were all silent for a while.

Then Grantley cleared his throat. "I'm sorry, but we seem to be right back where we started from. Since Marvin couldn't have committed the murder, there's nobody left but—"

"Goddamn right!" McBride raised his head, and his eyes glittered. His little lapse into humanity was over, on his face was the usual cocky belligerence. "Ann sweetie, you know what you just accomplished? You cleared me, and you made your client look guiltier than ever! Thanks a lot!"

Ann waited patiently until McBride's laughter had died down. Then, quietly and cheerfully, she said. "Actually you're wrong about that, Marvin. What I've accomplished is to scrub away one layer of lies. One more coating that's been preventing us from seeing the truth underneath."

"The truth underneath," McBride said, "is that this bum busted into that whore's bedroom, she caught him while he was trying to rip off her jewelry, and he killed her.'

"I'm glad you mentioned her jewelry," Ann said. "That brings me to the next layer of lies. We'll scrape *it* away now, and then, with a little luck, we *will* be able to see the truth."

She turned to Harry Stubbins. "Don't you think you should tell us about that ring?"

"I told you." Stubbins seemed to shrink back from her, though she hadn't moved from her seat behind the table. "Somebody gave it to me. Put it in my hat. Some kind charitable soul who wants to see me in the gas chamber."

Ann gave a sigh, then she launched into the chain of reasoning that Mom had tried out on Roger and me the night before. . . .

"The funniest thing about this ring," Mom said, "isn't that the Stubbins fellow had it in his pocket. The funniest thing is that he didn't get rid of it two minutes after he noticed somebody put it in his hat."

"I suppose he was planning to sell it or pawn it or something."

"You're right, ordinarily this is what he does with the things people give him. But this wasn't ordinarily. How come he wasn't scared out of his pants he should find it in his hat in the first place?"

"I guess I don't follow that, Mom."

"Look at it from his point of view already. He falls asleep in this woman's bedroom, he wakes up and somebody killed her, and the police arrest him for the murder. And what happens a couple days later? He looks into his hat after a hard day on the streets begging, and in there he finds this gold ring with the green stone in it, which somebody stole from the dead woman and which he saw her wearing the night she got killed. We know he saw her wearing it because the first conversation you ever had with him he described this ring to you, along with the rest of her jewelry. And now, all of a sudden, this same ring shows up in his hat.

"He's an old drunk, yes, but he isn't exactly a dope. You're telling me he didn't right away recognize this ring and ask himself some questions: 'What's it doing in my hat? Who put it there? *Why* did they put it there?' And could he ask himself these questions without he should come up with the obvious answers? 'It's no coincidence this ring got into my hat. The murderer stole this ring from Edna Pulaski, and the murderer put this ring in my hat—not by accident but on purpose. Because this murderer wants the police to find this ring on me. Maybe he's even tipping them off they can find it on me, because he's trying to make it look like I killed the woman. Maybe they're looking for me right this minute.'

"Where I'm driving, Davey, as soon as this Stubbins sees the ring and figures out somebody is using it to put him in a frame-up, how come he don't throw it away? Into the garbage, into the sewer, anyplace at all as long as it couldn't be connected with *him*? How come, knowing this murderer is planting such a big piece evidence against him, he carries this ring around with him all day long and into the nighttime?"

"He's an old drunk. He gets befuddled, he forgets about things. What does the reason matter? He *did* carry it around with him, he *didn't* throw it away, that's a fact!"

"Who's disagreeing with you? He carried it around with him—which to me means he *wasn't* afraid the police got a tipoff they should search him, he *didn't* worry this was a frame-up against him. And why wouldn't he have this worry? Because he *knew* the murderer didn't put the ring in his hat, *nobody* put it there. In other words, he stole the ring from Edna Pulaski himself."

"Wait a minute, Mom, have you come around to believing Stubbins *did* actually kill her?"

"Positively not. A killer he isn't. But a *goniff* he is. You know what's a *goniff?*"

"A thief, isn't it?"

"Good, good. You didn't forget everything yet from the language of your ancestors. He's a thief, and also a little bit of a liar. Not such a big liar as some of the other people in this case, but definitely a *little* one. He gets knocked out in Edna Pulaski's apartment, he wakes up from the old mother's screams, she goes running away to call the police, and he looks around to see how the land is laying. And he asks himself is there anything valuable he can take with him so this whole visit shouldn't be a total loss? What he sees is this big green ring on her hand. Why not take it, maybe he can pawn it for a few dollars later on, and after all *she* don't have any more use for it.

"Didn't you wonder, Davey, how come the police were in time to catch him? Like this Captain Delaney told you, it was five minutes from the phone call to when the squad car got to Edna Pulaski's house. Add on to that maybe another two three minutes while the old lady ran down the stairs and yelled in the street until somebody came along that would telephone the police for her. So what was Stubbins *doing* in these seven, eight minutes? He knows absolutely for sure the police are coming along soon, he certainly don't want he should be found on the scene, so what's he plotzing around for? Why isn't he running out of there a lot sooner?

"The answer is, he's trying to take that ring off the dead woman's finger—which isn't so easy to do if the ring's been there a long time. It takes him a lot longer than he expects, by the time he's got the ring in his hands the police sirens are making noises in the street. So he throws the ring out of the kitchen window, he'll come back for it later, then he goes down the stairs and out the front door and into a policeman's arms. And the next day, when he's out on bail, he comes back to the alley under Edna Pulaski's kitchen window, he crawls around looking through the dirt, and lucky for him the ring is still there.

"So ask him about this. He don't exactly sound like a tower from strength. Act like you know for sure what he did, and I'm predicting he'll fall in like a soufflé when somebody slams the kitchen door. He'll tell you everything. . . ."

And he did, of course. Ann had hardly finished her reconstruction when Stubbins started blubbering. And then, when you could make out words in between the blubbers, they confirmed everything Mom had deduced.

"I'm not a thief," he kept saying, giving little flounces that, I suppose, were meant to be gestures of dignity and pride. "I've hardly ever stolen anything from anybody in my life. Only out of the most pressing need—"

On he went for a while, the rest of us not quite wanting to look at him. Finally he was out of words, and the blubbering subsided into soft, almost inaudible sobs.

And McBride said, "Okay, so what? He could've killed her that night and still stole her ring in the morning. Nothing about this means he couldn't be the killer."

"Except the part," Ann said, "that tells us who the killer really is."

She milked the resulting silence for all it was worth. I ought to bring Mom and Ann together some day; there's a large streak of ham in both of them. Then Ann went on just like Mom had done last night. . . .

"So do you see already how useful this is," Mom said, "clearing away the layers of lies? Once we know this—that Harry

Stubbins stole the ring from Edna Pulaski's finger before he ran out of her apartment—this tells us who killed her."

Mom looked back and forth from Roger to me, but our faces were blank.

"You're not thinking so sharp tonight," she said. "I didn't make the coffee strong enough. So I'll tell it to you in simple words—since Stubbins stole the ring before the police got there, it's easy now to understand why it wasn't with Edna's things when they got returned to her mother from the morgue. It couldn't be with those things because it was never with them in the first place, it wasn't one of the items the police took away along with her body. So—if this is a fact—tell me please how Grantley, your assistant district attorney, could say he saw this ring on her finger at nine in the morning, just before the people from the morgue took her body away . . . ?"

"How about it, Leland?" Ann said, turning her gentlest smile in his direction. "Got any explanation for that?"

NINETEEN

"I'll be fucked!" said McBride. And practically for the first time since we entered that room, he stopped looking at Ann. He turned his gaze to Grantley now, he didn't seem to be able to get enough of looking at him.

After a moment Grantley made a little huffing sound, half bewilderment and half irritation. "Excuse me, Ann, is this supposed to be a joke? I'm afraid I don't think it's either funny or in very good taste."

"It's no joke, Leland. And this has gone way out of Miss Manners's jurisdiction."

Grantley got to his feet, snapping his papers into a briefcase. "I'll leave you now. If you need me, you'll find me at home."

"Sit down," Ann said, before Grantley could move from behind the table. "The policemen outside the door have orders to stop anybody from leaving this room."

"I happen to be the assistant district attorney—"

"Their orders apply to you especially."

"Who gave such orders? You have absolutely no authority—"

"They come from Captain of Homicide Patrick Delaney," I said. "He's acting head of the police department while the chief is off hunting this weekend. I spoke to Pat on the phone this afternoon, and he's happy to take the responsibility."

Grantley's face was suddenly very white. He dropped into his chair.

189

Ann went on talking, addressing herself to all of us. "Once you're willing to take a serious look at the possibility that Leland Grantley is behind these murders, it's amazing how many fuzzy details suddenly click into focus."

Then Ann ran down the list, just as Mom had done for Roger and me the night before. Ann's language was probably more elegant, but the logic and the observation were strictly Mom's. . . .

"One—" Mom raised a finger; she liked to use her fingers to keep track of the points she was making. "We'll begin with this slip he made about the ring. This Grantley did see the ring on Edna Pulaski's finger, but it isn't possible he could see it there on the morning she died, while he was looking over the body, because by this time the ring was gone. He saw it on her finger eight hours or so earlier, when he went to the room and killed her. He mixed up the two times in his head, he got a little careless—a natural mistake, since he's been spending a lot of time with her the last six months, and she made a habit of wearing this ring, he was *used* to seeing it on her finger, he didn't notice when it wasn't there.

"Two—" Another finger in the air. "How could this Grantley meet such a woman like Edna Pulaski in the first place? A stuffy fellow like him that never lets himself relax? We know the answer already, he met her the same way and at the same time that McBride met her. The police made a raid on her massage parlor six months ago, they brought her in for questioning, and McBride eventually questioned her—but first, like he told you himself, 'she was questioned by some of my lower-echelon people.' Which people from the lower echelon? (What's an echelon, incidentally?) Who else but the assistant district attorney?

"This is when he met her, and she gave him little signals, like she did to McBride, that she'd be happy if he followed up on the acquaintance. He called her, like McBride did, and pretty soon he was in bed with her once a week—one of the nights when McBride *wasn't.*"

"So Grantley and McBride were having affairs with her at the same time?" I asked. "Did they know about each other?"

"A woman don't go out of her way to tell one man he's in competition with another man. You ask my opinion, Grantley never found out about McBride and McBride never found out about Grantley. When you finally tell them both about it, you should keep your eyes open how they react, their faces will be very interesting.

"Here's another piece evidence Grantley was having an affair with Edna Pulaski. Call it my three." Another finger stabbed the air. "When you talked to Doris Dryden, she told you a story how McBride got mixed up when he cross-examined a witness, he thought he was cross-examining a completely different person in a completely different case. All right, it's possible this didn't even happen, it's possible Doris Dryden made it up. Only when Ann Swenson mentioned it to Grantley, he gave a reaction that showed it *did* happen. So we have to ask, don't we, how did Doris Dryden find out about it?

"Like she told you, only two people in the courtroom realized what was going on—McBride and Grantley. This is one story, you can bet money on it, that McBride wasn't talking about to his girlfriend—it made him look too foolish—so Grantley was the one that opened his mouth. Who did he open it to? The same spy that was giving Doris Dryden her information from McBride, isn't it obvious? Edna Pulaski—is it so surprising?—was doing to Grantley the same as she was doing to McBride. The information she got from him in bed she was selling to the political opposition.

"Which brings me to my four." Yet another finger in the air. "Grantley got nervous about this affair finally. It was getting closer to the election, reporters and TV people and the opposite candidate, Doris Dryden, are sticking their noses around for information that could make McBride look bad. His assistant district attorney having hanky-panky with a prostitute, this is something that could maybe be embarrassing.

"In other words, McBride told you the truth when he said his affair with Edna Pulaski was going along fine, with neither of them trying to break it up. Grantley was the one that told her he wanted to break up. Grantley was the one she was talking about when she told Harry Stubbins what schmucks men are, how she was going to get even with the man that was betraying her, how she threatened him she was going to give the whole story to the newspapers.

"This shouldn't be any big surprise, if we give a little thinking to the psychology of these two men. McBride is the type somebody threatens to expose his hanky-panky, he laughs and says, 'Go ahead, expose!' Between him and the voters is a love affair, or anyway he thinks so. They'll love him even more, he thinks, on account of he turns out to have a human weakness.

"This Grantley, on the other hand, he's got a completely different psychology. From what you told me about him, he never did this type thing before. He's got no experience with hanky-panky. He's got no confidence he can be a success at it. From the beginning, if you ask me, he's expecting the whole thing will explode in his face some day. So anyway, once she tells him she'll expose him, he don't think he can stand the publicity. It could be the end of his career, the end of his marriage—and without his high-society wife, maybe he can't afford to live in the same style he's used to.

"Also he isn't the type—like McBride is, for instance—that can sit patiently and wait to see what'll happen, telling himself that whatever it is he'll figure out some fancy story to wriggle himself out of it. She makes her threat to him on Saturday morning, maybe, and for Grantley it's necessary he should right away do something. And the only thing he can think of is he has to get rid of the Pulaski woman, before she has a chance to tell anybody what's going on between them.

"So right after the dinner, he goes down to the Pulaski woman's house, he gets there around twenty-five minutes after eleven. He sees from her window that the light is on, he's got a key to the downstairs door, so he goes inside and climbs the stairs. Very quiet—because he don't know she's given her girls the night off. He gives a knock, and walks into her room. Maybe he's got no plans to kill her—in his head is only a vague idea—but then he sees something that makes up his mind for him.

"Sitting in a chair next to her bed is this old bum, this Harry Stubbins. He's looking like he's drunk, he's fast asleep, Grantley is positive this bum never got a look at his face. It's like a gift from God on high, no? The perfect person to blame for Edna's murder. What's this type person called? A fall guy. So to put a long story in a nutshell, he pulls off his necktie and he strangles her with it.

"And then—I'm up to five, no?—" Mom brought her thumb into the story. "—it comes to him that everybody knows the type neckties he wears. Plain, dark, one color, like he's always on his way to a funeral. They see this type tie around the dead woman's neck, he thinks, they'll know right away who killed her. So he unwraps the tie from around her neck, and he takes it away with him. But you shouldn't bother to look for it, he already threw it away somewhere.

"We don't know yet, naturally, if he killed this Ron Pulaski with another one of his dark ties. Whatever he used, he also had to take it away from the scene of the crime, because everybody is blaming Stubbins for the murder, and it should look like the second murder was committed by the same person that committed the first."

"Why did he kill Pulaski, though? Have you figured that out yet?"

"It's my number six, what else?" She started on the fingers of her other hand. "The second murder, this whole business with the ex-husband Pulaski—this makes sense only if Grantley was the murderer. Why did this Pulaski have to be killed? Because he saw something that would point the finger at somebody for Edna Pulaski's murder. So what was it he saw? Pulaski was in front of his ex-wife's house at midnight, half an hour maybe after the murder, what he saw could only be somebody walking at twelve o'clock or so out of Edna's front door—somebody that shouldn't be there. Pulaski said it to his girlfriend, you remember? 'I saw, I saw—not supposed to be there—' Except that Pulaski didn't realize what he saw, he didn't recognize the person that came out of Edna's house, he didn't understand why it was important—till after he found out Edna was killed.

"*How* did he realize it already? At eleven o'clock on Sunday morning he finds out about his ex-wife's murder from a news broadcast. This broadcast goes on a while—and all of a sudden he jumps up from the bed and runs out of his house, telling his girlfriend he's going to the district attorney's office to give information. What happened all of a sudden that produced in him this big reaction? Right away I knew it had to be something about this news broadcast, something he found out from it.

"Was it something he *heard* or something he *saw*? This was the important question. This was why I told you to ask this Pulaski if he got the news from the radio or from the television. And when I found out it was from the television, how many more doubts could I have? What *was* there on that television news show? The woman's dead body? This couldn't be it. Pictures of McBride? This couldn't be it either, everybody knows what McBride looks like, all the time he gets his picture in the papers. Pulaski would recognize him the night before if he saw him walking out of Edna's house.

"What Pulaski saw on the television was the assistant district attorney, Leland Grantley, making a statement how the killer was found on the scene of the crime and was arrested by the police and justice would be done even though the victim was a prostitute and so on and so on. And watching this on the television, Pulaski recognized Grantley. *This* was the man he saw leaving Edna's house before the murder.

"You want more proof of this? Didn't it hit you what a peculiar thing it was what Pulaski did next? He's planning on blackmail, no? He's planning to ask the murderer for money so he won't expose him to the police? So what's the first thing he does? He *goes* to the police! He drops in front of them big hints that he knows who the murderer is! Is the man a total *schlimazl* or what? Suppose the police decided to arrest him, he's obstructing justice, they'll hold him in jail until he tells them what he knows. No blackmailer in his right mind is going to take such a chance. So I had to ask myself, why didn't this Pulaski go to the murderer first?

"And pretty soon I saw what the answer was. He *did* go to the murderer first. Going to the assistant district attorney, this *was* going to the murderer. When they were alone in Grantley's office, Pulaski didn't drop any hints about having information for sale. He told Grantley straight out what he saw and asked for money he should keep his mouth shut. And Grantley maybe didn't give him a straight answer, he hummed and hawed a little, he said he had to see how much cash he could raise.

"Which is the only thing, incidentally, that explains what Pulaski said to his girlfriend when he got home again. 'Wouldn't the police like to know what I saw! Maybe I'll tell them, maybe I won't. It all depends on that assistant DA.' Not meaning, you understand, that he was going to sell his information to the assistant district attorney if the murderer didn't buy it. Meaning that he was going to sell his information to the police if the assistant district attorney—who was also the murderer—didn't buy it.

"So after this talk with Pulaski, what was Grantley thinking? What else could he be thinking except 'If I let this bloodsucker get away with it, he'll squeeze me for the rest of my life, I won't have no more blood left in me than a turnip.' There's only one way for Grantley to handle the situation. Pulaski has to be killed, just like his ex-wife was. And this time it'll be easier to do than it was the first time. Murdering people is like any other bad habit—it's always easier the second time.

"So Grantley makes an appointment with Pulaski, he'll come to his house on Wednesday afternoon, he'll bring the money with him for the blackmail. He gets to Pulaski's house, and because Pulaski is practically passing out from drinking—he's celebrating his big stroke of luck, the money that's suddenly coming into his life so he can go back to Philadelphia—Grantley don't have much trouble killing him.

"No, no, don't say anything yet, I didn't tell you my number seven—the biggest giveaway of all. When Stubbins was falling asleep from the coffee, he got just a quick look at somebody, maybe a man or maybe a woman, that was coming into the room. He didn't see who this somebody was, but he heard Edna Pulaski talking to this person and saying out loud a name."

"Wait a second, Mom, Stubbins didn't tell us that. He never mentioned that she said the murderer's name."

"This is because he didn't know it was a name she was saying. You remember maybe what he heard her calling out?"

"Sure. It was something about the shows they're always rerunning on television. 'Rerun! Had enough rerun! No more!' Something like that, wasn't it?"

"It's a pleasure to see it, your memory is still good even though you're getting older. You repeated them exactly, the words Stubbins heard her say to the person at the door. He heard them, but he didn't understand them. It don't make sense, at such a moment why should Edna Pulaski express her opinion about television reruns? It has to be she was saying something different."

"What *was* she saying?"

"She didn't speak English too good. She spoke it with an accent, one of these Asian accents. And what's the biggest mistake that Asian people, Chinese and Korean and so on, make when they're trying to pronounce English? The letter *L* gets all mixed up with the letter *R*, the two letters are always turning into each other."

"Sort of like *V* and *W* in a Yiddish accent?" I couldn't resist saying.

Mom went on as if I hadn't made a sound. "In ordinary conversation, somebody mixes up *L* and *R*, you wouldn't have any trouble figuring out what they're saying. This is because you know ahead of time what's the subject of the conversation, you're expecting to hear certain words and not to hear others. But what Edna Pulaski said to the man at the door, Stubbins was hearing this without any clue to what the conversation was about. So naturally his ears have to make up for this, he has to give her words a meaning that fits with the *last* conversation he was having with her. She was talking a few minutes before about television reruns, so Stubbins, without anything else to go by—and remember he's already getting a little dizzy from the pills—thinks she's still talking about television reruns.

"Only she wasn't. What she was doing was giving a Chinese accent to Grantley's first name. She was mad at him, on account of he just broke up their relationship. 'Leland!' she was saying to him. 'No more, Leland! Had enough!' "

And Mom settled back in her chair with a pleased smile on her face. . . .

Not too different from the smile on Ann's face as she finished her summing up in that gray basement room.

The long silence that followed was broken finally by McBride erupting. "Jesus, Leland! You been humping Edna all this time? You been poaching on my preserves all this time?" Oddly, though, McBride didn't sound particularly angry or hurt. There was a mixture of surprise and admiration in his voice. "And I thought butter wouldn't melt in your mouth! Jee-*sus!*"

Grantley turned his head sharply in McBride's direction. "I won't dignify that remark with an answer. Let me just go on record as saying that this whole absurd theory is a tissue of lies from start to finish. You haven't got one shred of solid evidence. And now you'd better call off your bloodhounds, because I *do* intend to leave this room—"

He was on his feet again, but he still didn't get to take more than a few steps.

"One more thing you ought to know, Leland," I said. "Pat Delancy is digging up the solid evidence right now. He's got the fingerprint guys checking every one of those unidentified prints they picked up in Edna Pulaski's room. He's been to your house too—with a warrant—picking up glasses and ashtrays and so on to find a good clear sample of *your* prints. The experts will make a comparison, and if any of those unidentified prints turn out to be yours—"

"That won't mean a thing," Grantley said quickly. "I visited the Pulaski woman's room on Sunday morning, in connection with our investigation. Naturally you'll find some of my fingerprints there."

"According to Delaney," I said, "you didn't set foot in that room until after the fingerprint guys had left. If some of your prints *do* show up there, I'm afraid you left them too soon—in fact, before you were supposed to know the room even existed.

"Delaney also has a couple of men showing your picture to Edna Pulaski's girls, and a couple more showing it to people in the neighborhood. It's my experience, you know, that there's no such thing as a clandestine affair. *Somebody* always knows about it. Somebody sees or hears something. You can be pretty sure Delaney will dig up that somebody. The cops in this town are good at their jobs, though sometimes the cases they turn over to the DA's office get botched in the courtroom—"

"Hey! Wait a second!" McBride barked.

"What Dave is leading up to, Leland," Ann went on, "he and I are officially police officers, so with great regret I have to tell you that you're under arrest. Dave, will you read him his rights?"

"Glad to. 'You have the right to remain silent—' "

He didn't remain silent though. It's amazing how many of them don't. It seems to be more important to them to tell their stories than to save their necks.

"It's not fair," he said. "I didn't want to kill her. If I'd been McBride, I wouldn't have had to."

"How the hell do you figure that?" McBride said.

Grantley turned to face him. "It's so easy for you, isn't it, Marvin? You're a roughneck, you're a natural-born slob. All that barefoot farmboy bilge! Nobody expects anything else from you. You can even be a drunk, and get away with it. People smile and say, 'Oh, that's Marv McBride! Good old Marv, he sure can put away the stuff!' There isn't a person in this town who doesn't know how much sleeping around you do. But they forgive you for it. They're *proud* of you for it. 'Good old Marv, it proves he's still got balls!' You won't lose one single vote from it.

"Unfair! No justice at all! *I* can't get away with *anything*. I'm the Harvard man. The serious dignified young lawyer who wears vests and never uses obscenity and has no sense of humor. Have you any idea what it's like living up to an image like that? Have you any idea what a *strain* it is on a man? And with a wife like mine too. Always rubbing my nose in that high-society family of hers. Always cutting me down.

"And then Edna came along. She seemed to really like me. She thought I was fun to be with, she gave me affection, she laughed when I made a joke. You can't understand what a relief it was, how wonderful it was to feel like a different man—"

Grantley broke off, and for a moment I was afraid he was going to start crying. I don't like it when murderers start crying. What right have the bastards got to make me feel sorry for them? Before the tears could flow, though, Grantley got hold of himself. He lifted his chin, there was a note of pride in his voice. "One thing I'd like to make absolutely clear. It was never part of my plan—originally, that is—to put the blame for Edna's death on that homeless old man. I have the deepest sympathy for the homeless, I have genuine respect—"

He turned to Stubbins and looked him steadily in the eye. "I give you my solemn word about that, Mr. Stubbins. I got to Edna's place on Saturday night, and— Yes, my intention *was* to—dispose of my problem—once and for all that night. When I went in, you were lying on the sofa, and she was fluttering over you, acting quite agitated, she seemed to be afraid that you were dead. I think she realized you'd taken her medicine by mistake, and she was worried the dose might be too large for you. My first thought was I'd have to postpone the purpose of my visit to her that night. But then it occurred to me—I had this terrible second thought—that you'd make a perfect suspect. The point I'd like to stress, it was purely a sudden impulse, I'm deeply ashamed of it now—"

Stubbins didn't give an answer. He just blinked at Grantley, bleary-eyed. I guess the whole evening was getting to be too much for him.

*　　*　　*

So Grantley was hauled away, and Stubbins was taken back to jail—he couldn't be officially released until the paperwork was done—and Ann and Roger and I took McBride up to the real world again. On the way up in the elevator, McBride gave a little laugh and rubbed his hands together quickly. "Well, now," he said. "We did it, didn't we? We nailed the son of a bitch."

He reached out to clasp Ann's hand. "Thanks—thanks to all three of you. I was the quarterback, but I sure as hell couldn't have done it without my backfield. You've earned my undying gratitude."

Ed Brock came up next to him and took hold of his elbow, and I could see that his grip was tight. "This is our floor, Marvin, we've got a lot of phone calls to make. We'll have to set up a press conference for you—tonight—just as soon as possible."

The elevator stopped, and Ed led McBride firmly through the doors.

As they shut again, and we started up to our floor, Ann said, "One thing about this case still bothers me. It kind of got lost in the shuffle, but it's been in the back of my mind, I wonder if you've got any ideas about it."

I asked her what it was, and she said, "Why did Edna Pulaski invite Harry Stubbins into her house for coffee in the middle of the night? That was an awfully generous thing to do, and it doesn't seem as if she was such a generous person."

Roger had asked Mom the same question last night, so now I gave Ann the same answer. . . .

"We'll never know for sure," Mom said, "but maybe I can make a guess. Early that day or the night before Edna Pulaski phoned her lover, this Grantley, and told him she was going to expose their affair and ruin his life. Not such a nice thing for her to do. So maybe she was feeling a little guilty about it, and maybe she wanted to prove to herself she wasn't actually such a bad person. It's human nature, no? You're doing something rotten, so at the same time you do something good. Even better if you can make a sacrifice to do it. Like Edna Pulaski hated people that got drunk, so her sacrifice was she deliberately brought an old drunk into her house and sat him down in her chair and talked nice to him. This is the type action that makes it possible you can live with your conscience.

"Like Goldberg, the landlord, when I had my apartment in the Bronx. Goldberg used to send big turkey dinners to the Salvation Army, telling them they should give his generous gift to homeless people. Always he did this just before he evicted some poor family from their home. . . ."

My answer seemed to satisfy Ann completely. She suddenly gave my arm a squeeze and said, "You never cease to amaze me, Dave. Your insight into people's feelings, your empathy, your sensitivity—there's something almost *feminine* about it."

"I can't really take credit for it," I said. "I suppose I must inherit it from my mother."

I lowered my eyes with the proper modesty, and also because I didn't want to look at Roger.

TWENTY

The Republican American's poll, which came out on election morning, made McBride's victory look like a forgone conclusion. It put him so far ahead that the editorial was already congratulating the voters on their wisdom and good judgment in following the newspaper's advice.

What clinched that election was the arrest of Leland Grantley, for which McBride, all over the TV screens and on the front pages, took sole credit. The timing was perfect. The great coup occurred before election day, but not too much before: no time for the voters to get over McBride's momentary triumph and start remembering his long-term record.

Poor Doris Dryden couldn't make any headway against this. As she said to the reporters, after the debacle, "If I had Mr. McBride's luck, I wouldn't need my brains."

Just one personal note: Early in the morning, before I drove down to the courthouse, I went to my neighborhood polling place, the nearest elementary school, to cast my vote.

I've explained already that, in spite of my conviction that all politicians are liars and crooks and there's nothing to choose among them, I do vote. I do it out of habit, because I've been brought up thinking I should. The way you might knock wood sometimes, even though you don't believe for a minute that it brings you good luck.

But then, when I got into that voting booth, a very peculiar thing happened to me. I started to say eeny-meeny-miny-mo, since it didn't matter which one of them got elected, when all of a sudden this strange little voice was in my head, telling me that maybe it *did* matter. In fact, maybe I really cared. On the one hand was Doris Dryden, that ruthless bitch, and on the other hand was Marvin McBride, that incompetent slob—and on the third hand (and in a situation like this who says you can't have three hands?) there was me, facing a machine and being forced to make a choice.

Human beings are built so they have to make choices, said my little voice—and by this time, believe me, I wasn't having any doubts about *whose* voice that was.

So I thought about it hard for a while, for all the world as if there actually *was* something to think about it. I weighed ruthless efficiency against easygoing sleaze, and then my hand pulled down the lever. McBride's lever, God help me.

What the hell came over me anyway? Deep down in my subconscious, was I sorry to see him go, was I afraid his departure would leave a void in my life, did I find his brand of bullshit more *enjoyable* than hers?

So much for my image of myself as a rational human being!

Just before noon on election day, McBride suddenly appeared at the public defender's office.

His official reason for dropping in was to thank Ann and Roger and me again for the "invaluable assistance" we had given him in apprehending Edna Pulaski's killer. Once he had unloaded himself of this formula, he was able to get down to what he really had on his mind.

McBride had come to offer jobs to all three of us. "I'll be needing a new assistant DA," he said. "As, of course, you know. My number-one assistant. Lots of responsibility. You'll go to court for all the big cases, Ann, the ones I don't have time for myself. At an appropriate salary, you understand. And just between us, it's a lot more than you're making as public defender. With a decent office too. A view out on the courthouse square. Your desk will be twice as big. Your own personal secretary. And if you want it to be the old biddy that's out there in your reception room now, that'll be fine with me.

"And what I want *you* for, Dave, is to be my chief investigator. A big raise in salary for you too, and you won't have to operate out of this hole-in-the-wall any more. You'll have a real staff under you, four or five trained detectives. And you too, kid—what's your name, Ralph? Robert? whatever—Dave can bring you right along with him if he likes. And he can decide how much you get paid. Within the city guidelines. So how about it, Dave? You used to be a real cop, isn't that so? Won't it do wonders for your conscience if you start working on the *right* side of the law again?"

None of us said anything at first, and then Ann put the question that was on all our minds. "What happens to the public defender's office?"

McBride gave a shrug. "The city'll appoint somebody else, I suppose. What's the difference? It's never going to be more than a penny-ante operation. One of the things I'll be doing, after I'm elected, is submitting next year's budget to the City Council. And what I told you a while ago, I don't happen to have changed my mind—I'll be asking them to make drastic cuts in the line items for the public defender's office. No raises for anybody, no more assistant investigators, lower operating budget. But why should I go into all those dry financial details with you? None of you is going to even *be* here by that time. You'll be part of my team on the second floor, in the *decent* section of this building. You'll be playing up there in the Super Bowl, instead of down in the cellar."

While he was chuckling at his own sense of humor, Ann and Roger and I looked at each other. Then, one by one, we each told McBride that we didn't think we were interested in his offer. "I'm happy down here in my cellar," Ann said. "It's humble, I admit, but from time to time we play a pretty nice game."

A few seconds later McBride went stamping out. He didn't look very pleased. I told myself I should have voted against the little jerk after all.

I spent election night with Mom, watching the returns on her TV. Roger came to her house too, bringing a date along with him. It was the first time he'd been willing to do that in six months, not since that unfortunate business that soured him on women forever. None of us had thought at the time that forever would turn out to be this long; we couldn't be happier at this indication that the kid was sweetening up again.

The girl's name was Beth, and she was a student at the School of Veterinary Medicine, a branch of the state university, located in the state capital about seventy miles from Mesa Grande. It was very encouraging that she should be willing to make that hour-and-a-half drive, on a weekday night, for Roger's sake.

From the moment she stepped through the door Mom hovered over her with innocent little questions, all of them with a hidden meaning. She asked the girl about her family (hidden meaning: what did her father do for a living, did they happen to be Jewish?); about her friends (hidden meaning: were any of them unmarried men?); about her career plans (hidden meaning: were they likely to stand in the way of marriage?). At the same time, Mom plied her with cake, fruit, pieces of candy, cups of coffee, glasses of the special Election Night punch she had made. "With just a little sniff from alcohol in it. It wouldn't hurt a baby."

Beth took all this without strain, answering Mom's questions good-humoredly, never showing any wear and tear on her patience. And best of all, from time to time she would dart a look at Roger and her eyes would glow with pleasure. I hoped the stupid kid knew how lucky he was.

The polls close at six o'clock in Mesa Grande, and sometimes it takes a long time to count the votes. We have the usual modern up-to-date machines, but human beings have to open them up in back, read the gadgets inside them, and make records of what they say. Since all this is done by little old ladies with trembling fingers and failing memories, it wasn't till seven-thirty that the first figures started coming in.

It was pretty clear from the start that McBride was winning by a landslide. It was barely eight-thirty when the TV station took us to Doris Dryden's campaign headquarters, a ballroom in the Marriott-Chinook, so we could see her concession speech. This ballroom looked like some scene out of a sci-fi movie, after the atom bomb has fallen and only a handful of human beings are left in the world.

You had to give Doris credit. She couldn't have looked cooler and more elegant, as she stood up in front of those weary blotchy-faced college types, the ones who hadn't already gone home in disgust, and announced she was conceding the election. A few ritual cries of "No, no!" came from the group—even with the best will in the world, you couldn't call it a crowd—but they were halfhearted and didn't last long enough for Doris to acknowledge them.

After she said the words that are expected on such occasions—how she was deeply grateful to the people who had worked for her, how they had all put up the best fight they could, how she didn't consider her campaign to be a failure but a true *success* because they had brought the issues before the public—a TV reporter stuck a microphone in her face. "What's your future in politics going to be, Mrs. Dryden? Are you going to run against Marvin McBride three years from now?"

"*Is* McBride going to run again three years from now? I seem to have missed that announcement."

The reporter looked flustered. "Well, I mean, if he does."

" 'If' is one of the biggest words in the language. I'll tell you my short-term plans though. Right now I intend to go home and sleep as long as I possibly can. I feel like I haven't slept for about a year. And tomorrow morning, assuming I manage to wake up that soon, I intend to go down to my office and get back to work. I'm a practicing attorney, as you know. I've got partners, clients who depend on me. Cases have been piling up on my desk. Some of them, no doubt, will bring me into court opposite my recent opponent Mr. McBride."

And then, after a pause, she couldn't keep herself from adding, "We'll see how well he does in front of *those* juries."

The TV station took us back to the main studio, and a few minutes later switched us to McBride's headquarters in the Richelieu, where he was ready to claim his victory.

We saw the great man in front of a hundred screaming applauding fans, waving his arms over his head, lifting himself up on his toes. Behind him stood Ed Brock, larger than life and beaming. McBride began his victory speech by saying how incredibly humble it made him feel that he, a poor barefoot farm boy, should be elected for an unprecedented fifth term to the august office of district attorney. He expressed his thanks to the people who had worked on his campaign, how proud he was that they had fought cleanly and fairly and stuck to the issues. He reassured those who had voted for him, and those who had not, that he would continue to run a strong district attorney's office and hold the line against the criminal element wherever it reared its ugly head.

He paused, then he said, "Now I want to tell you one of the first matters I'm going to attend to when I start my new term of office.

"Ann Swenson and her terrific staff in the public defender's office gave me a big assist in clearing up the tragic murder case that came along in the last week of the campaign. I developed a new respect for their ability, competence, and dedication. So I want them—and all the people of Mesa Grande—to know that I intend to fight, with all the vigor at my command, to strengthen that office by asking our City Council to approve a ten percent across-the-board increase in the public defender's budget. That doesn't come close to what they deserve, but I hope it'll allow them to maintain an even higher level of service to the public than they've been maintaining through the years. A strong public defender's office, ladies and gentlemen, is one of the bulwarks of democracy."

A little later McBride came to a stop, his fan club exploded, and Mom turned off the TV.

My God, I found myself thinking, the impossible has happened. There actually turns out to be a spark of honesty and gratitude inside that little dynamo of phoniness? Could politicians possibly be as complicated and unpredictable as other human beings?

You can bet I didn't say any of that out loud to Mom.

I expected Roger to be more vocal though. Dryden had been his candidate, his knight in shining armor, his hope for a better tomorrow. Now that she had gone down to defeat, I steeled myself for one of his idealistic laments about the ignorance of the poor misguided voters.

He didn't say a word, and then I realized that he hadn't unloosed a single lament all night, even as the news about his candidate got direr and direr. The reason was obvious, now that I thought of it. He had been too busy watching Beth, making sure her glass was refilled, pushing himself close to her on the sofa. One of the best things love can do for a young fellow, I decided, is to take his mind off politics.

Later in the evening Roger and Beth left to go dancing. Mom and I, sitting next to each other on the sofa, had a last glass of punch together.

"So how are you feeling about the election, Mom?" I asked. "You voted for Dryden, I guess?"

After a pause Mom said, "I'd like to tell you something, Davey. Maybe it'll be to you a surprise. The fact is, I voted for McBride he should be the district attorney."

I couldn't say anything for a moment. Then I put on the shocked tone of voice that I knew she was expecting from me. "For God's sake, why? You know as well as I do, looking at him in the most generous light, he's stupid, incompetent, a liar. You're always telling me how important it is to make a choice. You haven't come around to believing it doesn't matter who wins?"

"No, no, this I could never believe. I made a choice. I thought about it a long time. The reason why I voted for him was Rabbi Schlossberg."

"I don't follow. Who's Rabbi—"

"He was the rabbi twenty years ago at my synagogue in the Bronx. Nobody was satisfied with him. He didn't have any ideas, he never did anything, he never accomplished anything, he only sat around. So we had a vote and we fired him, and we hired Rabbi Pearlstein instead. *He* did things. Such an accomplisher he was! In six months everybody in the congregation hated him, twenty families walked out, the head of the religious school had a nervous breakdown, the cantor who had a voice like Richard Tucker quit his job and Pearlstein replaced him with a cantor who had a voice like an old car that's having trouble starting on a cold morning. And on top of all this, the treasury was all of a sudden ten thousand dollars in the red. This is why I voted for McBride. Because twenty years ago I made a big mistake and I wouldn't make it again. This much I owed to Rabbi Schlossberg.

"All right, I know what you're thinking. Some choice, you're thinking. It would've been just as good I did it your way—shut my eyes and pushed down the first name I happened to touch."

In justice to myself, I have to say that I felt at this moment a definite pang of guilt. Not so painful, though, that it was accompanied by the slightest temptation to blurt out the embarrassing truth about my *own* voting behavior. Confession may be good for the soul, but certain feats of moral strength you just can't ask a mere human being to perform.

One more incident that's connected to this case, and then I'm finished:

The morning after the election, I parked my car in the courthouse parking lot and was walking to the front entrance when I became aware of a figure sidling up to me on the sidewalk. "Lovely day, isn't it?" the figure said in its usual hoarse croak. "Slight chill in the air, but that's the season. I'm all in favor of the seasons."

"How are you, Harry?" I said, slowing up a little, because he was still just a bundle of rags and bones who couldn't keep up with other people. "What're you doing around here? This isn't your usual place of business."

"Now it is," Stubbins said. "Changed my place of business. Working the courthouse steps and environs from now on.

Much better class of clientele than what I used to get. Changed my place of residence too. That alley on Arizona Avenue—hideous unsanitary slum!" Stubbins made a face, as if he were smelling something rotten. "Just moved into a cozy little spot—pleasant secluded cul-de-sac behind the courthouse, lovely view of the back of the jail."

"Any particular reason for all these changes in your life?"

"Matter of convenience." He gave me a grin, a flash of yellow teeth with a couple of gaps in them. "What I feel is, it's reassuring—very reassuring, in case of emergency—being located so near my attorney."

EPILOGUE

Excerpt from Mom's Diary

Dear Diary,

I'm feeling foolish already, and I only wrote two words in you.

When I was a girl I never kept any diary. . . . So tell me please, what am I doing with one now? At my age, after seventy-five years keeping such foolishness out of my life? The answer is, since I moved to this little town . . . in the shadow of the Rocky Mountains—where my son is investigating murders and other crimes for the public defender—I'm giving him more help with his cases than I used to do back in New York even. . . .

And it sometimes happens there are deductions I'm making about these cases, ideas coming into my head, that I can't tell him about, it would be dangerous or embarrassing he should know them. But I have to get them off my chest, no? Everybody has things they have to talk about to somebody. So that's you, dear diary, you're the one I'll be doing my talking to.

Like now, when I know something I never want Davey to know about these murders that all the politicians got mixed up in. . . .

Actually it took me the last three months to catch on to the truth. Being fair to myself, I have to say that I had a certain feeling about this all along. Something else was there, something nobody was seeing. Even while I was making my brilliant deductions, this itch was inside me, it wouldn't leave me alone.

But for three months I didn't do anything about it. I pretended to myself that I wasn't itching. Until finally, a couple days ago, I decided I had to scratch. I was watching the five o'clock news on television, giving the jury's verdict in Leland Grantley's trial. Grantley was indicted three days after the election, and for a month now he was standing trial. Like he promised the voters, District Attorney McBride personally took charge of the prosecution.

He botched it so bad that the judge wouldn't even let the charge be first-degree murder. He reduced it to manslaughter—for both murders yet!—and even when the jury found Grantley guilty they recommended a light sentence. (The judge took the recommendation and sent him to prison for five to ten years, which means, for some reason I don't understand, he'll be out in three.) Some of the people from the jury were interviewed on the television, and what they said was, McBride never convinced them that the idea for killing Edna Pulaski didn't come to Grantley on the sperm of the moment, when he saw Harry Stubbins passed out from drinking her coffee.

I turned off the television right then and there.

The coffee, I said to myself. My God, the pills in that coffee! All this time, up till this moment, I was taking it for granted, like everybody else did, that Edna Pulaski put the pills in the coffee herself. She was taking her nightly heart medicine, and she lost track and put in too many.

What a *schlemiel* I was! How could I believe it, even for a few minutes, that this explanation made sense?

Now, all of a sudden, I could see what was wrong. Edna Pulaski could maybe forget how many pills she put in her coffee, but could she forget she put *any* pills in it? Could she give the cup to Harry Stubbins, knowing all the time her heart medicine was in it? And she didn't get two different cups mixed up with each other either, because in the pot was only enough coffee for one cup.

Another peculiar thing. She told Stubbins she poured the coffee for him out of the pot. All right, Edna Pulaski would maybe put her heart pills in her coffee cup—but in the *pot?*

214

This woman brews up her medicine in a *pot?* Excuse me, but positively not.

I could see the answer now, it couldn't be clearer. Anybody takes a look at what actually happened, and they'll see the answer too.

Edna Pulaski goes into the kitchen to pour out coffee for her and Stubbins. In the pot she finds enough coffee for only one cup, so she lets him be the one to drink it. But what if Stubbins didn't happen to be there that night? Who could doubt that Edna Pulaski, sooner or later, is going to drink that cup coffee herself?

And if she drinks it, what's going to happen to her? In the coffee is the medicine she takes for her heart condition, only it's three or four times the usual dose. If somebody that don't have a heart condition, somebody like Harry Stubbins, swallows such a big dose, nobody can be sure it'll do something terrible to him. But if somebody that *does* have a heart condition, like Edna Pulaski, swallows such a dose, it's absolutely certain what it'll do to her. It'll kill her, no two ways about it.

So now, dear diary, it's clear, isn't it, what was actually going on with that coffee? Somebody put those pills into it, without letting Edna Pulaski know about it. So why? Because the idea was to kill her. The person that did it was in her apartment earlier, dropped the pills into what was left in the pot, and went away, expecting that later on Edna Pulaski is going to die from an overdose of heart medicine. Only Harry Stubbins showed up and drank the coffee instead. And a little bit later, Grantley comes in, and we know what happened after that.

In other words, what we've got here is *two* murderers, both of them wanting to kill Edna Pulaski. The first one didn't succeed. The second one made a better job of it.

So who was this first murderer—this almost murderer—that put the heart medicine in the coffeepot? I'd like to think it takes a genius to figure this out, but it don't. It's much too simple. What are the qualifications this murderer has to have?

It has to be somebody with an opportunity for poisoning the coffee—that is, somebody that Edna Pulaski would let into her apartment that night and also would give permission this person should be alone in her kitchen.

It has to be somebody that knew about Edna Pulaski's weak heart, and also knew which medicine she was taking for it. Most of all, it has to be somebody that was willing to do what I noticed from the beginning, when Davey described to me Edna Pulaski's apartment. On Saturday night, a few hours before Stubbins got to her place, she had dinner, but by the time Stubbins got there the dinner dishes were cleared up, there was no sign of a dirty glass or a crumpled-up napkin. She didn't have a dishwasher, but even so everything was cleaned and polished and put away where it belonged. Who did this? Not Edna Pulaski herself. She was the world's messiest housekeeper. Everybody who knew her said what a slob she was. It's unbelievable she suddenly reformed and got rid of the bad habits of a lifetime.

Who *usually* did Edna Pulaski's cleaning up for her? Who was her regular unpaid cleaning woman, the person that came in early every morning to do her housework? Her mother, the old lady, Mrs. Kim.

And isn't it logical to suppose the same cleaning woman came in on the night of the murder? In other words, the old lady wasn't telling the truth when she said that the last time she saw her daughter was Saturday morning. The truth is, she was there on Saturday night. And why would she lie about this? There's only one reason I can think of. Because this was when she put the pills in her daughter's coffee.

So I'm asking myself what was her motive. And this is the answer I'm getting. By this mother's standards her daughter was leading a shameful, immoral life. She was disgracing herself, she was disgracing all her living relatives, and her ancestors, and maybe even future generations. For Korean people, if they were brought up like this old lady, family is everything, ancestors are everything, honor is everything—this is what her great-niece said about her.

Plenty times, for plenty years, Mrs. Kim tried to persuade her daughter she should change her ways. They had loud arguments about it. On Saturday night Mrs. Kim came to make another try, and while they talked, the old lady also cleaned up the dishes from dinner. This is how it is if you're a natural-born fusser and cleaner, you have to keep your hands busy. But the daughter didn't listen to what the mother told her, she laughed at it like always.

And then, maybe when she's cleaning up the bathroom, old Mrs. Kim sees the heart pills in the medicine chest. Also she notices there's still some coffee left in the coffeepot. And she can't hide from herself no more that her daughter is never going to change. The honor of the family is never going to be pure again, unless she does something about it. It's a thought that was in her head plenty times before—of this I'm positive— and now, because all of a sudden the opportunity is in front of her, she decides she'll finally do it. So quick she puts some of the pills in the coffee, and a few minutes later she says good night to her daughter and leaves the house.

This isn't the end of it though. The worst part she still has to do. On Sunday morning, at seven o'clock as usual, she has to show up at her daughter's house, and she has to pretend she's surprised and full of horror to discover the dead body. She stays awake all night maybe, getting herself ready for this. So she does find the body, only it's strangled not poisoned, and the man that did the killing is right there in the room, or so she thinks. Dear diary, I don't like to think what a shock this was to her!

This is the only way to explain it, something the old lady said to Davey when he questioned her later in the day. What she said was, her daughter's murderer robbed her of "the only joy I still had to look forward to in life." What she meant, everybody thought, was the joy of spending her old age with her daughter. But her daughter *wasn't* giving her any joy in her old age. Her daughter, on account of her way of earning a living, was giving the mother nothing but tears. So the old lady's statement don't make sense if you try to explain it that way. What she *really* meant by it had to be something different—that the murderer robbed her of the joy of personally giving her daughter the punishment she deserved.

Yes, I know it, dear diary, this is a terrible thing I'm saying. An old lady, a mother, trying to murder her own child in cold blood! How could such a thing happen?

The truth is, it happens all the time. Davey told me this years ago, he's seen the statistics, but anybody that knows anything about human nature knows it has to be true: The majority of murders happen in families, with people who are closely related. Most of these murders are husbands and wives killing each other, but even more are parents killing their children. When it isn't children killing their parents. And it's not so surprising, if you come to think of it. If the emotions are strong in politics, where what's driving at people is only being ambitious or greedy or egotistical, how much worse it's going to be in families, where along with these ordinary emotions is also love.

So now, dear diary, you can see, I hope, why I couldn't tell Davey about this. What's the point? Is he going to arrest this old lady for attempted murder? Even if he was crazy enough to do it, who could ever prove anything against her? What district attorney, even a stupid one like this McBride, is going to prosecute her for it in court, and not only lose the case but also the whole Asian vote in the next election?

Besides which, who did this old lady kill, when you get right down to it? She *thought* about killing, she dropped some pills into a coffeepot, but what crime did she *actually* commit? Only being a mother. It isn't easy being a mother. The emotions that are inside a mother's heart, they're very complicated sometimes, very mixed up, they come out in peculiar ways. Leave her alone is what I say. She's old. Soon enough she'll pay for her mistakes.

So now I'll say good night to you, dear diary, and we can both get a little rest.